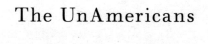

The UnAmericans

The UnAmericans

Stories

Molly Antopol

FOURTH ESTATE • *London*

Fourth Estate
An imprint of HarperCollins*Publishers*
77–85 Fulham Palace Road
Hammersmith, London W6 8JB
4thestate.co.uk

First published in Great Britain by Fourth Estate in 2014
First published in the United States by
W.W. Norton & Company in 2014

1 3 5 7 9 10 8 6 4 2

ISBN 978-0-00-754881-1

Book design by Lovedog Studio

Printed and bound in Great Britain by
Clays Ltd, St Ives plc

MIX
Paper from
responsible sources
FSC www.fsc.org   FSC® C007454

FSC™ is a non-profit international organisation established to promote
the responsible management of the world's forests. Products carrying the
FSC label are independently certified to assure consumers that they come
from forests that are managed to meet the social, economic and
ecological needs of present and future generations,
and other controlled sources.

Find out more about HarperCollins and the environment at
www.harpercollins.co.uk/green

For my parents

Marcia Antopol

Jeff Moskin

&

Paul Johnson

Contents

The Old World

No one wants to listen to a man lament his solitary nights—
myself included. Which is why, on an early fall morning four
months after Gail left, when a woman breezed into my shop
with a pinstriped skirt in her arms and said, "On what day
this can be ready?" I didn't write a receipt, tell her Tuesday and move on to the next customer. Instead I said, "Your
accent. Russian?"

"Ukrainian."

"The Jewel of the Baltic! I've read a lot about it," I said.
"The art, the food, those ancient fishing villages!" On and on
I went—though I had not, in fact, read about it. I had, however, caught a television special once, but I remembered little
more than twisted spires, dreary accordions, plates of pink fish,
pocked and shiny.

"Ukraine," she said slowly, "is not on the Baltic." She had
a wide pale face, full lips and short blond hair dyed the color
of curry.

"Ah," I said, and swallowed.

But she didn't walk away. She squinted, as if trying to see me better. Then she leaned across the counter and extended her hand. "Svetlana Gumbar. But call me Sveta."

"I'm Howard Siegel." Then I blanked and blurted, "You can call me anytime you like." She smiled, sort of. The lines sketching the corners of her eyes hinted she was closer to my age than to my daughter's, for which I was thankful: it was too pathetic a jump from the twentysomething girlfriend to the earring and squirrelly ponytail. I laid out her skirt, examining it for stains, and when I finally worked up the nerve, I asked her to dinner.

❀   ❀   ❀

"What are you doing picking up women on the job?" my daughter said that evening over chicken at her place.

"What's wrong with that?"

"There are better places to look for them. I know two women from Beit Adar who would love to meet you."

Beth was still lovely—dark and freckled with eyebrows too thick for her face—but the silk kerchief covering her hair would take some getting used to. So would the mezuzahs hanging in every doorway of her new Brooklyn apartment, the shelf of Hebrew prayer books I doubted she could even read. This was, to say the least, a recent development. And what timing. Right when I was trying to learn how to live alone after forty years of marriage, Beth had left for Jerusalem. And, worse, she came back born again—and with a fiancé, Ya'akov, who happened to be a fool.

"Listen," I said, "I've got a feeling about Sveta. You trust my taste in women, don't you, Beth?"

"But why rule out other prospects?" the fool said.

"I'm the one who has to spend an evening with these women, making small talk!"

"Still," he said, "give them a chance." Ya'akov was small and wiry, with agitated little hands and a kippah that slid around his slick brown hair, like even it didn't know what it was doing on his head. He was from Long Island. He had once been Jake "The Snake," pledgemaster of his fraternity. At the wedding his brothers from Sigma Phi had looked as flummoxed as his parents, as if everyone were waiting for Jake to confess that his religious awakening was just an elaborate prank.

"All my wife's trying to say," Ya'akov continued, "is that we know plenty of nice women."

"Maybe you could let Beth speak for herself, *Jake*."

"But I agree with him," she said. "Why not let us fix you up?"

"I just want to meet someone the normal way," I said. "Shopping for romance after services just doesn't sound like love."

"What do you think love should be, then?" Beth asked.

✵ ✵ ✵

OUTSIDE THE coffee shop windows, the swell of late-nighters sauntered past, their gazes concentrated and steady. Sveta looked so much more serene than the rest of the city, tiny and smiling in the big green booth, holding her tea mug with both hands. I sipped my coffee and listened to the goofy beat of my heart.

"You ask every woman you meet in cleaners on dates?" Sveta said, swallowing a bite of cheesecake. Her blouse was the same salmon shade as her lipstick, and riding up her wrist were gold bracelets that clinked when she set down her fork.

"Absolutely not! I've worked there my entire life and you're the first."

"You work at cleaners your whole life?"

"Not just one cleaners—I own five. The original store on Houston, one in Murray Hill," I said, counting them off on my fingers, "two on the Upper West Side and the one on 33rd where you met me. It's been in the family since my grandfather. He was a tailor in Kiev, came here and started the business. If my grandfather had been a brain surgeon, I'd be a brain surgeon now, too."

"*You* are from Kiev?"

"Not me, my grandfather. I've never stepped foot there."

But Sveta didn't seem to be listening. "*I* am from Kiev!" She reached across the table and squeezed my hand. "Our people are coming from same place."

Our people? My people were from Ditmas Avenue. My people had left Ukraine before the Cossacks could impregnate their wives. As a boy, I'd been dragged to visit my grandfather in White Plains, where our family kept him in assisted living. I'd been forced to sit on the tip of his bed, the smell of green beans and condensed milk heavy in the air, and listen to his stories of moldy potatoes for dinner, of the village beauty's jaw shattered by the hoof of an angry horse. I'd heard stories of windows smashed, of my great-grandparents' tombs knocked on their sides, the stones broken up and used to build roads. I'd imagined pasty faces wrapped tight in babushkas, soldiers charging through the streets with burning torches. I'd heard those stories so many times that they became only that to me: stories.

But I didn't say that to Sveta. I didn't say that, until I met her, I'd studiously avoided so much as looking for Ukraine on a map. I said, "What an amazing coincidence!" because I could understand how happy she was to meet a man who shared her roots on this side of the globe—and mostly because she was still squeezing my hand, and I would have done anything to stop her from letting go. "What brought you here, then, from the marvelous land of Ivan the Terrible?"

"My husband found work here."

"And your *husband* doesn't mind your going out with every dry cleaner you meet?"

"How would he know? He's dead." She spooned sugar into her tea and—was this really her deft way of changing the subject?—read the quote on the tea bag aloud like it was something to ponder.

"If you are a minority of one, the truth is the truth," she read. "What you think it means?"

I had no clue. And anyhow, I wanted to hear about the dead man. "You know where they come up with these quotes? At some warehouse out in San Francisco. Same place they make the Chinese fortunes for the cookies. The person who wrote this knows jack about truth."

"This person," said Sveta, "is Gandhi."

Of course I'd opened my mouth just when our hands were touching. It was during these moments in life that I feared I'd become one of those old men I always saw here in the coffee shop, alone at a table, slurping soup.

The check came and we both reached for it. "Let me," we said in unison.

"I had good time," Sveta said, slapping down a bill before I'd even opened my wallet.

I assumed she said it out of politeness after my Gandhi comment, but when we walked outside, she grabbed my face with both hands and kissed me, hard. "Where you are living?" she whispered. I pointed west, toward the Hudson. "Good," she said, taking my hand.

Inside my apartment, I led her to the kitchen. Not the sexiest room, but I really wanted to show off the view above the sink: I rarely had the opportunity anymore for guests to see it. While Sveta stared out at the boats dotting the river, the bright white lights of Jersey in the distance, I looked at her full cheeks and jagged teeth, remnants of lipstick escaping the corners of her mouth. In one long slow moment the room went quiet. I pulled her close. We were quick with each other, untucking, unbuckling, unzipping, until we were pressed naked against the dishwasher except for socks and watches and my glasses, which Sveta, at the last moment, set on the counter.

We stayed up so late that gauzy yellow light filtered in through the blinds and I could hear the garbage trucks outside, making their runs. Sveta was curvy and round, with a scatter of moles across her hips. And here I was, sixty-three, paunchy and balding, wondering how I had gotten a woman like Sveta into my bed, wondering even more how to make certain she stayed, and still completely clueless about how to keep things casual. "How long," I said finally, "has your husband been gone?"

"Eleven month."

"And am I too nosy if I ask how he went?"

"No, not nosy," she said, propping a pillow behind her head. And then she told me their story. She'd met him fifteen years ago, in her late twenties, just as they were finishing graduate school. They'd both been deep into their research—Sveta's dissertation was on Kiev's Golden Age, and Nikolai, a chemistry Ph.D., was researching Chernobyl's long-term impact on the nearby city of Pripyat—and there was something so comforting, Sveta told me, about those early years together. "It was the first time," she said, "I really knew what happiness means." Whenever they were together, even just reading side by side or walking down the block for groceries, the sky seemed a little brighter, the sun a little warmer, the world turned up a notch. They were both obsessed with their work, introverts at heart, and it had felt, once they were married, that she no longer had to try with other people, that what everyone else thought of her was of little importance. Of course they still went out with friends, but there was always a moment toward the end of the evening when they'd share a look across the bar, a silent understanding it was time to leave, to be alone again. That was a look I knew well, one Gail and I would notice between other couples, at dinners or parties, a look that always made us feel defensive and exposed. After those evenings, we'd find ourselves dissecting the relationships of our friends, picking apart their dynamic until we felt better about our own, standing beside one another at our twin sinks, brushing our teeth.

Nikolai had been exposed to Chernobyl's radiation every day for six years while he researched the disaster, Sveta continued, but it wasn't until he accepted a fellowship here and they moved to a safe, quiet street on Staten Island that he walked outside to rake the leaves one morning, clutched his chest and collapsed right there in the driveway. "Nobody had idea about his heart," Sveta said. "We were knowing nothing. Murmur condition is affecting something like one in every million men, and it has to be my Nikolai." Sveta was left alone in a new house in a new country with only Galina, a cousin she'd grown up with in Kiev who now lived in Chicago, to talk to.

I ran a finger along the inside of her wrist, creamy and warm and marbled with delicate veins. My own problems, the ones I had wallowed in for months, were nothing compared to hers. It occurred to me that she was stronger than I was. "Why not go home to your family?"

"I have no child, and my parents die long time ago. My grandmother raise me, but when Nikolai and I marry, she do aliyah to Israel. Move back home?" She shook her head. "At least here I can learn English and get job in accounting. It's more easy being in U.S."

"Oh, Sveta." A throwaway comment, but the only thing I could think to say.

"How you say here? Shit it happens." She laughed, but it sounded startled and strained—the laugh that carries over everyone else's in a crowded restaurant.

I, in turn, tried my best to hint at what an unbelievable catch I was. I told Sveta about growing up next door to Gail in Brooklyn, how she went from being my playmate at school to my best friend to my steady girlfriend. I told her we married at twenty-three and scrimped for years, finally landing our dream apartment on Riverside Drive. I told her Beth's birth was undoubtedly the most important day of my life. I told her how even as a little girl, Beth seemed more like a friend than a daughter. And I told her what a terrific time we had over the summer, after Beth finished law school and moved home to save money while she studied for the bar. What bliss: we ordered in most nights, matineed on Sundays, sat up late talking in the kitchen—it was as if she had never been gone.

I didn't tell Sveta how painful it was to hear my daughter announce, at the end of the summer, that she had no idea what she wanted to do with her life ("Neither do I!" I'd said. "And

I'm sixty-three!"), that she'd chosen this career simply because she was terrified of never discovering what she *did* want—only then to run off to Jerusalem and return with Ya'akov. I didn't tell her how even walking from the subway to Beth's new apartment made me jittery and cold. I felt like I was walking back in time, back to when I was still a religious kid living in Brooklyn. Back when my family had enough money for a silver kiddush cup but not for new winter coats, back when we were just another poor family with too much faith in God.

Everything felt so new and fragile with Sveta that I didn't want to make the mistake of oversharing too soon. There was a huge part of me, hearing Sveta talk so openly about her marriage, that didn't want her to know my own had failed. And I knew my closeness to Beth—whom I'd always felt understood me better than anyone else in the world, including her mother—might sound odd if I attempted to describe it to another person. So I didn't tell her how Gail would snap about some mess I'd left in the kitchen and Beth would catch my gaze and roll her eyes: she had a way of making me feel she was on my side without ever explicitly saying so. I didn't tell her that when Beth wasn't around and we were left without a buffer, Gail and I could barely share a meal without a blowup. Everything I did ignited a fight: the way I chewed my food, the way I folded laundry, the way I made love. I told Gail it was impossible to live with someone so critical; Gail said it was impossible to live with a man who dealt with emotion by avoiding it altogether. But I had wanted to work things out—if not for us, then for Beth. I suggested counseling; Gail flew to Burlington and fucked a retired architect she had met online.

"The fantastic thing about Gail is that we're still great

friends," I lied. "I couldn't imagine not being in touch after sharing so much."

Sveta touched my face. "I told Galina I wasn't ready for new somebody, but she said there were many other people out there."

I waited for her to finish the thought, but she didn't. She tucked her body around mine and shut her eyes, as if there were nothing left to say.

※   ※   ※

FOR THE next few weeks, I'd close up the shop near Herald Square and wait for Sveta to finish her English class. I'd had this same view of a bodega and a produce stand for years and never thought much of it—but now Sveta would come gliding around the corner and even the asphalt would shimmer.

"But be honest," the fool said, "aren't you the tiniest bit worried you're just a rebound?"

I was, yet again, at Beth and Ya'akov's for Friday night dinner. It was the only time I saw them: they wouldn't ride the subway to visit me on Shabbat, they wouldn't eat in my kitchen because it wasn't kosher, they wouldn't eat at kosher restaurants near my apartment because they weren't kosher *enough*. Who does the hashgacha at this place? Ya'akov always wanted to know.

"I mean, how long has it been since this guy died?" Ya'akov held up his hands, as if they were supported by logic. "Tell me you haven't considered this."

"What do you know about loss?" I said.

"Actually, a lot. When I was in Jerusalem I did home visits with my yeshiva to bring a little tikva"—already he and Beth had begun to pepper their sentences with Hebrew, their inside jokes with God—"back into the lives of people who had lost family in the bombings, and—"

"Ya'akov." Beth shot the fool a look he deserved. "My father knows what he's doing. He's a grown man."

"Thank you, Beth," I said. "Listen, why don't you come over tomorrow and spend the day with me and Sveta? Lightning won't strike if you miss services just this once."

"I *like* going."

"But why?"

"I just do. Why do you care so much?" She suddenly sounded like the old Beth, and I had a glimpse of how she might have been as a lawyer, her delivery so sharp I felt my own voice wobble when I said, "No, really. I mean—what about it do you love?" I honestly wanted to know.

"Something about stepping into that sanctuary where people have been singing the same melodies for hundreds of years. It's like I finally belong somewhere," she said, her tone softening, and though I expected her blue eyes to be wild with fervor, they were bright and calm. "All these people in shul, they're like my safety net," she said, and I stood there blinking: wasn't it enough to fall back on me?

"Now that you're here," she said, "I wanted to tell you that—"

"We're pregnant," Ya'akov said, coming behind her and stroking her flat belly.

He gathered me into a hug, his skinny arms tight and firm, while I stood there, my feet cemented to the floor. I swallowed a pain in my throat, but it came back up again.

"What news!" I said, sliding out of Ya'akov's hug. "Does Mom know?"

"I haven't told her yet," Beth said. "I wanted you to be the first to hear."

"Well," Ya'akov said, "after Reb Yandorf and the rebbetzen, you're the first."

I kissed her cheek. She even smelled like a mother, of sweat and cooking oil and a dozen oniony dinners. "I'm so happy for you," I tried. "That's wonderful."

"Thanks." Then she glanced at me with more concern than a daughter should. "You're really sure Sveta's making you happy, too?"

That was the understatement of the century. I loved waking up beside Sveta, watching her rub sleep seeds from her large brown eyes. I loved how quickly we slept together, as if neither of us could muster a reason to hold back. And I loved the sex itself, which was undeniably, almost unbelievably, good. I loved watching her face scrunch up and then go slack, and I loved the moment right after, when she would huddle into the nook of my arm and run a hand over my hairy chest, calling me her big bear. I loved that she came to Friday night dinner at Ya'akov and Beth's and never let her eyes glaze during the blessings, though I'm sure she was bored nearly to sleep. I loved that she was kind to them, and I loved the quiet dignity she maintained when refusing to join in on the prayers—letting them know that growing up, she hadn't been *allowed* to learn them—rather than snapping at Ya'akov, as I often did, to hurry up already so we could eat. Those moments at the dinner table, I felt as if Sveta were teaching me something important: that I didn't need to make every opinion known, didn't need to be filterless, that sometimes the best thing was to sit quietly and smile and sip my wine. I loved the weekends, when we would take the paper to the park and spend all day lazing around the meadow, watching the neighborhood parade by with its strollers and dogs. I loved kissing her in that meadow, on the street, on the subway platform, just before the train roared into view—as if we were the only ones who existed, as if the entire city were being carried away in a tornado, and we were caught smack in the center of its glorious gray swirl.

Of course there were nights when I heard her slip out of bed after the lights had been off for hours. As my eyes settled into the darkness of the room, I'd see her standing by the window, lifting a book or a paperweight off my shelf. Not really looking at the object, just turning it over in her hands like she'd forgotten its function. Usually I rolled on my side and fell back asleep, knowing at some point she would return to bed—after all, when Gail first left, I'd found myself wandering the rooms of my apartment, opening cupboards or flicking on lights, then forgetting why I had entered the room in the first place.

But one night—it was October, a work night, two weeks after I'd learned Beth was pregnant—I put on my slippers and followed Sveta's footsteps down the hall. I found her on her knees in the bathroom, face cupped in her hands, weeping. She was in one of my undershirts, so baggy it reached her knees, and the sight of her on my bathroom floor was—well, it just *was*. The room was dark, but there was enough moon coming in from the window that her skin lit up white. I had no idea what it meant to find her hunched on my tiled floor in tears, and to be honest, I didn't *want* to know—who would interrupt a moment like that to ask if she was having, like the fool would suggest, a meltdown?—so I knelt beside her and stroked that soft ambiguous space between her back and her behind. I wiped her damp face with the heel of my hand, and then I asked her, just like that, and she said yes.

❊   ❊   ❊

WE'D BOTH learned that the big things you plan in life never live up, so we kept it small at a nearby synagogue. I would have preferred to sidestep all the Orthodox malarkey and have the wedding at City Hall, but then Beth wouldn't have come, and Sveta, maybe because of her secular background, said she couldn't care less where the ceremony was held. Sveta's cousin Galina flew in from Chicago and carried flowers down the aisle. She looked older than Sveta, late forties at least, with dark curly hair and delicate wrists that suggested she had once been slender. I hated thinking she had probably been at Sveta's first wedding, too, wearing that same puffed pastry dress, so I concentrated on the clacking sound my Oxfords made as she scattered roses across the room.

Under the chuppah Sveta looked especially flush-faced and pretty, wearing a silky dress that stopped at her ankles. Saying the vows was much easier the second time around. While the rabbi droned on about the seven blessings and the history of the ketubah, Sveta started to cry: not enough to smear her makeup, but enough for me to notice. For a second, I wondered if she was scared to be going through this again. Or, worse, if she feared the whole thing was all wrong. But then Sveta gave me one of her smiles—just a flash of teeth, and then it was all about that lower lip—and I thought, *My God*, this woman has tears of joy for *me*. I raised my foot above the glass and the guests broke into applause.

✿ ✿ ✿

THE NEXT afternoon, we were off on a honeymoon to Ukraine.
Beth and Ya'akov drove us to the airport. The women were
quiet in the backseat: Beth nauseated and pale, small hands
stroking her stomach; Sveta dozing with her cheek against the
window, still tired from the wedding. Sunlight caught her gold
band and I twisted my own; when Sveta slipped it on the night
before it was as if it had always been there, as if there was never
an interim when my finger was bare. We veered onto the Tri-
borough Bridge and the skyline rushed into focus, so miniature
and grand. I nudged Sveta to look up, but she was groggy and
slow, and by the time she opened her eyes it had disappeared
from her view.

We pulled into Kennedy, and Ya'akov and I unloaded the
trunk while Sveta went with Beth to the bathroom.

"I've got to hand it to you," Ya'akov said, setting our luggage
on the curb. "You move fast."

"Would you let it go already?" I said.

"I'm sorry." He clamped a hand on my shoulder. "Sveta's
great and I didn't mean for it to come out that way."

"How did you mean it, then?"

I stared hard at that bony hand, perched on my shoulder like
a proud parrot, but Ya'akov didn't remove it. He met my eyes.
"We just want what's best for you. Forget what I said and enjoy
the honeymoon. We'll look forward to the photos," he said, and
I wondered if I would ever be able to hear that *we* without
feeling my throat clog.

Then it was time to go. Sveta and I said our goodbyes to

them and slogged through security, and soon we were taking off. By her feet was a handbag full of magazines, but she just kept staring out the window. I followed her gaze but all I saw were clouds, the kind that look sturdy enough to nap on. The sun set. I thought about how if the plane flew in the other direction, the sun would set and set and set.

At Charles de Gaulle we took a shuttle to a dinky terminal and boarded a little plane with orange vinyl seats and no leg room. As it taxied off the runway and bumped through the sky, I reached for Sveta's hand. It felt lighter than usual, and warm with sweat.

"You're afraid of flying?" How odd to think I didn't know this about her.

"Not so much," she said, but her cheeks had blanched. "It's just these tiny planes, they frighten me."

I thought to say, but you're the one who wanted to fly half-way around the world. A month ago, just days after I'd asked her—I'd still been rolling the word *fiancée* on my tongue, tasting the sound of it—Sveta had come home with a Ukrainian guidebook. "You can imagine more perfect honeymoon?"

"Terrific!" I had said, though I'd been hoping for Tahiti.

I must have seemed underwhelmed because she'd looked at me, her round face more serious than usual, and said, "I haven't been back to Ukraine since Nikolai. My whole life— it was there." I think I understood only then how infuriating it must be for Sveta to translate feelings this complicated. "I know your life in U.S. I want my husband to know place that make me. Please," she said. "Anyway, we have nice time in Kiev. You can see my flat from youth, my school. And what a treat for you to see where your people are coming from."

There was no point in telling her I'd never had much desire to explore the city my relatives had fled. All my life I'd tried to look forward, not back. My grandfather worked for years in a factory until he had enough money saved to open a tailor shop. My father took over the shop and added a dry-cleaning business, and when it became mine, I hired more workers, bought a quality steam press—all in the name of moving forward. I kept the shop open on holidays to increase profits—all in the name of moving forward. But sometimes, when I was locking up the shop or drifting to sleep, I'd think about how everyone around me seemed to be regressing. Beth returning to the Brooklyn shtetl I had abandoned, Gail acting impulsive and smitten and happy—nothing like her age, nothing like I had known her to be. And now me, vacationing in Kiev. Still, what could I say but yes?

❊　❊　❊

SIX HOURS later the sun was coming up and we were in a taxi, swerving through Kiev. Everything was calling out to be photographed—the dark choppy water of the Dnieper; pine trees that lined the road, so green they were almost blue; even sights as commonplace as a mother and daughter on the corner, clutching plastic grocery bags and peering down the block as their bus came closer—until Sveta sighed and tucked my camera back in its case.

She'd seemed almost annoyed with me the moment the plane touched down and we had to split into separate lines at customs. And now she was acting as if there were an invisible person between us in the taxi whose space we needed to accommodate, her body pushed against the passenger door, the window down, her arm hanging out.

I figured she was tired, and didn't want to bother her. So I opened my guidebook and leaned toward the driver. "Vy hovoryte—"

"Yes," he sighed, "I speak English."

"Maybe you can show us some sights? Some old KGB stuff?"

Sveta's face cleared and she cringed. Through the rearview, she muttered something to the driver, and though I didn't speak a word of Ukrainian, I recognized her expression—the international look of *I'm sorry*.

As we made our way down a thin, cobbled street, she said something else to the driver and we stopped. Outside the window was a department store, glass-walled and wide, with mannequins in dresses and heels.

"This used to be the shop where my grandmother work as stockwoman," Sveta said, more to her lap than to me. "Now looks like Bloomingdale."

"That's a good thing, no?" I said.

The taxi started up again.

"Maybe," she said, but she stiffened. Then she sat upright, silently watching her city blur past, and all I could concentrate on was the way her nostrils widened and closed as she breathed.

✧　✧　✧

OUR HOTEL room in Kiev was just a sunken bed, a mini fridge and a green floral armchair pushed against a window. This was what the travel agent had called four-star? I opened my mouth to complain, but stopped. With Gail I would have said something, but maybe that had been part of the problem. On the second go-around I knew to keep things breezy.

"Smile," I said, pulling the camera from my fanny pack and aiming it at Sveta.

"Stop with photos," Sveta said, flopping on the bed. "How are you not feeling jet lag? My ears haven't even popping."

I knelt beside her. The carpet was pale brown, the kind we had in my living room growing up. I kissed her. She let me. I read this as a go. I tucked my hand under her sweater.

"Howard, I'm smelling like airport."

"So?"

"What I'm needing is rest," she said, blinking into sleep.

I looked around the room, at our unpacked suitcases and the old floral chair and the brown carpet, and told myself not to overanalyze—there was nothing wrong with Sveta wanting a nap. I lay down and wrapped my arms around her, and then the exhaustion hit me, too.

I wasn't sure how long I'd been asleep when I felt her slip out of bed. She tiptoed into the bathroom, closing the door behind her. The clock on the nightstand read 12:18, but with the heavy drapes, was it A.M. or P.M.? I yanked open the curtains, cracked the window and the cold air jolted me awake. Afternoon; we still had most of the day.

When I turned the knob, Sveta stood at the sink, wiping her eye makeup off with a tissue. In the mirror her face looked weathered and puffy, older somehow—as if the flight had aged her. She stepped out of her sweater and jeans; I stared at a body still so amazingly new to me: her full white hips, the swelled curve of her upper arms. Her back was like some secret object being unveiled.

She began to take off her bra when she saw me in the mirror. Then she hooked it back on. "You're needing the toilet?"

"I wanted to see if you're okay." I hoped my voice didn't sound as pleading to her as it did to me.

"I'm fine, thanks." She turned to face me and I was stunned by her expression: she seemed genuinely startled to see me standing there. "But you're let all the cold come in."

"I'll go check out the shops downstairs," I said, walking out, not knowing what else to do. Just before the room door slammed shut, I saw Sveta step out of the bathroom and pick up the phone.

"Galina," she said after a moment.

I waited. I pressed my ear to the closed door, but all I heard were hiccups. Then the hiccups broke into sobs.

❧ ❧ ❧

DOWNSTAIRS LOOKED like an American hotel lobby: potted ferns, gloomy nautical art, a pretty concierge tapping away with long pink nails on a computer. Men in glossy black loafers and dark mustaches—I had never seen so many mustaches—whispered into cell phones, conducting business I sensed was enormously important. I sat on a sofa and watched them, but after a while I gave up trying to understand their conversations and wandered into the gift shop. There I found all the presents I needed to buy without ever going outside: a matryoshka nesting doll for the baby, a set of bath towels with the hotel name stitched in Cyrillic for the fool, a scalloped wooden jewelry box for Beth.

Back in the room, Sveta was still on the phone, wrapped to her chin in blankets. She nodded at me and cradled the phone to her cheek, suddenly responding to the other end in only *nyet*'s and *uhuh*'s. Her voice was low and wavery; I knew not to mention the hotel's long-distance rates. I sat beside her on the bed and opened up the matryoshka doll. A smaller doll was tucked inside. I opened up the next one and the next one, until there were five little dolls lined up on the bedside table.

Sveta placed her hand over the mouthpiece. The look she shot me made me swallow, hard. "Go enjoying the day," she whispered. "I think I'm wanting to stay in."

I sat there, staring at my wife, with her short rumpled hair, bare toes peeking out from the heap of blankets. I wanted to ask what that look was for. It was even worse than the one I'd gotten in the bathroom: it was the terrified look you'd give an intruder barging into your hotel room. But I had a feeling I knew the answer, and the last thing I wanted to hear Sveta say was that she had made a mistake. I knew it was ridiculous to be threatened by a dead man, but I couldn't help it. Nikolai had been the kind of man, I decided, whom people in America had never referred to as Nick. The kind of man who would have seemed ten times more charming and intelligent than I did, simply because of his accent. A man who would have looked dashing in his white radioactive gear, wandering the Chernobyl countryside while women fell at his feet. A man who made love like a pro, a man who was probably—oh, God—the *original* big bear.

And yet I knew, deep down, that it wasn't only him. It was the way Sveta had closed into herself this morning as we passed that department store. It was the bewildered way she'd looked out the taxi window, as if her city had gone into hiding. It was the fact that she'd called her cousin when she felt this bad, rather than turning to me. I hadn't even had time to mess up in the ways I'd anticipated, ordering stupidly in a restaurant or bumbling in front of her friends. That moment in the taxi earlier, when apparently I'd said something embarrassing I still couldn't pinpoint—those sorts of things I had worried about, of course, but had believed they'd all seem inconsequential once we returned home to New York. But this felt different. As if the moment the plane landed in Kiev, Sveta was no longer certain I belonged in her life.

All at once I felt crowded and dizzy and nauseous. I took in some air, what felt like all of it left between us, and said, "How about showing me your old school?"

"Not now."

"Later, then. When you're off the phone we can go."

"Howard," Sveta said, "I'm not wanting to give tours now. Why don't you go seeing some sights yourself?"

"It's fine, I'm in no rush." I sensed I was talking my way into a hole, but I couldn't stop. I never fucking could. "Relax now and we'll go out for an early—"

"Stop, please." She muttered something to Galina, put down the phone and led me to the door.

"Listen," I said, reaching for her arm—but as I said "listen" she said "have fun" and closed the door. I stood outside the room, noticing, for the first time, the view of a soccer stadium from the open hall window. Amid the bleats of horns below I could hear the faint cheers of the crowd in the distance. I leaned against the wall and said "No" out loud.

Then I knocked, twice, and Sveta opened the door.

"You're my wife," I said. "Just tell me. Did I do something, anything, to make you feel—"

"It's nothing like this."

Then I said it: "You thought you loved me, and it turns out you don't."

A maid wheeled her cart by. Down the hall, a vacuum hummed. "I'm so sorry," Sveta said. She stared at the carpet, then thrust a guidebook at me.

❊ ❊ ❊

THE DAY was blue and crisp. Trees were still bare but the snow had melted, visible only in tiny patches along the sidewalk. I stuffed the guidebook into my fanny pack and roamed the streets, mapless and lost. I looked up at the blocky rows of concrete tenements, wondering if Sveta had lived in one of them, if she'd had a balcony crisscrossed with clotheslines and dotted gray sheets, like the ones billowing up now in the breeze. Two boys played tag, zigzagging through a row of parked cars, and I wondered if Sveta had been the kind of girl who would have hitched up her school dress to play with them, or if she would have stayed upstairs with her grandmother, avoiding cuts and bruises. I didn't know, and I felt ridiculous standing there in the narrow alley. So I followed the walking tour in the book instead, moving onto cleaner, bush-lined roads. I visited Lenin's statue and St. Volodymyr's Cathedral, the Taras Shevchenko Museum and Golda Meir's childhood home, caring less about the significance of each place as the day dragged on.

Down a skinny brick road I wandered into a square, elegant stone buildings towering over me: this city really was much more glamorous than I had expected. Women in dark wool coats shouldered past, swinging department store bags, leaving behind whiffs of perfume I didn't recognize. A grocer sifted through a bin of tomatoes, chucking the rotten ones into the gutter. Back home, it was morning. The storefront metal grates would just be coming up along Broadway.

I needed something to show Beth and Ya'akov, some proof I was even here, so I walked through the square, snapping photos. Through the viewfinder I stared at the grocer's green eyes and light skin, exactly like my own. Of course some of the people here looked like me: if my grandfather hadn't had the foresight to sneak onto a cargo ship almost a century ago, I too might be out here while some silly tourist photographed me. And this was if I had been lucky. I knew this was the moment I was supposed to lock eyes with the grocer and think, Could he be a distant, forgotten relative? (Or, just as likely, the person who had beat the hell out of a distant, forgotten relative?) But the only thing on my mind was how I had gotten here, halfway across the world to the city my grandfather had escaped, with a woman I barely knew. I wondered where Beth was. Probably still in bed, in her dark, cramped apartment in the city I had fled, sleeping beside a man she barely knew: the things we do when we're lost.

But maybe Beth was truly happier living a poor pious life with the fool. Maybe in religion, Beth really had discovered a way never to be alone. Maybe *I* was the only lost one, wandering the streets of Kiev, competing with a dead man. I hated to think the fool had been right about Sveta and me all along— that perhaps the fool wasn't such a fool after all.

Across the square I found a restaurant, the entrance winking with fairy lights. I took a seat in the corner and flipped through the menu to see what I could stomach. Chernobyl was about an hour away so most vegetables were out, and the guidebook warned that restaurants didn't refrigerate their meat. I settled on a chocolate babka.

A waiter appeared. "Something to drink?"

What I really wanted was a glass of Chianti, but when in Rome. "Vodka?"

All around me, people sat clustered together, clinking glasses and leaning close in conversation. I wondered how I looked to them: an aging man dressed so obviously like an American, wearing spanking white sneakers and a baseball cap. How had I let myself become just another sad old man at a table for one?

My drink came and I gulped it like water. Outside the window, the sun was going down, spreading over the city as evenly as butter. I ordered another and watched people stroll arm in arm through the streets. Watching them disappear around corners in the shadowy light—it was beautiful, and for a moment it comforted me to cradle my drink as the city faded and grayed.

But then the sky got dark and the streets went quiet and the group beside me paid and walked out. Soon, I knew, the restaurant would close and I would have to leave. But when I thought about returning to the hotel and listening to a crying Sveta apologize again and again as I wheeled my suitcase down to the lobby, when I thought about the long flight home and the freezing taxi line at Kennedy and the silent apartment that awaited me, the helplessness that rushed at me was so real I felt it move through my fingers and hair.

So I tried the only thing I could think of. I put down my head and prayed. It felt like the fakest thing in the world and at first I didn't know what to say, or even who to say it to, but then I closed my eyes and tried. I prayed for calm in the world and for joy, I prayed for Beth and Ya'akov and the baby, for Sveta and even for Gail, but inside I knew I was praying mostly for myself. I was praying for a way out of this sadness.

And when that didn't work, when the waiter cleared my glass away and the restaurant emptied, I prayed for that safety net of people to appear. They would be just as Beth described, reverent and serene, and as they sang in unison about God's grandeur and His pity, they would move closer together until their shoulders were touching and stretch their arms open wide, ready to take me in.

Minor Heroics

It wasn't even noon, and already the heat was so strong that the other moshavniks were tarping the vines and escaping inside. I wished I could head home and take the afternoon off before I returned to the base and began another week as Lieutenant HaLevi's personal driver: possibly the least essential job in the Israel Defense Forces.

But there were dozens of tomato plants left to prune, and I didn't want my mother, the production manager, stuck doing it alone. So I knelt in the dirt, the sun burning my shoulders right through my t-shirt, while in the distance my older brother and his girlfriend lazed in the pomelo groves. My mother would have called me a schlub if I'd skipped a day of work, but she was too relieved Asaaf was home from Hebron to care what he did. Last Sunday he was discharged, and all week it's been, *Let Asaaf sleep in, Give Asaaf the remote control.* And I've been nice about it. But watching him now, his head in Yael's lap, her fingers running through his hair, already beginning to grow out of its buzz cut—seeing him

27

with her got to me even more than usual, and I yelled, "Could you get off your ass?"

He flipped me off and turned back to Yael. But after a second he hopped onto the tractor and I thought, *One point, me.* And the truth was that we really did need his help. If the temperatures continued to climb through summer we'd have to worry about calcium deficiencies and blossom end rot eating away at the tomatoes, making them unsellable; I could already see the vines beginning to wilt as Asaaf rode past me and down to the squash field. His shirtsleeves were rolled to his shoulders, revealing his bulky brown arms, and I wondered why, even when he wasn't, my brother always seemed to be showing off. Behind him stretched dunams of farmland, marked by stucco clusters of other kibbutzim and moshavim that rose out of the valley, then dropped away just as quickly. The day was so quiet all I could hear was the hum of the tractor and the chickens squabbling in their coop, and I was suddenly reminded of how pretty it was out here. My brother plowed through the fields and down to the sunflowers, and then I lost sight of him as he cut behind the dairy. When he reappeared he was chugging down a hill, and then he must have hit a root, or a rock, because the tractor tipped. Just a little at first, and I waited for it to steady out. But it teetered some more and I watched Asaaf, small as an action figure, fly right off and tumble down the grass. From that distance, the landing seemed so soft that I waited for him to pop up and take an exaggerated bow. But he didn't, and that's when the tractor started to roll, over and over, until it stopped at the bottom of the hill, right on top of him.

I started running. By the time I made it over, my mother and Yael were already trying to pull him out. His eyes were closed, his face was scrunched and I wondered if the pain was knocking the breath out of him. There was blood on the tractor, on the grass, on my brother. "It's okay, it's okay," my mother murmured, to Asaaf, or to herself.

But he wasn't moving. The wheels were still spinning, spitting out dirt and weeds. I looked out at the empty hills and screamed for help. But I knew no one could hear me, so I ran to the work truck parked outside the dairy, keys dangling from the ignition as always, and started it up. I grabbed a chain from the back of the truck and hitched one side to the bumper and the other to the tractor's chassis, inching forward until my mother and Yael dragged Asaaf out and wrapped a work shirt around his leg. His right one looked okay but the left one was destroyed—his jeans were ripped off and the skin of his calf was slashed wide open, all the way down to the muscle and bone.

"Call an ambulance, Oren," my mother yelled, and when I didn't move she yelled it again. But I knew it would take the paramedics at least twenty minutes to wind up the mountain—and anyway, why had the army made me memorize every shortcut in this country, every side street and alley, if not for a moment like this, so I grabbed Asaaf under his arms. I must have looked more determined than crazy, because my mother and Yael helped me lay him across the seat of the truck. I slid into the driver's side and they climbed into the flatbed among the chains and spades and tarps, and then I was speeding down the dirt road, past the vines and rows of sunflowers, out the moshav gates and down the hill into town.

Asaaf's head was in my lap, and I kept one hand on the wheel and the other on his waist to keep him from sliding off.

His yells were starting to sound like sobs, and he was shaking, and the blood was soaking through the shirt so quickly that at the first stoplight I reached for a towel on the floor to cover it. But I thought about the dirt and gasoline and who knew what else was on that towel so I threw it off, then wondered how I could possibly be waiting for the light to change now anyway. When I looked through the rearview, my mother was mouthing for me to *go, go,* and I knew how terrified she must be that I'd blank under pressure: the whole reason I'd wound up with such a crappy army assignment in the first place.

But then something happened, and it's like a map overtook my vision and I knew I could speed through that light without getting hit. I knew to gun the engine, weaving past a delivery truck, then back into my lane before the light changed. I'd done practice drives like this on the base, but never when it mattered—and here I was, with only one free hand to steer, zipping down Dekel Boulevard and making a left onto Sapir Street without ever slowing down. I knew to avoid the highway, bottlenecked with Haifa commuters even this early in the day. I knew to zigzag past the bus depot, where traffic always clogged, and onto Arlozorov Road. Then down a side street, and another. Past the open-air market on Hanassi where people threw up their hands as I sped through a crosswalk, and down an alley to the back of the ER, where the two medics outside took one look at my brother and wheeled him straight into the operating room.

❋ ❋ ❋

FIVE HOURS later Asaaf was out of surgery and knocked out on painkillers. Visiting hours were over. I waved to the receptionist as my mother checked in with the doctor once more, and when we stepped back into the parking lot, it stunned me that it was still light out. I was exhausted, but it felt important to drive home, and my mother and Yael crawled into the passenger side of the pickup without a word, as if they barely registered the blood splattering the floor and the vinyl seats. As I turned down Hanassi, shopkeepers closed up their stalls, wheeling out barrels of unsold strawberries, folding card tables back into vans. It seemed impossible that I'd sped down this road only earlier today. I rolled down the window, hoping the air might slap me awake, but it was hotter outside than in the truck.

As I steered onto the highway, my mother and Yael pulled out their cells and began a phone tree to spread the news. "They had to amputate below the shin," my mother announced before even saying hello. "But, for an accident like this, it's the best-case scenario." Those were the surgeon's exact words, and by her clipped tone I knew the situation wasn't real to her yet. I didn't think it was for me, either. I'd almost passed out when I saw Asaaf after surgery, lying on that narrow hospital bed with his left leg bandaged and half-gone. He was attached to all sorts of bleating monitors and a pain pump he kept pushing, and every couple minutes a religious guy would peek inside, trying to get us to pray. Normally my brother wouldn't have waited a second before telling that guy off, but he was too drugged to notice—and still, I knew this *was* the best we could hope for. That's what I'd heard all day: if I hadn't gotten my brother to the ER so quickly he would have lost too much blood and probably would have died. Everyone had said it—the doctor, the nurses, the surgeon, even the receptionist—and each time, my mother gathered me into a hug and thanked me, over and over.

And now she thanked me again as she scrolled through every one of her contacts, and by the time I parked outside our bungalow, the entire moshav was waiting on the porch, along with guys from Asaaf's unit and even his best friend Dedy, who still had three days left of service and must have finagled time off and driven up from Gaza. My mother still sounded composed as she led everyone into the kitchen, but when she got to the part about the amputation, her voice got stuck in her throat.

"Anybody thirsty?" I said, to say something, and all at once everyone—there must have been thirty people—sprang into action. Uri from the dairy turned on the kettle while his wife Hadas sifted through our cupboards for tea. Dedy uncorked a bottle of Arak and passed glasses around. "To Oren," he said, lifting his drink, and when everyone turned to face me, I caught my breath. The last time I saw Dedy, at a barbeque Asaaf had dragged me to in Rosh Pina, he'd spent the whole night hassling me for pouring beer in the bonfire. All of Asaaf's friends treated me that way: like the group's collective little brother, knocking me around but still letting me tag along, though at twenty-one I was only a year younger than they were. "It was nothing," I said, clinking my glass to his, then quickly setting it down, suddenly afraid I was showing off.

"Bullshit," he said. "You were going what, one-fifty?"

My mother came behind me and rested her hands on my shoulders. "It's not just the speed, it's knowing all the side roads."

I could have stayed in that conversation all day but knew to shrug sheepishly, though really I'd gone one-sixty, one-sixty-five in the valley—and it was only then that I remembered my commander had no idea about the accident, and was expecting me at the base in the morning. I took the cordless to my bedroom. As I dialed his cell while everyone in the kitchen carried on without me, I suddenly felt too large for my twin bed, with its striped comforter and solar system decals above, too important to be calling a commander I couldn't stand, even though his voice softened when I told him what happened.

"Take two weeks of emergency leave," he said. "Two and a half if you need it." I knew just where he was: outside the dining hall, hocking watermelon seeds into a bucket while his soldiers filed out from dish duty. "Yigal or Stas will cover for you, no problem."

"I appreciate it," I said, though really I'd have been happier if he told me I'd never spend another day in the army sedan, carting Lieutenant HaLevi to his meetings. We always went to the same places, down to headquarters in Tel Aviv or up to the air force base in Haifa. Sometimes he'd even have the gall to order me to pull over and get him a Fanta at one of the stands along the highway, and I'd wait in line at some roadside hummus place, picturing my brother doing real work in the territories.

Before he was discharged, Asaaf had commanded a unit guarding a settlement in Hebron, and was away a month at a time—so different from how I had it: home every evening, weekends working in the crops or feeding the chickens. Sometimes I'd be cleaning the coop and think about Asaaf setting up roadblocks with an M16 across his shoulder, his uniform matted with dirt and sweat—then feel like an idiot for glamorizing work I knew he hated. There was nothing worse than guarding land he just wanted to give back, Asaaf was always saying, nothing worse than having one of those Americans stop by his station to tell him, in English, that he was doing holy work. But he didn't want to be jailed for refusing to serve and also didn't have it in him to lie to the army, pleading insanity, the way many others got out of duty—and even signed on for an extra year at his commander's urging. Asaaf was like that: he'd spend the whole weekend back home cursing the war, but right when he had to return to it, he'd snap back into soldier mode, standing up a little straighter as he buttoned the uniform my mother had just ironed, pulling his gun from underneath his bed without a word. I think there was a part of him that liked to hate what he did, to have something to bump up against.

Asaaf was forever telling me I should be grateful I hadn't been placed in combat, and that what he really wanted was to get out of the country and be someplace quiet. Lately all he'd been talking about was his post-army trip to the U.S. with Yael: spending four months on an organic yoga farm in California and then another two driving down the coast and into Mexico with Dedy; they were supposed to leave in a week. When I asked why he'd take a sixteen-hour flight to spend more of his life picking fruit and mucking cow shit, where he'd be forced to do *yoga*, for God's sake, my brother smiled— not the wide white grin he walked through the world with but a smaller one, more with his eyes, and said, "Yael's been obsessed with this farm for months," and that's when I knew he really loved her.

And then, last week, Asaaf sauntered through our front door in his civilian clothes for the first time in four years. The entire time he was in the army, my mother and I ate dinner in silence while the radio played, waiting for news of clashes or casualties. When it came on she'd put down her fork and wait, taking off her glasses and working a finger into the corner of her eye, letting out a long slow breath when the broadcast was over. But that night with Asaaf back home, she flicked the dial to the classical station instead. She prepared his favorite meal, schnitzel and fries, salad and rice, and they quickly fell into their private discussion about the prime minister and the upcoming U.N. negotiations, the sort of things she probably spoke about with our father before he died, back when I was still an infant, long before Asaaf assumed his place at the table—and by the time I came up with something to contribute, they were two or three conversations beyond me.

Asaaf slept late and spent afternoons tooling around on the tractor or strolling through the citrus groves. As he and Yael walked through the property, moshavniks popped up from the crops and congratulated him on his medal of valor. Asaaf had told my mother she was being ridiculous when she made a show of hanging it from the living room shelf, but out there he nodded humbly, thanking the workers, though later he told me they were fools if they believed medals meant anything. They'd never have known; he had a way of talking to people that made them feel both witty and important, and sometimes I wondered if I was the only one on earth who knew his other, judgmental side: repeating their words under his breath as we walked away, twisting their compliments into something crass and idiotic. I watched him and Yael zigzag through the squash and tomatoes and down to the dairy, and when he leaned in to kiss her, I felt my heart cave.

He'd always had girlfriends, but before Yael they'd been the kind who lounged inside on their cell phones rather than working in the fields. I'd known her for years—back in high school

we used to ride the bus home together while Asaaf stayed after
for track practice, sharing vending machine junk, playing cards
and road games I knew were childish but liked because I usually won. It would be inaccurate to say I enjoyed those rides
together, when I always felt both terrified and thrilled sitting
beside her as the bus bumped through the valley. She was more
serious than almost anyone I knew back then, as if she were
constantly looking beyond school, our neighborhood, even the
country. That she believed she deserved a different, better life
than the people around her hadn't even struck me as snobbish,
simply because she made whomever she was talking to, myself
included, feel as though we deserved it too. Still, whenever I
was with her I felt as if I were on uneven ground, that I could
say one stupid thing and she'd find someplace else to sit.

But that never happened, and those rides carried through
to graduation, which was right around the time Asaaf noticed
her. She'd never seemed his type—not just that she was always
in sweats and flip-flops; more that she didn't even seem to exist
within the same orbit as the other girls he usually dated, the
ones who threw as much of themselves into getting his attention as he did into winning the hundred-meter dash. But then
he went for her, without a thought that I might be interested
myself, and she surprised me by falling for him as quickly and
gushingly as all the others. And just like that, our time together
seemed blotted-out and forgotten, as she lay beside Asaaf on
our sofa, watching TV at night, or scrambling eggs in the morning while he leaned against the counter in his boxers, swigging
juice straight from the carton. But that wasn't the worst part.
It was that they actually made sense together. She made him
nicer, he made her more relaxed, and together they were like

some strong, unstoppable force, breezing through life on a sleek and glorious ship while the rest of us watched from the shore.

She was the one girlfriend of his my mother could stand, the one girl who helped around the house, the dairy, in the garden, sifting through the mud for nightcrawlers. That's disgusting, Asaaf had said as the bugs skirted down her fingers and into the compost, but Yael shook her head. You see their pink bellies? They're kind of beautiful, she said, and in her hands they actually were.

✳   ✳   ✳

AND NOW, for the second time this week, I welcomed Asaaf back home. He was in a clean white t-shirt with the medical tag still dangling from his wrist, and my mother had to swerve his wheelchair around the driveway to avoid potholes. His face was the same—three days in the hospital hadn't paled him—but his eyes were sleepy and red from the painkillers, and his left sweatpant leg was folded over neatly, like the flap of an envelope.

Asaaf squinted up at me as my mother ran back to the car for his duffel. "What are you looking at?"

"Nothing." I wanted to stare at him for a long time, but looked at the ground instead.

He tried to tip himself back to get through the open screen door, but the wheels banged against the raised wood I only now noticed separated the porch from the kitchen. He grunted and pushed again, but the wheelchair didn't budge. "Here," I said, reaching for the arms, "let me help." But he swatted my hand away, and for a minute I just stood there, listening to the wheels hit the threshold over and over.

Behind us, people trickled up the driveway, carrying foil-wrapped cookies and cakes. Dedy and the neighbors were here again, along with high school classmates Asaaf probably hadn't thought about in years. I'd made a dozen family visits like this one—earlier this month, even, when a soldier from the moshav had been wounded in a raid on his base—and knew to wheel Asaaf to his room and stay out of the way while the guests lined up to see him. But every one of them came forward and slapped my back and asked about the drive—and as I stood beside his bed, the only thing stopping me from holding court all day was knowing I'd seem even more impressive if I didn't.

As the crowd shuffled into his room I followed my mother, hoping to be of use. She moved quickly, making sure guests' glasses were filled and then rushing outside to pull our good napkins and tablecloth from the clothesline. She'd always been this kind of worker, quick and impatient, and I saw it reflected throughout our house: in the sagging shelves filled with paperbacks and my father's old Yehoram Gaon records; in the herbs she repotted in anything she could find, coffee cans or olive oil tins. It felt good working as a team, and for the first time she didn't seem annoyed as I trailed behind her: handing me cucumbers to dice into a salad, asking me to drag over the picnic benches from the groves so there was enough seating in our yard.

When I checked on Asaaf, he was in bed with the guests all around him. His bandaged leg was propped on a pillow and hidden beneath a blanket. The shades were up, and his bedside table, which a few days ago had held gum wrappers and cigarettes and keys, was now cluttered with orange prescription bottles and rolls of gauze.

"It's good it was below the knee," Dedy, self-proclaimed expert on everything, was saying.

"Better for the prosthesis," Yael said. She twisted her long dark hair into a braid and curled up beside Asaaf. I had no idea how she could seem so unfazed. Maybe it was hearing guns fired all day as a shooting instructor in the army, or maybe she was just tougher than I'd thought.

"And that won't be a problem," Asaaf said. "I'll be so bored by tomorrow I'll be doing laps around the house." This was the solid, capable tone he always used in public, but when he sat up to face the group, his blanket slid off. Everyone stood there, silently rocking back on their heels, looking as if they wanted to leave but didn't know if they should. They all had to know what a bandaged leg looked like, and anyway there was nothing to see, just that sweatpant leg pinned back. But still they stared, and suddenly the last place I wanted to be was in that room, so I slipped out the front door.

Outside the moshav gates, the brown roads were almost desolate: just a few kids selling sunflowers at the bus stop. Sheep huddled together in the open yellow field, as if desperate for contact, and above them, far beyond, ran the long barbed fence tracing the Syrian border. Being in these hills reminded me of all the days Asaaf and I spent playing out here as boys. Other times it made me miss a part of my life I couldn't even remember, before I lost my father to a mine while he was on reserve duty, almost twenty years ago. I imagined a different mother then, sleepy and smiling, leaning into my father's knees like in the photos she kept shelved away in albums.

Across the road, I climbed down a hill and peered into the

valley. Lake Kinneret glittered below, dotted with figures so small I couldn't tell whether they were swimmers or ducks bobbing along in the ripples. If I stood still in this spot, sometimes my voice would bounce off the hills and I'd yell things I couldn't say to anyone, like for my mother to get off my back or for Lieutenant HaLevi to drive his sedan off a cliff.

But this time I didn't know what to say. I stood there, looking out at the water, then down at my feet. Finally I yelled, "Fuuuuck!" which felt so good that I yelled it again. I threw it out into the distance, but nothing came back.

❊   ❊   ❊

THAT NIGHT every sound jolted me awake: the insect chorus outside my window, my mother's slippers flapping down the hall. I wanted to say it was thoughts of Asaaf that kept me up, but in truth I was too amped from the past couple days. I'd never gotten so much attention in my life—and before I could stop myself, I let my thoughts speed to where they always wanted to go, sliding a hand into my boxers, thinking about Yael.

I finished off and walked into the bathroom, and there she was, brushing her teeth. Her hair was long and loose and crinkly from the braid, and she wore one of Asaaf's t-shirts and a pair of his sweatpants, folded low at her hips.

She spit in the sink. "I'll be out in a second."

I turned to leave, but didn't. Shadows rimmed her eyes, and though they could have been remnants of makeup, I saw the exhaustion behind them. "He asleep?" I said, pulling my toothbrush from the medicine cabinet, as if this were our nighttime ritual.

"He's taking up the whole bed. I don't want to move him over, not like it would work anyway, he's so knocked out, and—"

"You'd rather be on the couch."

She scrutinized her face in the mirror. Her beauty had always seemed like more of a distraction to her than anything else, though she had to be aware of it—everyone knew the army placed the best-looking girls at the shooting range so the guys would perform better. But now I saw how mottled her skin looked beneath the yellow lights, the way her mouth cinched together.

"God, listen to me," she said. "I sound horrible. But it's just—you know tonight I had to scoot him over so he could reach the bedpan? He can't even do that by himself." Then she let out a long slow breath I hadn't even known she was holding, and all at once it was as if something inside her had split straight open, and there she was, this whole other Yael, drained and exhausted and quiet. I thought about pulling her into a hug, but wasn't sure she wanted me to. She could back away, or, worse, stand stiffly until I let go. But then I went for it, just like that. Up close she smelled fresh, like a bar of soap just unwrapped from its package. Her cheek was warm against my shoulder, and under the lights I could see the pink gleam of her scalp. She was tiny inside Asaaf's t-shirt. Her hair was falling over my arms, and as I held her, I felt the night expanding. Moths were banging into the window, sprinklers were tinkling through the grass, but all of that seemed distant and irrelevant. Everything real was happening right here, inside this blue-and-white tiled bathroom, as if we were reaching some different, newer kind of intimacy that had nothing and everything to do with my brother, and the longer I stood there, the more I wanted him to stay sequestered in his bed, drugged and dependent, so my life could finally roll into place.

Then she let go. "Thanks, Oren," she said, squeezing my arm. She picked up her toothbrush and opened the door, and though that squeeze felt more sisterly than anything else, it was something. "Anytime," I said, and slipped down the hall back to bed.

❊   ❊   ❊

It was still dark that night when I awoke to my brother's screams. When I ran into his room, my mother and Yael were standing at his bed, trying to wake him. His shirt was pushed over his stomach, and he was sobbing in his sleep, reaching for the place where his leg used to be.

"We think the Dilaudid wore off," Yael said, "but not the sleeping pills." I could see what she'd meant about sharing a bed with Asaaf: he consumed the entire mattress, his one leg splayed and his arms out on either side of him, as if in a permanent stretch. His eyes were closed, and he still smelled like the hospital, of bleach and rubbing alcohol. My mother shook him by the shoulders. "Wake up, Asaafaleh," she said. I hadn't heard her call him that since elementary school, but it seemed to work. He looked up, as if he recognized us but was in too much pain to nod. He was crying, but that wasn't how I knew he was hurting—I could see it in the way his eyes rolled back, the way he gripped the sheet with both hands. "Sit up for a second while I give you a pill," my mother whispered, and when I glanced at Yael, hunched beside him with her arms across her chest, I swiped a pillow off my brother's bed and set her up on the couch.

✵   ✵   ✵

BY THE time I woke the following morning, my mother had already talked to Asaaf's doctor, a nurse and an orthopedic surgeon up at Rambam Medical, who suggested he be switched to morphine. When she asked me to pick up the prescription while she waited for the nurse to stop by, I happily agreed: anything to get out of the house, even for an hour. I was unlocking the door to my mother's hatchback when Yael ran out. "Okay if I tag along?"

I hadn't left the moshav in days, except to go to and from the hospital, and as I pulled onto Sapir Street now, it felt good to speed again, my foot pressing effortlessly onto the gas. I'd always liked the mornings best, before the heat settled in and mist hovered over the valley. But today the sun was so strong it felt as though a hot-air fan was blowing right in my face, and all the workers along the road were already taking a water break. I turned on the AC as Yael fiddled with the radio dial, and for a few minutes we rode in silence. Then she said, "Your mom's so on top of things. Makes me feel a little guilty."

"She makes everybody feel guilty," I said. "That's her thing. She's just good under pressure."

"I guess she did raise you two alone."

"Yeah, but I'll bet she was always that way. When a bunch of our neighbors got jobs outside the moshav, she just took on more farmwork," I said. "And you know she used to work folding chutes? If she messed up even once, some soldier could have died." I regretted the words before they'd left my mouth. There was no point in reminding Yael that I was the only one doing immigrant work in a family of commanders—

starting with my grandfather, who'd escaped Vilna, fought in the Givati Brigade back in '48 and helped found the moshav, back when it was four families dredging a swamp. No point reminding her that I'd failed my placements while my brother was out collecting medals. The physical part hadn't been so tough, but ever since I was little I'd frozen during exams—and during the interview, I'd stared at the officer's boots tapping the linoleum floor to a quick, steady beat and gone completely blank. Then my army assignment came in the mail and I had to hand that letter over to my mother—and the worst part was the nonchalance she'd feigned, saying, "Everyone's good at different things," and I'd had to pretend to believe her bullshit answer.

Yael and I had forty minutes to kill at the mall before Asaaf's prescription was filled, so we flipped through magazines at the newsstand, then rode the escalator up to Ozen HaShlishi and listened to music. I bought chips and we shared them on a bench. A guy I knew from high school walked out of McDonald's and was halfway down the escalator when he turned and saw me. I waved, grateful someone noticed us.

"So you're really just going home when you're discharged?" she said, and I stared at her: she talked this way with my brother, sharing random bits of conversations that must have been running in her head and assuming he'd understand. It had always made them seem so close, as if every sentence were some intimate, privileged thing. Of course I wanted to go traveling. But the other drivers in my unit couldn't afford vacations like the U.S.—Amare had already lined up a job with Nesher Cabs at the airport, and Stas was saving up to visit his family in Odessa.

"Who told you that?" I said.

"Asaaf. He was worried you didn't have anything going on."

"When did he say that?"

"I don't know. A month ago?"

I hated thinking about them pitying me—as if my life could be sketched out so easily, going straight from finishing the army next month to tilling the same fields for sixty years to being one of those old moshavniks who was too arthritic to milk the goats but still hung out by the dairy, just to have a place to spend his days. "Maybe I *like* the moshav." I was filled with a sudden need to let her know I'd be missed if I left. "I help put on the harvest fest in September, and it's nice how quiet it gets during the winter."

"Asaaf can't stand the winter there," she said. "He goes crazy during the rain."

"Asaaf doesn't do shit during the rainy season. He just likes to complain."

She smiled. "He *does* like to complain, doesn't he?"

"You have no idea," I said, getting excited. "The moment he's back in civilian clothes he's a fucking baby. I still don't know how you got him to agree to another farm."

"Oh, he whined," she said. "But it's totally worth it—the woman who runs it does biodynamic everything on land twice the size of yours. Everybody pitches tents and sleeps out there too, not like here where the moment the sun's down we're all in front of the TV." It was just like her to have found this place, some secret part of America I never would have known to look for myself, beautiful and forested and calm, where people slept in the middle of a field, unafraid of anyone or anything coming after you. Suddenly she looked like the Yael I'd always known, so enthusiastic that on any other girl her earnestness might have embarrassed me, and before I could stop myself I said, "What's with California now?"

"I'm not going without him."

"What does he say?"

"That I should, of course. But there's no way he means it."

"He does," I said, and knew it. I wondered what it was like to love someone so deeply their happiness overpowered your own. I had no idea—I only knew that right then, sitting beside her, I was seized by a genuine moment of boldness and wanted to use it, before it disappeared.

"I'll be discharged in a month," I said. "Let me come with you."

"You?" she said. And then she didn't say anything else. She wasn't even looking at me. I followed her eyes, but all I saw was the never-ending line of people outside the mall entrance, waiting for the guards to scan them through. We were so close I could see all these things that should have made her less beautiful: the faint fuzz above her lip, the constellation of acne scars on her jawline. It was requiring a lot of effort to breathe, and I hadn't realized I was flicking at a hangnail until my thumb started to bleed.

"This is all so crazy," she said finally. Her voice was flat and small, and I didn't even know which part of the craziness she was referring to.

Then she turned to me. "Just promise," she said, swallowing, "that when we're out on the farm, you'll let me win at cards at least a couple times."

She smiled, and I saw something pass over her face, a flash of recognition—and the thought that all this time she'd remembered those rides gave me such a jolt that I stood up. I took her hand and led her to the escalator, as though we were about to navigate a dangerous intersection. Then I let go, stepped onto the moving stairs and she followed right behind. I could feel her gaze on me the whole ride down to the pharmacy but knew not to turn around, not even once—a move I'd seen my brother make on a hundred occasions but was only now, for the first time, pulling off perfectly myself.

❊   ❊   ❊

THE MORPHINE worked for Asaaf's pain but made him nauseated. He threw up his breakfast, then his lunch. The three of us hovered over him, fluffing his pillows, feeling his forehead, offering dry toast and seltzer, which he threw up as well. His shades were down, blocking out the sun and everything else, and even in the dim, cool room with the AC on high, Asaaf was visibly sweating. When he rolled onto his back, his penis slid out of his boxers. All three of us saw it, all three of us said nothing, and I wondered if Asaaf was too drugged to even know. Finally my mother pulled the sheet to his chest and she and Yael stepped back into the hall, but I couldn't stop watching him. It was horrible, seeing a guy once so in control of his body rolling and squirming and dry-heaving now that everything he'd ingested was in the wastebasket beside him.

"Would you get the fuck out of here, Oren?" he said finally, opening one eye. He'd never talked that way to me before and it stung more than I wanted to admit, and when his new crutches arrived in the mail later that day, I devoted myself to putting them together, grateful to have a project that kept me out of his room. My mother had ordered them from Jerusalem, and they were about a thousand times nicer than the junky pair the hospital had given us, with aluminum legs and removable handgrips. I'd always liked these kinds of tasks—when I was little I used to take apart our answering machine to see how it worked, then screw it back together—but it was distracting having Yael next to me, reading the instruction manual aloud, and I kept putting the underarm pads on backwards.

By late afternoon, Asaaf's food was staying down and Yael went to check on him. She didn't have to say anything: as she walked slowly down the hall, I knew she was going to tell him. She stepped into his room and closed the door behind her. I stared at the instructions and told myself the least I could do was give them privacy. Outside the window, my mother paced up the driveway, talking on the cordless. I took a deep breath, let it out quick. Then I tiptoed down the hall and pressed my ear to the door.

"I'll be here when you're back—it's not like *I'm* going anywhere," Asaaf said. He laughed, but it sounded breathless and raw, like he was blowing out a match.

"And Oren?"

"Why would I give a shit? You can nerd out on the farm together."

"Really?"

"Really," Asaaf said, and when Yael didn't respond he said it again, and again, until they fell into silence. I pictured them on the bed, neither of them knowing what to say next. Maybe they were holding hands. Or maybe Yael had tucked her head under his armpit, the way they used to lie together, as if her body were an extension of his. Finally the television flicked on; I heard the false ring of a laugh track. Amid its buzz was the rustle of sheets, a few muffled breaths, and then it got quiet. I heard Yael apologize.

"It's okay," Asaaf mumbled. "Let's try again."

"Like this?"

"Maybe this way. Be patient?"

And she was, until they were hushed for so long I assumed my brother had fallen asleep. I imagined him taking up the entire bed, Yael sequestered to the side, sweaty and anxious and wondering how long she had to stay in that vomitus room—and then I imagined her walking out and finding me at the door, so I went into the kitchen, where our neighbors Uri and Hadas were coming in with dinner platters.

"Tonight we've got salad, beets and a kibbeh," Uri said. "Your mom says that's your favorite, right, Oren?"

I nodded, genuinely touched.

Yael walked in and gave everyone a halfhearted wave. She rubbed her eyes, as if she'd just stopped crying or was trying to keep the tears from coming out at all.

"How's the morphine working?" my mother asked.

"Better," Yael said, "but he was complaining about itching."

"I'll go check on him," my mother said, but Hadas stopped her and said, "Let me. Why don't you all relax a minute?"

I did what I was told. I sat on the couch and Hadas handed me a soda. Uri turned on the oven and set the tray of kibbeh inside, and as the smell of onions and cinnamon filled the room, I circled an arm around my mother, the other around Yael and waited for my dinner.

❉ ❉ ❉

THE NEIGHBORS' visits lasted two more days, through Shabbat. Then another week began, and Uri hosed the blood off the tractor and worked the fields himself. My mother went back to the vines, and that evening, when no one came by with a hot meal, we cooked the same hurried dinner we always had. Once again we ate with the radio on, this time tuned to the weather as temperatures climbed into the forties and there was talk of the heat wave not letting up for weeks. Now that Yael had decided to go to America she was around less: driving around buying gear or seeing her parents in Yoqneam. And with only a week to prepare for the trip before I was back in the army, I was busier than I'd been in years. It was as if we were all desperate for a reason to escape the house—but Asaaf, who needed fresh air more than any of us, refused to leave his bed. His TV was always on, like a never-ending soundtrack, and though he should have been on crutches by now, they were still leaning against his dresser, unused. Every time my mother peeked into his room and tried to get him to start doing exercises, warning about blood clots, he'd say he wasn't ready. And when I suggested we take a walk, even up the driveway and back, he snapped that his room was off-limits and to get out. The sound of the TV, and his smell, began to stop bothering me—and even seeing him in bed started to feel normal, as if he had become as much a part of it as the mattress and box springs.

It cost too much to pay a nurse for more than Sunday home visits, so now that my mother and Yael were running around all day and I still had another week of leave, it was my job to check on Asaaf and to cook for everyone. But on Asaaf's ninth day back from the hospital, my mother didn't come home to eat at noon, or at one, and finally at two I went out in the fields to look for her. I found her hunched over the tomato vines. She was in her work clothes, cutoffs and sneakers and a ratty green t-shirt, and when I knelt beside her I saw the blackened bottoms on the tomatoes. I walked through the rows of vines and checked every piece of fruit—just to do something, really, since I knew she'd already inspected the entire crop, probably twice. Only about half the fruit was black, but blossom end rot spread quickly enough that it would be on every tomato by the morning.

"I left a message at the canning factories in Sederot and Kiryat Gat," my mother said. The open-air markets wouldn't buy blemished produce, so at this point all we could do was sell them for sauce. But if end rot was happening here it was affecting every farm in the north, and the others probably had the sense to call the canneries the moment the first black splotch appeared. Usually my mother would have been five steps ahead and it frustrated me that no one on the moshav had picked up her slack this week—but I had a feeling they'd tried and she just hadn't let them.

"Tell me what I can do," I said.

She was staring at the vines with the same strained expression I'd always assumed she reserved for me, and as I watched her now, I knew my mother wasn't harsh—she just had the face of a person who'd spent too much of her life looking at terrible things.

"Nothing else to do out here," she said quietly. "But Asaaf needs his lunch," so I ran home and brought him a glass of grapefruit juice and a sandwich.

"The crop's rotting," I said, unfolding the legs of his tray. "Think there's any place that'll take them?"

"How would I know?" he said, more to the basketball game on TV than to me, and I blinked: he'd always at least pretended to know the answer.

"We're pretty much screwed out of thousands of shekels," I said.

"Oren?"

I stepped closer.

"I just want to be alone. Would you shut the door behind you?" he said, closing his eyes and falling into a sleep so deep and fast it had to be false.

I roamed the house, wondering if I should go back outside but knowing my mother would want me home with Asaaf. I opened the refrigerator, scrutinizing the cool shelves until the motor kicked in. Outside the window, Uri chugged by on the tractor, cutting through the fields and up to the toolshed. Finally I flopped on the living room sofa, settling on the same basketball game my brother had on two doors down.

Israel was up 76 to 48 against Montenegro, but one of our players was still running to the sidelines and waving his hands in the referee's face, arguing over the basket, when my mother returned. Sweat lined her upper lip and the neck of her t-shirt. When she knocked on my brother's door and he yelled "Sleeping!" her shoulders sagged and she went into the kitchen. She pulled a mug off the dish rack, her hand rattling as she stirred in Nescafé. "The canneries aren't buying anymore," she said. "I tried all four." She kicked out the chair beside her and I sat down. "We'll lose fifteen thousand shekels, easy. And this one," she said, nodding toward Asaaf's closed door, "he can't even *try* to get on his crutches?"

She pressed her fingers to her face and rubbed her temples, and I noticed the lines fanning the corners of her mouth. I hadn't seen her show this much of herself since I found her on the couch after a bad first date, years ago, listening to Yehoram Gaon with her knees tucked beneath her. I took her hand now, callused and tanned with rims of dirt wedged beneath her nails. "Listen," I said. "I know it's been rough. Let me know what I can do."

"Thanks, Oren," she said, squeezing back. "You know what you *can* do?"

I looked up at her. I smiled. "Anything."

"Start tackling these dishes. They've been piling up all week and I've got to find Uri and Hadas."

I wasn't sure what I'd expected, but going from a lifesaving drive to dish patrol in under two weeks wasn't it. But I had a feeling that drive no longer mattered to my mother. There would be no more praise, no bravery medal engraved in my honor to hang from the living room shelf. Mine were minor heroics, at best, and when I returned to work, I knew the lieutenant would continue to ignore me as I turned out of the loud, dusty base and onto the highway. No one was thinking about my drive anymore, and in a week we wouldn't even be thinking about the tomatoes: there would be something else to deal with, and something after that—the way it had been since I could remember, and sensed it always would be.

So I stood up and cleared the table. My mother kissed my head and walked outside, and a moment later I watched her bicycle wheels kick up dirt and wind down the narrow drive-way, growing smaller until she was just a glittery black speck in the day.

I hadn't even finished scrubbing the pans when it was time for Asaaf's next round of pills. When I let myself into his room, his sheets were tangled on the floor, giving me my first real look at the stump. A plastic brace kept his leg in place, and covering the bottom was an ace bandage, wrapped tightly up his thigh. He saw me watching and I turned away.

"It's okay," he said. "I don't care if you look." He sat up and unwound the cloth.

Up close, freckles of dried blood circled the wound. The skin around it was red and puckered, and the stitches were starting to fall out. I didn't know what I wanted more: to touch the ripples of raised skin, running my fingers over the bumps, or to bolt from the room. "Does it still hurt?"

"The first few days? Like a motherfucker. Now, not so much." Maybe it was the morphine making Asaaf forget his room was off-limits, but still I edged onto his bed. "Another month and they'll fit me for the prosthetic."

I tried, but I couldn't imagine something so pink and slick attached to Asaaf's hairy thigh. "Why not get it sooner?"

"If I put weight on the stump before it's healed, it could crack."

"Nasty."

"Seriously nasty. Only grosser is if it gets infected," Asaaf said, and for a moment he seemed not to be talking about him-self anymore, but as if he were examining the stump like a specimen, the way we would light ants on fire with a magnify-ing glass as kids, watching them crackle and siss.

"Is Yael here for dinner tonight?" I said.

"Depends on how long it takes in Jerusalem—she's getting her passport renewed."

I didn't know what to say. The socks Yael must have kicked off in her sleep were balled on the floor. I picked them up and tossed them in the hamper, and when I turned around Asaaf sat all the way up. "Listen, Oren, before you start buying things for the trip, go through my closet. I just bought a good backpack, a sleeping pad and a fleece—"

"Why are you alright with this?"

"What do you mean, why?" He looked right at me. "You saved my life, right? Even though you're too weird to ever say it. So take all the gear I bought before you start charging things you know you can't afford."

Asaaf was saying all of this as casually as if he were offering me half his sandwich, and as I sat beside him, I'd never hated myself more. "I'm in love with her," I blurted. "I have been for years."

For a second he was quiet, as if considering every one of my words. Then he said, "Everybody knows, Oren. There's a reason they didn't put you undercover."

"But I'm spending the next four months traveling with your girlfriend, Asaaf, and the whole time, while you're here in bed, I'll be thinking about how to make something happen with her." I couldn't believe I was telling him these things, but once I'd started talking it was like a valve had opened, and I couldn't screw it closed. "And the thing is," I said, realizing as I heard my own voice that it might actually be true, "I think something could."

Asaaf shrugged. "Who knows? Maybe it will."

"What are you even talking about?" I said. "She's your *girl-friend*. Doesn't this situation seem fucked to you?"

"A lot of things seem fucked," Asaaf said quietly, then turned back to the TV.

He'd never sounded like such a defeatist. The brother I knew would have found his way onto that plane to the U.S. The brother I knew would have wheeled himself down the bumpy path to the yoga farm and spent the next four months sleeping on some uncomfortable floor mat, just to be with her. The brother I knew would have told me I was a betraying little fool for making a move on his girlfriend—not, he would add, that I had a fraction of a chance anyway—and then would have kicked me out of the room, yelling not to let the door hit me on the way out. Any of that would have been better than this, so I said, a little wildly, "If you wanted things to be good with her, maybe you shouldn't have asked for her help taking a piss."

Finally he faced me, and it wasn't the anger I expected but genuine bewilderment. "She told you that?"

"Who do you think she's been confiding in?"

"Get out."

I didn't move.

"I mean it, Oren." He tried to kick me off the bed with his right leg, but I scooted out of his reach. He tried again. Only the breakfast tray rattled.

"I'm warning you to get out right now," Asaaf said, but it was so hard to take his threats seriously that I couldn't even look at him. I stared at the TV, watching a player sprint across the court, and that's when Asaaf grabbed me from behind and knocked me to the bed. I smelled his sweat on the sheets and when I rolled over, he hit my jaw, then my nose. The punches seemed to be the best he could muster, and I had a feeling they were hurting him more than they were me. But he kept at it. He climbed on top, teetering on his right side for support, and when he hit me between the eyes my head pulsed and my vision went blurry. In my spotty white haze I saw how easily I could push him over and take the upper hand. But I didn't. I lay back and took the hit, and then another, because for that second I had my brother back, towering over me with those dark muscled arms, his green eyes bright and flashing and victorious.

My Grandmother
Tells Me This Story

Some say the story begins in Europe, and your mother would no doubt interrupt and say it begins in New York, but that's just because she can't imagine the world before she entered it. And yes, I know you think it begins specifically in Belarus, because that's what your grandfather tells you. I've heard him describing those black sedans speeding down Pinsker Street. I've been married to the man almost sixty years and know how he is with you—he makes every word sound like a secret. But he wasn't even there. He was with his youth group by then and even though I *was* there I don't remember being scared—even when they knocked on our door, I didn't know what was happening. Even when they dragged us outside with our overstuffed suitcases spilling into the street, shouting through megaphones to walk in the road with the livestock, I still didn't know. I was thirteen.

The story really starts in the sewers. Everybody in the uniform factory whispered about them, and everybody had a different theory. Some said they were an escape route a plumber had spent years charting, an underground system of tunnels running from Poland to Belarus to Lithuania. Others said they were an impossible maze with no way out. But the truth was that when my mother pulled me aside after only six days in the factory and whispered that she'd worked out a plan for me—smuggled vodka for the guards, a shoulder bared, my poor father, a lifetime of loving a woman who knew just how to spark another man's sympathy—I simply stood there, taking notes in my head. After dinner, she said, I'd slip past the guards and down the street, around two corners and up a road where I'd see the slats of a sewer. The grate would slide off easily, she said, and she and my father would find me soon. I had no reason not to believe that was true, no way of knowing the sewers would lead me to the forest—that night all I knew, as I climbed inside the manhole and down the metal ladder, was that it smelled worse than anything I'd imagined, of shit and piss and garbage.

It was black in there, and dank and cool, the ceiling so low I sank to my knees and crawled. I just kept following the crowd of voices—in Yiddish, which was both comforting and horrible, hearing that language forbidden in the factory. Then there was a rumble, and water rushed in and knocked me down. I gasped and tried to wade forward. The sewer started filling up and I felt around in the slimy water for the person in front of me. But everybody seemed far ahead, and it took me a minute to realize dinner must have been ending aboveground, everybody washing dishes and taking baths and pouring water down the drain all at once.

Soon I had no sense of how long I'd been underground. My eyes grew accustomed to the darkness and I saw the shapes around me. The woman up ahead, the hunched slope of her back, the walls of the sewer. The shadow of a rat before it ran across my arm. Then my whole body started to wobble and I knew I wouldn't make it through a wave of morning dishwashing, so when I saw lines of light through the grate, I stopped.

Keep moving, the woman behind me whispered.

But I couldn't. I waited for the group to go by and when I heard nothing above, I slowly lifted the grate and climbed onto the streets of a village that looked as if it had been passed over by the war. I wasn't used to the sun after an entire night in the sewers—it was just rolling up over the houses, and the forest beyond was so bright it looked painted. Dirt, river, sky— everything stunned me. That the wooden cottages lining the road were still intact, that people were feeding their horses and selling vegetables and sweeping leaves into the gutter.

A man walked past with his young daughter and she stared. The father took one look at me, yanked her arm and hurried down the road. I knew not to spend another minute standing there in the daylight, so I crossed the road and entered the forest. It was cold and dim, and when I leaned against a tree trunk, exhaustion came right at me.

I wasn't sure how long I'd been asleep when I heard footsteps. I opened my eyes and stared up—into the barrel of a gun. I swallowed, hard, refusing to make eye contact. That much I knew. I looked at the sticks and pinecones littering the forest floor and thought up a story. I was lost, searching for mushrooms, and could he help me find my way back? But how to explain the smell, or my work uniform, and before I opened my mouth, a boy put down the gun and said my name.

How odd that the first word I heard in the forest was my

own name, and for a minute I wondered if that night in the
sewers had made me crazy. Then I looked up. I know how
you see your grandfather, sweet and smiling, always insisting
that we put on a movie after dinner and then dozing on the
sofa halfway through. Your chess partner, your theater date,
the man who checks out the minute your mother and I start
up. You wouldn't have recognized him. His long, bony face
splotchy from the sun, his light brown beard growing in sparse,
threadbare patches—he was only fifteen—and his straight hair
obviously hacked off with a knife. But even with that terrible
haircut, even with a rifle over one shoulder and paper sacks
swinging from the other, he still looked like the same Leon
Moscowitz I'd grown up with.

It was one of the great miracles of my life, finding someone from home, right there, in the middle of the woods. But I
won't lie and say he was the person I'd wanted to see. I barely
knew him back in our village. He was two grades above me
and had struck me as bigheaded and bossy, one of those boys
who always raised his hand in class. I hadn't been the shiny
student he was but had been a good girl, a rule-follower—and
your grandfather had not only seemed the opposite, it was like
he saw anyone *not* challenging every point made in class as a
weakling. His whole family was like that. His father had been
a professor, and the one time I'd gone to his house to make a
delivery from my parents' tailor shop, I remember how dark
and dusty it was, books pulled from the shelves and strewn on
the floor in a way that must have made them feel intellectual
though to me it just looked sloppy, brown drapes so thick you
immediately forgot about the sun outside. That past year your
grandfather had stopped coming to school one day, but I wasn't

surprised—so many were fleeing by then that I hadn't spent much time wondering where the Moscowitzes had gone to hide.

You look like shit, Raya, he told me then.

I know, I said.

No, he said, eyeing me more closely. You have actual shit on you.

I came from the sewers, I said, and he nodded, as if I wasn't the first he knew who had, then said, And your family?

Back home. In the uniform factory.

Your grandfather nodded again. He reached into a paper sack, but when he handed me a loaf of bread, it was so heavy I almost dropped it.

When's the last time you ate? he said, and I had no idea. I didn't know what time it was, or even where I was. As I followed your grandfather through the brush, he talked. His family had escaped to a city in the north that past winter, he said—this was all happening in September—where he and his three younger brothers had trained with a youth group. The entire family had gone from there to Palestine, but he had met a plumber, Yosef Zanivyer, who'd seen something special in him (I couldn't help but roll my eyes that even then, in these silent, deserted woods, your grandfather had to let me know how fabulous he was) and asked him to stay. Yosef was the plumber who'd engineered the sewer route I'd just come through, he said. For the past few months, your grandfather and his group had been roaming a labyrinth of tunnels, committing them to memory for an evacuation and supply route they'd use to smuggle weapons and food into the forest.

He led me through a zigzag of uncleared scrub and over so many marshes and creeks I couldn't count, until finally we reached the densest part, a cluster of trees so tall and thick it suddenly felt like evening—an area protected enough by branches, he told me, that no military plane could spot us from the air. He took my hand and we elbowed our way around trees and bushes until an entire village emerged. There were blanket tents held up by logs, what looked like an infirmary, a makeshift kitchen surrounding a fire pit. About forty people, all teenagers, almost all boys, unbathed and bedraggled, were at work in different stations. Everybody was speaking Yiddish and the whole scene was so stunning I didn't know what to look at first. But your grandfather just kept leading me forward, as nonchalant as if he were giving a tour of our school back home.

This is Yussel, he said, pointing to a squat, suntanned boy. He was a medical student and runs the infirmary here. And this is the kitchen—here he handed me a potato, still hot from the fire—and this is where we run drills after dinner. He waved to a bigger kid, this one fifteen or sixteen, oafish and freckled with red, flyaway hair, the parts of a gun spread out on his lap. That's Isaac from Antopol, he told me.

Isaac, your grandfather said, meet Raya. We grew up together.

I'm trying to concentrate, Isaac grunted without even shooting me a sideways look, and your grandfather shrugged and said, He'll grow on you.

Then your grandfather stopped. Can you cook?

Not really. My mother cooks. I could barely say it.

What can you do, then?

I thought about it. I can do ballet, I said. I can play the flute, and that was when your grandfather started laughing. Wow, he said, throwing his hands in the air, thank God you're here, and I wanted to smack him.

But your parents are tailors, right? he said. So I'm guessing you can sew, and I can't tell you how much it meant to me right then that there, in the middle of the forest, someone knew this basic fact about my family.

Yeah, I can sew.

Good, he said. We already have a tailor, but if you're quick with your fingers, you can go in the armory.

So that afternoon I went to work, learning how to repair broken rifles and pistols, how to mend cracked stocks and replace the worn and rusted parts. He was right: all my years helping my parents sew on buttons and rip out seams made the job come easy. I was grateful I was good at it, and for many hours I sat alone, a little relieved Isaac was such a grump that I could work in silence. Your grandfather was running around, stopping at every station. It seemed obvious he was the leader, which I learned for certain that night at dinner, when five new boys arrived at the campfire.

They were young, your grandfather's age, and had just come back from a mission. Your grandfather crouched beside me and explained. Everyone here was part of a brigade, he said, called the Yiddish Underground. He'd started it back with his youth group, doing combat training in basements around the city. In the beginning, they'd slipped into nearby villages and robbed peasants for food and tools and blankets. But every day the war seemed to be getting worse, he said, and now the brigade was traveling farther to carry out attacks. They torched cottages and stole guns. When they ran out of bullets, they sneaked into cities with empty shotguns and long, straight branches, which, from a distance, could pass as rifles. They chopped down tele- phone poles, attacked supply depots, burned bridges to disrupt military routes—and that night, the five boys at the campfire had just returned from dislodging two hundred meters of rail line.

And? Your grandfather said then, turning to one of the boys.

And the conductor stopped the train, the boy said, spearing a sausage from the fire. And I walked right on and shot four soldiers in the dining car. They didn't even have time to put down their forks.

Your grandfather clapped the boy's shoulder like a proud parent, and I just sat there swallowing.

I told the other passengers to tell the police the Yiddish Underground was responsible, the boy continued, and your grandfather nodded. Everyone on the train was so scared, the boy said, and I just kept saying it as I walked through the cars, taking all of this, he said, gesturing at the suitcases and sacks of vegetables and bread by his feet.

Perfect, your grandfather said, and when he flicked on his radio, everyone put down their food to listen. He tuned through static until an announcer came on with word of the day's casualties. But when the announcer described the ambush, he said it was the work of Russian guerilla fighters, communists camping out in the woods. The Yiddish Underground wasn't mentioned at all. All around us were these kids, huddled together in stolen coats, waiting for their commander to speak. Your grandfather cleared his throat. He'd looked his age for that second, wide-eyed and serious and more than a little frightened, and I'd had a flash of that same boy in the schoolyard, the market, walking his younger brothers down Pinsker Street. I'd known that whatever he said, inside your grandfather felt as lost as every one of his fighters. But he stood up. He switched off the radio and said the only way they couldn't ignore us was to plan bigger. We have to let them know, he said, that there's a secret army they can't touch, soldiers fighting back with weapons taken from them, then retreating deep into the forest to plan their next attack.

※　※　※

THIS IS the part of the story where I know you want to hear how we fell in love. I understand—don't think I haven't noticed how you're always free to visit your grandfather and me, even on Saturday nights. How five years out of college you're still living like a student, still alone in that shoebox studio. Even when you were little, it was your favorite part of every story. It used to kill me when I'd overhear you asking your mother those kinds of questions about your father, this young chubby you with long blond braids and a dreamy expression, as if with your eyes half-closed you could envision a time your parents weren't sneaking around your living room at night, scribbling their names into each other's books, or storming after each other outside your old apartment, fighting over who got to keep this ceramic fish-shaped platter your mother said she made at summer camp but which your father claimed he made at an Adult Ed class at the Y—a fish, he yelled, that held his nachos just right.

And I remember after he left, you and your mother piled all of your possessions into a taxi and headed over the bridge to our apartment in Queens, where the two of you moved into her childhood bedroom, sleeping side by side on her trundle bed, surrounded by her spelling ribbons and stuffed-animal collection, as though you were living in a permanent exhibit in the museum of her life. And I remember all the dates she'd bring back, Philip and Hugh and the one who wore his sunglasses inside, how she'd parade those men into my home with the same defiance she had in high school, only she was thirty-six then with a four-year-old daughter eating dinner with her grandparents in the next room. From the kitchen the three of us would listen to her carrying on, her voice high and clear and always drowning out the other person's, which probably made her a good teacher during rowdy assemblies but not such a hit on those dates. There were so many nights when I'd watch her crawl into bed beside you after her date had left, her back to the wall, her bare feet wrapped around yours, holding on to your stomach so tightly it was like she feared the distance you might fall was so much greater than from the bed to the carpet.

I want to tell you mine was a great love affair, but the truth was that the only reason your grandfather started coming into my tent at night was to protect me. There were so many things to be afraid of in the forest. Not just the soldiers but bears and snakes and wolves. Russian communists who lived in other parts of the woods, coming by our camp, offering bullets for a night with one of the girls, sometimes taking one even if refused—men who disliked your grandfather but respected him enough, even as a boy, not to touch the one he was with. Anyway, it was almost winter—I will always remember that as the coldest season imaginable, the winter I watched hot tea freeze in a cup—and when your grandfather climbed inside one night and lay beneath my blanket, his hands roaming up my shirt and into my pants long before he thought to kiss me, it didn't feel romantic—more like a basic physical need that had little to do with me.

We'd already seen each other naked, anyway—we all bathed around each other, there was no other choice—and even though I was thirteen years old and he was my first kiss, I wasn't so naïve to believe your grandfather was in love with me, though for a lot of my life I did believe our relationship wasn't so bad. We had no one but each other when we first arrived in the States, and a big part of me wondered if I had another option. We never even talked about marrying—we just did it. I think your grandfather and I both wanted to forget everything that had happened and try to be as normal as all our neighbors on Dinsmore Avenue. It was only years later when you and your mother were living with us that I had to listen to her opinions on how I would never be normal, my fuse was just too short, she'd never met a person who could go from zero to sixty so quickly. From the beginning it was like that with your mother and me: even in the womb I think she was kicking me on purpose. Whenever we argued, your grandfather would walk out the door and around the block, as if your mother and I had taken up all the air in the apartment. But you would always stay. It used to drive me crazy, watching you watch *us*, as if our fight were being transcribed and filed away in the Dewey decimal system of your mind. But the truth was that there were moments when I'd look at you—you always resembled me more than your mother, especially when you were young, with your light hair and cheeks that went red no matter what the weather—and think that you reminded me of an alternate version of myself.

I too might have lived in my head if, when I was a girl, I'd had a school to spend my days in and an apartment for my nights, rather than a tent and a bed of pine needles that

I shared with your grandfather. But to his credit, he never once tried to pretend ours was some sweeping romance. At fifteen, he'd already had a life separate from our village, a life of organizing and combat training and falling in love with Chaya Salavsky, whom he called the most brilliant thinker from his youth group and promised to reunite with one day in Palestine, where she had gone with his three younger brothers and most of their brigade. After the war, he said, he'd join his brothers on the collective they'd started, and every day he'd swim in the sea and eat grapefruits and lemons that grew wild from trees. You can come with me, he'd say, always an afterthought, but during those talks I'd be lying quietly beneath the blanket, trying to convince myself that if anyone in a uniform factory was going to stay alive it was tailors like my parents. I'd heard reports on the radio that the soldiers were finding themselves ill equipped for the Russians, and since winter was coming, they'd put more people to work sewing uniforms and fixing weapons and equipment. I held on to the belief that my parents were safe for as long as I could—it would be another eight months until I knew for sure they were not.

When your grandfather wasn't talking about Palestine he was talking about the war. The rules were changing every day, he said—soldiers patrolling nearby villages in grimy work clothes, passing as farmers; military planes flying so low we'd hear their engines rumbling. And the day before, Isaac had been on watch when he found a teenage boy wandering the woods, claiming he was looking for blackberries, when anyone from the area knew they weren't growing so late in the year—

it was halfway through November, I'd been in the forest two
months by then. Your grandfather felt it was time to move, to
scout another location in the woods to set up camp, but first
he wanted to plan one more mission, and he wanted me to
come. With my light hair and green eyes I could easily pass
through town unnoticed—and anyway, your grandfather said,
who would suspect a girl so young?

I didn't want to go. In those two months I'd found a routine
that made me feel almost safe: cleaning barrels and collecting
spent shells from the forest floor, going to target practice after
helping the other girls clean up dinner, or working with Yussel
in the infirmary, where he was always concocting a new treat-
ment out of herbs and pig fat and other loot the fighters brought
back. But the forest had become home to me, the brigade a
kind of family, and—I know this will make you uncomfortable,
so I'll say it very quickly—in many ways your grandfather was
beginning to feel more and more like an older brother than a
boyfriend, even those nights together in the tent. I think that,
at thirteen, I still needed to be taken care of, to have a hand
guiding me through the forest, and if your grandfather felt I was
ready for a mission, I believed him. So I sat and listened the following night as he and Isaac strung together the plan in the dugout beside the kitchen, where they always held their meetings.

The train, your grandfather told me, would carry sixty-four
soldiers and two cars' worth of supplies. At nine-fifteen the
following night, it would stop in Haradziec, where I'd have
already laid out explosives.

It's a stupid idea, Isaac said, crouching low in the dugout—I
was the only one short enough to stand up straight under the

ceiling of blankets. Maybe she'll go unnoticed, he said, but she'll slow us down.

Secretly I agreed with Isaac, but your grandfather ignored him. He had a way of dismissing people without angering them, simply by pretending he hadn't heard them to begin with—a trait I appreciated then and now can't stand: sometimes I feel like he's walking around the apartment wearing earplugs. But that night I admired it, watching him roll out a map on the dirt floor, the yellow light of the lantern flickering across his face, which was getting thinner every day. It was an old map, one I remembered from school, when my village was still part of Belarus. Right then I didn't know what was what. I stared at the names of towns, trying to will them to memory as your grandfather dragged a finger along our route.

We won't have to worry about snakes in this weather but watch for bears, he said, passing out pistols and bullets to Isaac and me.

I'd never pointed a gun at anyone. I'd held plenty: in the armory workshop and at target practice, and back home my father had a rifle above the fireplace but I'd never seen him load it. I touched the slide of this one now, feeling my way to the trigger.

A pistol's entirely different, Isaac said, and I sensed he was right: I'd been using shotguns during practice, but these would be easier to hide. You know how to push your weight against a shotgun, remember? he continued. With this, it'll be twice as hard to have the same accuracy.

I wrapped my hands around the grip. Even before Isaac could criticize me, I knew my stance was wrong. My shoulders were hunched, my arms stiff. I hated the way your grandfather looked at me then, as if he suddenly recognized every risk in bringing me and was embarrassed for thinking the plan up at all.

But he just sat beside me and said, Push the magazine all the way up until you hear a click, then pull back the slide to chamber a round—that's the only way to know it's loaded for sure. You probably won't need it anyway since you'll be with us. And remember that if you *do* hear something, don't shoot. It might just be an animal.

I nodded. I knew the rules. They'd been hammered into me since my first day there, your grandfather reciting them around the campfire every night: Don't get cocky with your weapon. Remember what happened to three of our fighters who were loud and overconfident on a raid and were gunned down from a window, their stupidity already forest legend by the time I'd arrived. If you kill an animal, make sure the carcass doesn't drip blood as you carry it back to camp: never leave a trail. Don't forget that many of the peasants in the surrounding villages are good people, suffering as well, some even risking their own safety to protect us. If you have to rob them, take only what you absolutely need.

These rules were important to your grandfather. To Isaac and some of the others, not so much, though they always listened. I didn't know if Isaac had always been gruff or if the war had made him that way. I knew he'd seen things I hadn't, that when he'd heard soldiers coming into his village, he'd been quick to scramble behind a barn and from there had submerged himself in a river to hide, and when he crawled out hours later, he found himself completely alone.

It was like Isaac was running on adrenaline to stay alive,

whereas with your grandfather it was something different. Even that night in the dugout, I knew he was considering morals only partly out of decency—mostly he saw himself, in his heart of hearts, as a boy with a legacy. A boy who, after the war was over, would be written about in textbooks, talked about in reverent tones: Leon Moscowitz, whose rebel army not only changed the course of the war but did so ethically.

I had never met a person so aware of his own voice, carefully stringing together sentences with the hope they would be quoted later, even as he told me to cup my hands as he passed out explosives. First a grenade, then six long sticks of dynamite.

This part's easy, your grandfather said. Lay the sticks flat on the tracks.

And then what? I said.

For God's sake, Isaac said.

Just before the train comes, your grandfather said calmly, hold the spoon of the grenade down with your thumb. Then twist off the pin with your other hand, and the moment you throw it, start sprinting toward the woods.

This is ridiculous, Isaac said. She'll get us killed. Why not stay back in the armory? he said, and right away your grandfather stood up, as if secretly grateful Isaac was running his mouth so he had a reason to lecture. Just this week a statement went out all over the country, he said, offering farmers two sacks of grain for every one of us killed. Do you think anyone else is wasting their time with these concerns, pondering the differences between kids and teenagers, girls and boys? he said, his eyes flicking around the dugout as though his audience were much bigger than Isaac and me.

Then your grandfather turned to me. If anyone stops you, he

said, you have to remember, even if you're terrified, to keep the Yiddish out of your accent. Okay?

Okay, I said.

You could be a Dina, he said then, looking at me.

Or maybe Henia, Isaac said. Henia from the north, visiting her family?

He handed me a stack of clothes, all from a previous raid. Folded on top was a knit brown hat, which I slipped over my head. Your grandfather pushed it back, scrutinized my face and said, There. Already she looks like a different girl.

Yeah? I said, fingering the hat. What about Sonya? Sonya Gorski, I said, sounding it out, almost beginning to enjoy our game. It was like the dress-up I used to play back home, my best friend Blanka and me goofing off in my parents' tailor shop, darting between the tall spools of fabric and draping the scraps around each other, pretending we were classy society ladies dressing for the opera, where our handsome, imaginary boyfriends would be waiting outside on the marble steps in suits.

❈   ❈   ❈

THE FOLLOWING day I got ready for Haradziec. A gray wool dress and coat, leather boots and thick brown stockings. The boots were too large but everything else fit so snugly it was as if I'd picked out the clothes myself. In my pocketbook were my pistol and a case of bullets. I clutched it under an arm as I followed your grandfather and Isaac down the dark, mulchy path. These woods I knew—it was where we foraged for shells and mushrooms. We were quiet walking through, your grandfather brushing the ground with a stick to cover every footprint. Then

Isaac called out to me, If the police stop you while you're cas-
ing the station—

I'm Henia Sawicki. Staying with my grandparents nearby.

And if they ask what you're doing on the tracks?

Looking for my ring. It slipped off somewhere.

These lies, I knew, were the easy part. But really, the entire
plan was simple. We'd walk along the edge of the forest—far
enough in the woods to go unnoticed, close enough to glimpse
the villages through the trees. In Haradziec, I'd slip out and
cross the tracks, set the explosives down, run back into the forest. Your grandfather had made it sound so effortless in the
dugout, but here I worried about keeping it straight in my
mind. If one wary soldier saw through my lie, that was it—I'd
be shot, your grandfather and Isaac probably next, or maybe
tortured in an attempt to be led to the brigade. So I was trying
to remember the plan—Henia, the ring, the grandmother—
while clonking around in my too-big boots, and that was when
I tripped on a rock and fell to the ground, twisting my ankle so
hard I couldn't stand up. There I was, splayed in the dirt with
my ankle throbbing, and even before your grandfather helped
me to my feet, Isaac was already moaning about how he *knew*
something like this would happen.

Twenty minutes out, he said, and your grandfather snapped,
Tell me, Isaac, one of us couldn't have fallen?

Before your grandfather could hoist himself back onto his
soapbox, I started hobbling along the route and all they could
do was follow.

Don't be stupid, Isaac called.

He's right, your grandfather said.

I was suddenly so angry: with your grandfather for always

acting like he knew what was best, with Isaac for being so hard
on me, with myself for botching the attack. For the first time
since the sewers, I felt utterly hopeless and alone. I had no
idea what to do, or who to *ask* what to do, because—and this
was the first time it really became clear to me—I had no one
left. The only people I had in the world were these two boys I
barely knew at all, who looked so unbelievably *confused* right
then, walking in their oversized coats, Isaac breathless and
spastic, your grandfather's cap falling over his eyes. Up ahead,
through a gap in the trees, I saw straw roofs, the jagged steeple
of a church. I kept limping down the path, and when an entire
village came into view, I slipped out of the forest. We were still
two hours from Haradziec. My ankle was swelling, my clothes
were covered in dirt, and I pushed through town, not even sure
what I was looking for. The streets were empty and so eerily
quiet it was as if something terrible had happened the second
before we'd arrived.

Your grandfather and Isaac hurried behind me, whispering
to get back in the forest. But I kept on, and that was when I
realized this was the town I'd crawled into from the sewers.
Huddled along the road were the same houses, the same barns
and mill and school, only now the buildings were deserted
and destroyed: broken windows, piles of bricks, rats darting
up stairways leading nowhere. The war, it seemed, had finally
arrived here. A few cottages were still smoldering. A man,
hard-faced and dirty, dragged a skinny horse past without even
looking up. This time, I knew, I was no more shit-stained than
anybody else.

Along the strip of shops was a bakery. The door was open,
and when I walked inside, the glass cases were smashed, the

shelves bare, only half the tables standing. But as I moved through the kitchen and up the stairs, I saw shadows flash beneath a door. I pulled out my gun, pushed the door open with my shoulder and strolled inside.

The room was small enough to take in all at once: just two wooden chairs facing the fireplace with a bed and dresser in the corner; a stove, sink and table against the wall. A mother washed dishes. She had a cinched little mouth like a balloon knot and dark hair twisted tight at her neck. A boy, eight or nine, bent over homework at the wooden table. The mother glanced at me and at my gun and put down the pot she was drying. The boy stared. My hands wobbled as I aimed at them.

I need something to wrap up my ankle, I told the mother. It was the first time I'd spoken and my words sounded loose and clunky in the silent room. And boots and a coat and your warmest hat and scarf. And gloves, I added greedily as she sifted through drawers.

She handed over the clothes and I peeled off my dirty ones. I didn't even have my tights off when the mother yanked the boy's head toward her chest, and it took me a second to realize I'd gotten so used to bathing around everyone in the forest that it hadn't seemed strange to strip down in front of this family.

Henia, Isaac hissed from the doorway, where he and your grandfather were standing. Let's *go*.

But I couldn't, not yet. As I sat at the table and tied a clean sock around my ankle, bruised and puffy but possibly only sprained, I looked at the math problems the boy had printed out neatly on lined white paper, and imagined, for just a second, what it would be like to have homework again. Not that I'd even liked math—it had been my worst subject, the one my father had to spend close to an hour correcting every evening. But to be at a table again with my mother, to have classwork and meals and chores—I had wished for my family every day in the forest, but never before had what I'd lost been flaunted so vividly in front of me, and I was filled with a sudden rage at this boy. This kid who had so little, whose father could be dead or at war or just not around, whose school was certainly shut down and whose mother was probably trying to keep up some semblance of routine by making him practice math in the middle of this chaos, and at that moment I resented them both.

What was for dinner? I asked them.

Soup, the mother said.

What kind?

Potato.

Fill three bowls for me.

It's gone, the mother said. She held up the empty pot she'd just dried.

What *do* you have? I said.

She handed over a potato and three turnips.

I pocketed the food as I walked the length of the room, opening cupboards, rifling through drawers, feeling under sweaters and pants for a hidden stash of *something*.

I need your money, I said.

We don't have any, the mother said.

Why should I believe you? I opened their closet, overturned pillows, shook out blankets.

I promise you, the mother said, looking at me pleadingly. It was already stolen. Everything was.

You'll be sorry, I said, if you don't give me your money. It took me two tries to pull back the slide, but it didn't matter, I realized, when I was the only one holding a weapon. I grabbed the boy, circled an arm around him and pressed the gun to his cheek. He was shaking, and his fine brown hair was damp with sweat. He felt like such a *child* next to me, his skinny arms tight at his side, his breath coming out in short, hot gasps.

The mother was blinking quickly, and she kept looking at her son, then back at me. A sound came out of the boy's throat, squeaky and remote, and I pressed the pistol more firmly against his skin. The mother closed her eyes. Then she crawled under the bed, ran her hand along the bottom of the mattress and pulled out a thin stack of bills. It was a small amount, enough for maybe two weeks' worth of food.

Give it to me, I said.

We'll starve, she said. Leave us something. Please.

Give it to me, I said again, and when she did, I let go of the boy. I waited for him to run to his mother's arms, but it was like his feet were nailed to the floor. The room was so quiet I could hear a horse's hooves clicking past outside. I walked backwards with the pistol still cocked, out to the stairs where Isaac and your grandfather were waiting.

They wouldn't talk to me as we made our way through the bakery and out the door, where the cold air chilled me through my new coat. We were halfway down the road when your grandfather caught up with me and said, That family did nothing to you.

He grabbed my shoulders and shook me, like a box my voice might fall out of. How could you take everything they had?

But I kept walking. I don't know how to explain it except that I was struck by a haziness where I could hear his words but they suddenly meant nothing to me—I will always mark that as the moment I stopped listening to your grandfather, and also as the day Isaac started looking at me with a curious, cautious respect. We were back in town, the same route we took in, and as we passed that row of gutted shops, I caught my reflection in a broken window. There I was, thirteen years old and stumbling around in someone else's boots, looking more hideous than I could have imagined. I hadn't been in front of a mirror since back home with my parents, I realized, and in that time I had become an ugly girl. My hair was greasy and knotted and so beaten by the elements it was a shade lighter. Black circles rimmed my eyes, scabs dotted my chin and forehead and lips, my teeth had gone as rotten and brown as tree roots. In only a couple months I had become a Medusa, a monster, a creature from the forests of a fairy tale.

I still see glimpses of that ugliness now. At the salon, when the hairdresser finishes my blowout and spins me around to face the mirror. Or sometimes on the subway, when the person across from me gets up and I'm shocked to see that same terrifying beast staring back at me in the scratched, blurred glass. But I want you to know it wasn't that way for everyone. Your grandfather did the same things, lost the same things, watched that same boy doing math at the table—and responded by patiently sitting with your mother the entire time she was growing up, helping her with algebra and history and even with spelling, though it pained him to sound out words in a language he barely knew. I'd watch the two of them hunched over her homework at the kitchen table and wish I was the kind of person who could be grateful I was still in the world to join them, rather than always standing a few feet from everybody else, slouched in a doorway.

Your grandfather, once the biggest loudmouth I knew, became a quiet, almost invisible man in America, stumbling over his English, bashful in public, shy to ask directions on the street after hearing some teenagers singsonging his accent. He was rejected for every job he tried to get, an immigrant without even a junior high school education. I was the one who found work first, in a clothing factory if you can believe it, back in a hot room sewing in zippers and finishing seams. Your grandfather was humiliated that he could provide for the brigade but not for his own family, humiliated when he finally *did* find a job, making deliveries for a beer distributor, just another tired man dozing on his subway ride to work.

Still, he found small parts of his life to genuinely appreciate: growing tomatoes on the patio, listening to the radio after dinner, taking the train to the city on weekends. And yet none of those things I could ever teach myself to love. Your mother and I may not have the easiest time together, but I'll admit when she's right. And though it pains me to say it, she told me something once that I know is true: I never stopped thinking people wanted to hurt me, even when they no longer did, and that rage would rumble through me during even the nicest times. Walking in the park with your grandfather on the first real day of spring, eating at a good restaurant on our honeymoon in Atlantic City, on vacation in Israel, almost forty years ago, when we could finally afford to go. Finally your mother met that side of her family, finally your grandfather visited his parents' graves, finally he saw his brothers, middle-aged by then, with wives and children and grandchildren. I remember sitting in your great-uncle Natan's backyard in Ramat Gan, drinking orange soda and picking at a plate of grapes, and right away your grandfather started asking about Chaya Salavsky. I hadn't heard his voice climb so high since his speeches in the dugout. Did they still see her, what was she up to, he assumed after all these years she'd married?

His mouth quivered on that last word, and when his brother said she'd died a couple of years ago, rather than taking my husband's hand and murmuring condolences while he blinked back tears, I started chewing on my lip the way I always did before saying something risky.

How dare you ask about her with me right beside you! I yelled, in front of all my new in-laws, in the backyard surrounded by the grapefruit and lemon trees your grandfather had dreamed about for so long. Get over yourself, I continued, though I wasn't actually angry, or jealous of a dead woman I'd never met, a woman he hadn't seen since he was a boy. I was simply filled with an urge to fight, so electric and immediate I felt my face flush. So I carried on, even as your grandfather cleared his throat and looked at his shoes and rattled the ice in his empty glass.

And no, I won't tell you the rest. You can guess. You can go to the library and read about the sixty-four soldiers killed that night in Haradziec, in a train explosion engineered by an unknown anarchist group. You can waste full days in the research room, ruining your eyes scrolling through microfilm. You can read about the attacks that followed—eight more before the war ended and your grandfather and I missed the quota to Palestine and were loaded instead on a boat to the States: not an option either of us had ever considered, a place that didn't feel real even as we docked at the immigration port and saw Manhattan glittering in front of us. You can even find stories about Isaac, killed a year after we left for New York when his homemade bomb went off prematurely, still on his way to some unknown mission. One of those kids who couldn't imagine living anywhere but Europe even once we were allowed to leave. Maybe because he was addicted to the fighting, maybe because he could finally go home but no one was there. Search for his story in the library—for that and everything else. But you won't learn what happened to that mother and son I robbed, because believe me, I've looked and looked and there's just no way to find out whether those two people survived the coldest winter of their lives.

I don't understand you. All your life you've been like this, pulling someone into a corner at every family party, asking so many questions it's no wonder you've always had a difficult time making friends. It's a beautiful day. Your grandfather's on the patio grilling hamburgers, your mother's new boyfriend is already loud off beer, she's hooked up the speakers and is playing her terrible records. Why don't you go out in the sun and enjoy yourself for once, rather than sitting inside, scratching at ugly things that have nothing to do with you? These horrible things that happened before you were born.

The Quietest Man

The news was waiting when I came home from class: my daughter had sold a play. Not the kind she'd put on as a girl, with a cardboard stage and paper-bag puppets, but a real one, Off-Broadway, with a set designer and professional actors— one of whom would portray me, because this was, Daniela said in her breathless phone message, a play about our family.

I set down my briefcase, stuffed with my students' blue-books, and hit rewind. Then I called Katka.

"She's twenty-four!" I said.

"So?"

"So when we were her age we were living under Husák, and *we're* not writing autobiographical plays."

"Your fatherly pride astounds me."

I wondered how the wife I had known when Daniela was first born—the quiet, sunken woman who read the Czech newspapers in the library every morning and then wrote long letters to her mother in Prague, letters Katka had known would be swallowed by security—could have become this confident voice on the line.

"I'm just suggesting," I said, "that Daniela may not know what she's getting into."

"Well, she's the one with the play, and you're an aging man who begins sentences with 'When we were her age.'"

"Ha," I said, and after we hung up I spent the rest of the evening calling Daniela, getting her voicemail each time. Finally, just before eleven, she answered.

"Congratulations!" I said. "I hope I'm not waking you."

"No, now that people are actually going to see the thing, I'm up trying to fix it."

So there was still time for revising.

"Why don't I fly down this weekend to take you out?" I said. "Dinner, a show, whatever you want."

"What about July?"

My yearly New York trip. "I'll come then also."

"You don't want to be down here," she said. "It's a hundred degrees and pouring."

I told her I'd fly her up to Maine, then. It was humid here for May, too, but being on the water was almost pleasant. She'd never been up and it was an easy ninety-minute flight; we could make a leisurely weekend of it, driving along the jagged green coastline, stopping at Ocean Street Pier for taffy. "They have this big machine," I said, "where they'll make your own flavor right in front of you."

"Sorry," she said, and my heart flopped: didn't she used to have a sweet tooth? I had no idea what she *did* like. I pictured her in her apartment on 103rd Street, a glum matchbook studio she had brightened up by painting it yellow and lining the sill with ferns. She would be on her bed, doing ballet stretches, and her hair, long and thick and the color of cola, would be falling into her mouth. "I've got a lot of work."

"So?" I said. "Me, too."

"I figured as much."

Ah, this directness was new. The young artiste emboldened by a sale. "I'm so proud of you, Daniela. I just want to celebrate," I said, and finally her voice softened and she said okay. I knew I was laying it on thick, but what were my options? I pictured a velvet curtain pulled open to reveal the stage. I saw that Queens backdrop: the low huddle of brick tenements with the metallic sparks of the city beyond. Under the spotlight sat a girl on her stoop, pudgy and pale with dark brown bangs cut straight across. She was waiting for her father. It was his weekend; he should have arrived an hour ago. She waited and waited. The theater lights brightened as the afternoon got hotter, and when the mother returned from the third house she'd cleaned that day, she took one look at her daughter and led her inside. The mother, tired and tall in bleach-stained sweats and sneakers, called the father long-distance as her daughter slumped on the sofa, still clutching her lavender suitcase with both hands. And when the father told the truth, that somehow the Saturday pickup had become Sunday in his mind, the whole strained story of their relationship was revealed in the way the mother drew in a breath to stop from yelling, before ripping open a package of cold cuts and making their lunch.

✲ ✲ ✲

I KNEW ANY good parent would have been thrilled. And I wanted to be. In some ways it would have been easier if I'd been a monster—at least I'd know what was coming. Instead, I just hadn't been around much. And so, for the next few days, sitting through office hours or doing laundry in preparation for Daniela's visit, all I could think about was being written into her life story—especially because I knew just where she had gotten her facts.

Daniela was two when Katka and I separated; she was bred on a lifetime of her mother's tales about me. Katka, I imagined, would begin by saying that I was the one who dragged her to America in the first place. In Prague we had written anonymously with our colleagues for the journal the *Chronicle of Our Time*. We wrote by hand—the government had a record of everyone who owned typewriters—and late at night I'd sneak into different university buildings to type the materials. Every time we finished an issue, we'd distribute it to people we knew, who then passed it along to people they knew, until we had thousands of readers throughout the country. But when the StB still managed to link me to a typewriter, I was brought in for questioning and fired from my teaching post in the political science department. At the time Katka had seemed like the lucky one: she was on maternity leave from the economics department that term, and so avoided suspicion. But it was my name people chanted outside the university. It was my name that made international headlines and reached the desk of Saul Sandalowski, the Collins College professor who campaigned to get me a visa and a teaching job to avoid imprisonment.

She'd tell Daniela about packing our entire flat in three days before boarding the long flight to the States. She'd talk about the brick faculty apartment that awaited us in Vermont: boxy and carpeted and new; a million times nicer than our flat on

Bořivojova Street, but dimly quiet without our friends crowded around the living room, chatting away the evening. She'd talk about how my assistant professor's salary barely covered our rent, let alone food or doctor's bills—and she'd talk about working the early morning shift as a janitor at the college, mopping the same mahogany classrooms I lectured in, emptying the garbage can full of my students' crumpled napkins and paper coffee cups.

Katka came from a long line of intellectuals. She was the one who was supposed to be offered a professorship in America. Her father had been shipped to a psychiatric prison for writing his own anti-government pieces when Katka was still a baby, and an enormous part of her childhood was watching her mother devote herself to getting him out. I remember meeting Katka back in university and trying to impress her with my big ideas, only to realize the political books I was reading for the first time were ones she had already dissected and gleaned an understanding of years ago. There was something so exciting, almost romantic, about watching this brawny college girl reduce my ideas to a lumpy pile of porridge, making me feel not like a rising star at the university but what I really was, deep down: a skinny kid from a family of uneducated dairy farmers in Moravia. A big part of me had always believed I was destined to ride *her* coattails. The only thing I had over her was fluency in English; I'd studied in London after college. I could see how hard the move to Vermont was on her. I could see it in the way she closed into herself when I dragged her to cocktail hour at the provost's house, the way even meeting me for a quick lunch before class made her anxious. The woman who had once stood outside Party headquarters, chanting "StB

Equals Gestapo," was suddenly afraid to order at the campus sandwich shop because she didn't understand the menu.

At this point, Katka would say the transition would have been difficult no matter what, but that I certainly didn't help. She'd say even when I was home I wasn't really *there*—at the dinner table, or lifting a crying Daniela from her crib, I always seemed to be silently working on another essay. How I ducked into my study at every possible moment, how birthdays and anniversaries slipped into a murky, irretrievable place in my mind—but how I never seemed to forget the dates of Saul Sandalowski's dinner parties. And she would be right. But those dinners! Saul, with his floppy, wheat-colored hair and shirtsleeves rolled to his elbows, clamping a hand on my shoulder as he led me inside. His stone house on Seminary Road, so mazy and grand I always got lost looking for the bathroom. I was the honored guest, the man with the stories scholars and journalists and philanthropists wanted to hear.

And so, over glasses of Borelo, I told them about the two StB officials waiting outside the political science department on U Kříže Street. "Tomás Novak?" one had said, and I had said, "Why do you need to know?" and they dragged me into a black service car. It was late April, sunny but cold, and as we pulled away from the curb, I saw people outside the university, staring away or feigning conversation so they wouldn't be witnesses. In the headquarters, the officials led me down a long hallway into a windowless room with white walls and a steel desk with a green-eyed, round-faced man behind it. He calmly asked me to name the other writers involved in the journal. I refused. He asked again. He asked again and again, so many times that the hours began to blur and I couldn't tell if we'd entered the next day. All over Czechoslovakia, writers were breaking down and naming names. But did they really believe sleep deprivation would crack a father with a newborn? I joked to Saul's guests—though I remembered the moment I'd started to cry, sitting in that hard-backed chair as I recalled stories of people brought in for questioning and never heard from again. The lights were bright and one of the chair legs was shorter than the others so I felt as if I was perpetually sliding off, and every time I nodded into sleep the man would slam his desk drawer shut, jolting me awake. But I continued to refuse. And when one of Saul's guests would ask where that bravery came from, as someone always did, I'd tell them we all had a reserve for when we needed it most. I believed that, though sometimes I wondered if I could ever depend on it again. When I was finally released, word spread and I became famous among other writers—they called me the Quietest Man.

Yet as I circulated Saul's living room, with Brubeck on the stereo and little salmon crudités being passed around, I understood I could finally name the names of the *Chronicle* writers without consequence. So I told them about Ivan and Michal and Dita, and most of all about Katka Novak. My brave, brilliant wife who unfortunately wasn't here this evening because we couldn't find a sitter, I lied—when in truth she rarely wanted to leave the apartment except to take Daniela out in the afternoon. My wife who, for the four days I remained quiet in the interrogation room, was anything but. With a newborn on her hip, she led rallies outside the university, marching through Nové Město and up to a podium in Wenceslas Square. She spoke with such force that she persuaded an American reporter to write a piece about me. So while people with less evidence against them were jailed, enough support came through that my family and I were given emergency clearance—and when I described Katka to Saul's guests, it was like she was back up on the podium, drawing so large a crowd that children climbed the trees to glimpse her.

But then Saul's dinners would end and I'd tiptoe into our silent apartment and find the new Katka in bed with the lights off. "You awake?" I'd whisper, a little drunk off the Borelo as I ran a finger along her pale, freckled arm. "No," she'd say, rolling over, and it was only hours later as the sun came up and I walked her through campus that she'd unlock the lecture hall with her ring of janitor's keys and say, "Imagine eating alone while *I* was at dinner parties." That's how Katka was: she'd pick up a conversation I thought had ended eons ago without ever reintroducing the topic. "I'm not saying we go home, I know we can't," she'd say, "but maybe New York." Somewhere, she said, with people like us. Somewhere that didn't feel like the edge of the earth. But before I could answer, the first students of the day would breeze past as if we were no more significant than the chalkboards and long wooden desks that filled the room.

Katka continued to push the idea of moving to New York, but things were changing for me, and fast: my two books of essays were translated and published by a university press, and I was invited to speak at colleges all over the Northeast, in Hartford and Amherst. Katka said I was being selfish. I told her I was working hard for all of us. She said I owed it to our daughter to be home more, that if I didn't consider her feelings she'd leave me and take Daniela to stay with her second cousin in Queens. I begged her not to, but there was a secret part of me that wanted her to go, that longed to be free from the responsibility of my family. I wasn't ready to leave Vermont—not when I felt my life there opening up, wider and wider.

Of course I didn't really expect a woman with no money and next to no English to leave, and it was only when I made the first custody drive down the Taconic that it actually felt real. Of course I didn't expect Katka to find steady enough work cleaning houses in New York, or that she'd parlay it into her own business with a dozen employees before eventually selling it and enrolling in business classes. And of course I didn't expect that three years after Katka left, communism would collapse and the work I'd dedicated my life to would be done. That the dinner discussions at Saul Sandalowski's would suddenly revolve around Bosnia and that a young female Serb would become Saul's newest honored guest—and I certainly didn't expect that same woman to win tenure over me. That my thirties and forties would be about mastering the delicate, tricky dance of pleading for adjunct work up and down the east coast—Albany, Durham, Burlington—and now, for the past two years, in Harpswick, Maine, which, if Katka thought of Vermont as the edge of the earth, would have made her feel she'd fallen off completely.

✳   ✳   ✳

DANIELA LOOKED different than I remembered. When I'd seen her the previous summer, she still had that self-consciously sloppy, post-college look. Gone now were the flip-flops and baggy hooded sweatshirt, and with that change I would have hoped—and, deep down, expected—that she'd have continued to take after her mother. I had expected her dark hair to be wavy and loose like Katka's. I had expected that she too would straddle the precarious line between fatness and fullness, settling on the latter, and that she would have the same thick black eyelashes that first caught my attention, more than thirty years ago, on the street outside the Clementinum Library.

The sad fact was that Daniela was turning out plainer than her mother, but she was certainly more polished and put together. Though the afternoon was hot and gray, she wore a white button-down, pointy sandals and creased jeans cuffed at the ankle. Her long hair was so flat it looked ironed, and her pale blue eyes—she had my eyes—were hidden by thin-framed glasses. Standing outside the arrival gate, she could have easily passed for one of the students who used to trudge slush into the classrooms Katka had just mopped. I'm certain that to anyone else Daniela would have appeared exhausted from her flight; rumpled, nervous and probably overwhelmed to be seeing her father after almost a year. But to me she looked like one of those girls, who, with one quick toss of her glossy hair, used to make me feel like an awkward foreigner with an ill-fitting sweater and tangled teeth.

"Daniela!" I got out of the car. I wondered if I should hug her. "You look . . . older."

"Thanks. You, too."

I glanced at my shorts and striped shirt, my stomach puffing over my belt. "You got in early," I said.

"There was a delay at JFK but the pilot said he made up for it in the air."

People rushed past us and through the automatic glass doors. Somewhere nearby, a car alarm went off. I looked at my daughter and she looked back.

"So," I said, just as Daniela said, "So," and then she said, "Jinx."

"What?"

"Nothing."

"Everything's good with you?" I said.

"Great."

"Good."

"Your semester's almost over?"

"Yup."

"That's good."

Ever since I could remember Daniela had been so bumbling and nervous around me, so desperate for my attention that she'd blurt anything. And now she was just standing there, looking deeply amused as I sweated through the conversation, her hip cocked and her leather suitcase at her feet. Finally I swallowed and said, "We just finished the Battle of Königgrätz."

"I don't know what that is."

"Ah," I said, and we fell into silence.

Traffic was light for Friday night. Alfalfa fields blurred past, dotted with the occasional farmhouse before the land seemed to give up altogether and retreat into marsh. As we made our way into town, I followed Daniela's gaze, trying to see what she did. There was the hardware store that doubled as a market now that it was May and apricots were everywhere; the movie theater, which for the past three weeks had been showing a film about a foulmouthed man trapped in the body of a baby; the fire department, which hosted pancake breakfasts every fall. I rolled down the windows and the soupy smell of algae swelled in. I liked living a block from the water, away from the perky bakeries lining Willow Road or the Neanderthal bars closer to the college. I remember taking long walks along the harbor when I first arrived and knew no one in the entire state of Maine, and I sat with some of the men who looked as old as the weathered wooden dock they fished on, making small talk that helped me feel less alone than I feared I was.

But when I pulled into the driveway and Daniela saw my small gray clapboard, when she saw the front yard, wild with tall grass and calla lilies and the rope swing the previous owners had left hanging from an elm, she said, "So this is it." And then her face opened into something between a smile and a smirk, as if anyone belonged here more than I did.

I was admittedly a bit of a slob, and in anticipation of her visit I had washed the floors, vacuumed the two butterfly chairs that faced the fireplace, even organized my record collection: the Ellington I'd coveted in my twenties, the Gould that had felt like required listening at Collins, the Billy Joel I played now that I figured I was old enough not to give a shit. I had wanted Daniela to see I was stable, homey and responsible. But now, leading her inside, I wondered if she was making mental notes for the script.

"You want to wash up?" I said.

"I'm okay, thanks."

"You need some time to settle in and unpack, then?"

"Not really," she said. "It's two days."

Daniela, it seemed, was going to revel in making me work for everything this weekend. She set her backpack in the entryway and I wheeled her small suitcase into the guest room. "We can walk out to the water," I tried.

"If you want."

"Or maybe you're hungry?"

"Not really."

"Daniela," I said, unable, suddenly, to control the shrillness in my voice, "just tell me what you want."

"Fine," she said. "Let's eat."

I brought cheese and a baguette and a bottle of wine out to the porch and dragged two Adirondack chairs together. "To my daughter the playwright," I said, filling her glass.

Daniela raised her drink, then took a long sip, as if unsure how to navigate the line between excitement and bragging. "The craziest part," she said, "is that they did Mamet on that same stage."

"Impressive," I said, a knot pressing into my chest. It hadn't occurred to me that she might actually be good.

"Or bizarre. Mom was worried—I was working on it every night after work, and I think she was nervous about what would happen if nothing came of it."

"Your mother's the biggest worrier around, isn't she?"

Daniela looked confused, or annoyed, as if she were searching for the joke in my words and couldn't find it. I knew putting down her mother would score me no points. Katka and I worked hard at keeping up a friendship, mostly for Daniela's benefit; sometimes I felt as if tolerating me was just another item on her long list of things to do for her daughter, right after making sure that the security system in her building worked and she was getting enough protein in her diet. I wanted to change the subject to something tame and tried to remember the name of the company Daniela had been temping for this year. While I had no real interest in the job, I liked envisioning my daughter at a desk in a bright buzzing office, staring out at buildings and sky. I liked imagining that she also chewed up

her pens and that she popped her knuckles while she wrote—
that she'd gotten certain traits from me that were irrevocable.

"You know when I heard, I didn't tell anyone the first day?"
Daniela said, swallowing a bite of bread. "Not even Mom. I
was convinced they'd made a mistake and that the producers
would call to apologize."

"I've always been the same way. The moment something
good happens I'm waiting for a bus to speed around the corner
and kill me."

"Mom said you had that side."

So, they *did* talk about me. "We're both just really happy
for you," I said, a little too fast. "Did I ever tell you that when
my first book was published here, your mother spent an entire
weekend making a celebratory meal?"

"Really?" she said, her voice beginning to rise. Daniela loved
stories about times she was too young to remember. When she
was little I used to catch her staring at this one photo of me
and a pregnant Katka outside our flat in Prague, as if looking
long enough would reveal what we were saying just before the
shutter clicked.

"She took the bus all the way to Burlington to get lamb and
then spent the next day baking dumplings," I said. "It was outstanding." That was a lie; Katka used ingredients from the Stop
& Shop and the dessert came out charred and inedible, but the
conversation finally seemed to be flowing and I imagined us
sitting up late, finishing one bottle and then the next, swapping
stories and secrets. At least I thought we would, until Daniela
stood up and said, "Is the guest bed ready?"

"It's not even ten." I hoped it didn't sound like a plea.

"It's been a long day."

I'd set her up in my study, just off the kitchen. It was my favorite room: wood-paneled and dark, with a wall of books and an old copper lamp I'd bought at a yard sale years ago. But when Daniela walked in, the space felt small and dusty, and I wondered if the futon, which I napped on every afternoon, would even be comfortable for her.

"Here are towels," I said, setting two on the desk chair. I hesitated, unsure how to say good night.

"Dad?"

Here it came. I blinked, twice, and stepped closer. "Yes?"

"I need to change into my pajamas."

"Right," I said, backing toward the door. "I'm out here if you need anything."

I spread my students' bluebooks across the kitchen table and listened as Daniela walked down the hall to the bathroom. The faucet turned on, then off, the bathroom door opened, the guest door closed. And then, finally, the band of light beneath her door went out. I opened the first bluebook and read the sentence "Austrian forces arrived near Sadowa" three times without registering a word. I got up, poured myself a glass of water, sat down. Then I took off my shoes and slid quietly through the kitchen, the living room, and into the entryway, keeping an ear out for Daniela. Her backpack was still leaning against the mail table. I coughed, masking the sound as I unzipped it. Then I thought about what I was doing, how easily I could get caught, and closed it back up. I told myself to go back to my bluebooks. But I couldn't. I crouched on the floor, unzipped her bag in a single motion and searched the entire thing. But there was no notepad or laptop, nothing at all resembling a play—just her running clothes, a neck pillow and the

Sunday crossword, and it occurred to me that Daniela wouldn't be stupid enough to leave the play out where I could find it; I'd kept every copy of the *Chronicle* hidden behind my medicine cabinet until we were ready for distribution. Or was I being too cynical? Could Daniela not even trust her own father? I shut it again and returned to the kitchen. But the last thing I wanted to do was read another student essay, so I took the cordless out to the porch. It embarrassed me that I was dialing Katka's number for a second time this week, when she never seemed to make these desperate calls—at least not to me.

"This is a disaster!" I said when she picked up.

"Tomás?"

"She's barely talking to me."

"You got in a fight?"

"Of course not." Right then I wanted nothing more than to confide in Katka about what I'd just done, but it felt too terrible to say aloud. "Daniela's impossible to read. And to be honest, she's getting on my nerves a little—the whole too-confident-to-notice-I-exist thing is a bit much. She's hardly asked anything about my life—and you two *talk* about me?"

"She's probably just stressed."

"What does *she* have to be stressed about?"

"I don't know, Tomás. Sounds like a relaxing weekend to me." Katka's voice drifted. She sounded bored. "Where is she?"

"She went to bed. What twenty-four-year-old is in bed at ten?"

"Can she hear you?"

"I'm outside," I said, but suddenly I worried that Daniela could. Living alone, I never had to consider this. I ran across the lawn and let myself into my hatchback. The interior still smelled like Daniela's buttery lotion. I reclined the seat and closed my eyes, the way I did after takeoff. "Have you been in all night?"

"Sam and I were at a concert earlier." Her boyfriend of the past few months.

I could see Katka as clearly as if she were in front of me, sprawled on her sofa in an oversized sweater and ankle socks, one of those crime dramas she liked on mute. It was always so comforting to slip back into Czech with her, and in the beginning I'd wonder if sitting on the phone long enough we could begin to feel like us again—not the "us" in Vermont but the "us" that was good, back on Bořivojova Street—but it never happened; she told me about Sam and all the other men she dated with loose, offhand ease, as if she could barely remember why she had married me in the first place.

"Listen," I said, "just tell me what the play's about."

"I honestly have no idea."

"You expect me to believe that? Daniela probably lets you read her diary." I looked out the window at the clear night. I caught my reflection in the glass, warped and blurry. The critics, I knew, would call the father character "unsympathetic" and "unreliable." My neighbors would read about it in the paper. My students would laugh. In one night in some dim Off-Broadway theater, Katka's version of the story would become the official one. My entire legacy as the Quietest Man would be erased and for the rest of my life I'd be known as The Egomaniac, The Itinerant or maybe, simply, The Asshole.

"I asked her," Katka said, "but Daniela said talking about her work too early would kill it." She said the last two words as though she were wrapping air quotes around them. But I knew it made her proud to hear our daughter trying to sound like an artist, and suddenly Katka seemed to be purposely flaunting their closeness. That's how I felt this past summer in New York, anyway, seeing them together at brunch. Over waffles Daniela had talked about her temp job and the new play she was working on. She'd just read *Catastrophe*, and watching her enthuse over Beckett, I remembered first encountering Anna Akhmatova's poems and feeling like I was sliding back into a conversation I'd been having for years with the writer. Even the new vocabulary Daniela was trying out—she kept talking about the "exhibitionist nature of the theater"—was offset by her genuine ease at the table: she was so animated, talking with her hands, moving the salt and pepper shakers around to enact her favorite parts of the play. Katka seemed to be reveling in every second of it, and for the first time I wondered if our daughter's desire to be a writer allowed Katka to finally accept the fact that she no longer was one. As I watched them, squeezed in the corner booth, swapping food off each other's plates without even asking, it seemed as though their relationship had morphed into a genuine friendship.

I knew that should have made me happy, but I hated the way Katka had kept mentioning Daniela's friends by name that morning. I hated the way Daniela talked about the professors she'd stayed in touch with after graduation, and when she said she was going to see one of them read at the National Arts Club, I wondered if she was intentionally rubbing it in that I'd never been invited to talk there (though how could she have known?). Even Katka's supposedly nice gesture of heading back to Queens to give us time alone had felt like an aggressive challenge: how would we fill the day?

But Daniela seemed to have it all planned out. The moment

her mother said goodbye, she led me down Amsterdam, pointing out her morning running route and the Greek diner where she stopped after work. We walked and walked, long after I craved refuge in some air-conditioned store, and before I knew it, we were in the theater district.

She stopped in front of a theater, small and brick with a ticket-seller who waved to her through the glass booth, then went back to reading his magazine. "I've been ushering here a couple nights a week," she said. "They let me see free shows."

"That's nice."

"The guy who runs it, he said he'll read my script when it's done."

She was staring up at the marquee, and I knew that if Katka were there, they'd already be fantasizing about her play being sold and all the glorious things that would follow. But I was afraid it would have been cruel to indulge the dream. This was the theater that would end up taking her play, but I didn't know that then. That summer afternoon, it didn't seem possible that my daughter would have her name up in lights. I didn't doubt she was intelligent—she'd always done well in school; all her life teachers had commented on how hard she worked, how creative she was, how nicely behaved. But she had always presented herself to the world in too apologetic a manner for me to take her ambitions seriously—because it hadn't yet occurred to me that it was different to be an artist or writer or thinker here in America. That one didn't need to be a persuasive speaker, or have a charismatic presence, as so many of my colleagues had back in Prague. Daniela simply needed to live as an observer, sitting discreetly in a corner, quietly cataloging the foibles of those around her.

"I know it's not one of the fancy places," she said. "But it has a history. Yulian Zaitsev did his gulag plays here."

"Zie-tsev."

"What?"

"*Zie*," I repeated. "You're pronouncing it wrong."

Daniela didn't respond. She looked like such a mess in a loose black t-shirt with her hands stuffed in her denim cutoffs, her face blotchy and raw in the heat. "This is my life," she said, quietly.

I could barely hear her. I felt as if we were on the loudest, most obnoxious street in the world. Cabbies were having detailed conversations with one another entirely through their horns, and throngs of people kept pushing past us, their foreign, sweaty arms rubbing against my own.

Daniela took a deep breath. "I'm trying to show you—my life."

"Yes," I said. "Thank you." I was hot, and tired, and I didn't have the energy to tell her she was twenty-three, that this wasn't yet her life, this was an unpaid job she did a couple days a week with a bunch of other theater kids lucky enough to live in New York.

I just wanted to get out of there. I hated midtown, especially in summer, and though I was a tourist myself, I didn't want to be surrounded by them, so I turned away from the theater and started up the block. The disappointment was all over Daniela—in her face, in the heavy way she walked—but the last thing I wanted was to have a conversation about any of this. All I wanted was to get through the rest of the day without making things worse, my flight back to Maine that evening the light at the end of the longest, most excruciating tunnel.

We just kept heading uptown, in the vague direction of her apartment, neither of us saying a word. She's just guarded around everyone but her mother, I tried to tell myself, but I saw the way her entire face opened up when an acquaintance called to her from across the street, how she joked so effortlessly with the lady at the coffee cart. I loaded her up with groceries and a new fall coat she didn't need, and after a while even the bustle of the city couldn't cushion our silence, so I suggested we slip into an afternoon movie. It would have seemed impromptu and fun if we were different people. But I could feel how depleted that afternoon was making us both. We passed popcorn back and forth and I studied her soft profile as the screen colors flickered across her skin, wondering if I could come up with anything new to say before the credits rolled and the lights came on.

✾ ✾ ✾

BUT NOW it was up to me. If I needed things to be relaxed, I had to make them that way. So when Daniela shuffled into the kitchen in the morning, still in her pajamas, I handed her a mug of coffee and said, in a tone I hoped wasn't too falsely cheerful, that I had the day all planned.

"I'll show you around town, and we can walk through campus. For lunch there's a decent fish place on the water," I said. "Or you can stay in and write, if you need to. You can even bounce ideas off me."

"No," Daniela said. "Let's check out the town."

But she didn't move. Instead we both sat there holding our mugs and staring at our laps, and suddenly it was like this could have been any one of our visits—in Burlington, Durham or, the last time she was allowed to stay with me as a kid, when she was ten and I still lived in Albany.

It was one of those interminable winters like the kind I'd known in Prague, where you don't see the sun for months and your life seems like it's being filmed in black and white. That year had been especially hard: Saul Sandalowski was hosting a South African performance poet, always apologizing for losing touch but things were just so busy. Even my old friend Ivan, who had immigrated to Toronto that fall, would go silent when I called and tried to talk politics. We'd been close friends since university and saw each other every week to work on the *Chronicle*, and at first I'd thought his silence on the phone was the residual fear of tapped lines. But after a few conversations I sensed he just wasn't interested—he was working double shifts at a sporting-goods store, trying to save enough to move his wife and sons to the suburbs, and after we joked around and updated each other, our calls grew shorter until they finally ceased altogether.

But in the midst of my self-pity, a small press in Minneapolis had asked me to write an introduction to a new anthology of dissident writings. It felt good to be on a tight deadline again, and what I really wanted to do the Sunday of our father-daughter weekend was brew a pot of coffee and stand at the sink eating cereal straight from the box, thinking aloud. But every time I walked into the kitchen Daniela was there, wanting a push-up pop or a cheese-and-cracker pack or some other kid-friendly snack I'd forgotten to buy. Or to show me the imaginary city she'd built out of water bottles and paper-towel rolls and my coffee canister, the grounds of which she'd spilled all over the linoleum. And when I snapped that I was busy, she followed me into my cramped office and said she'd work then, too.

So she crouched on the carpet with her Hello Kitty pencil case and began, amid my piles of papers, a story. It was hard to stay annoyed while she sat writing with an eraser tucked behind her ear: her vision of an academic. I loved watching her bent over those pages, and I even loved the smell: the room smelled fresh with pencil shavings. We were quiet for hours. Every so often she'd sense my presence and look up, but then, just as fast, she'd return to her story, and I loved that, too. I loved it because I got it. I knew that feeling of wanting more than anything to stay uninterrupted in your head, because there your thoughts came out with confidence and ease, as if, at that moment, a little bit of your life was lining perfectly into place.

But when I looked at her story that evening, I was disappointed: she was merely writing her way into a book that already existed—*Daniela, the Witch and the Wardrobe*—without even changing the other characters' names. And I was more than disappointed when I discovered that the paper she'd used to write and illustrate it on were the first eighteen pages of my introduction. These were still the typewriter years; I'd have to retype the entire piece before the morning deadline, and I still had a stack of student essays to grade.

Daniela saw my frustration and crawled onto my lap, still in her pajamas, her breath warm and a little milky. But she was too big, and beneath her weight I felt hot and crowded, and at that second I'd known what I had feared all along: I just didn't have it in me to take care of another person.

"Get out," I said, pushing her off. "You just gave me about five more hours of work."

But Daniela didn't move. Instead she stood there swallowing as if willing herself not to cry. Her hair was falling into her face and she kept pushing it back with her hand. I carried her into the spare bedroom and slammed the door, then walked into the study and slammed *my* door, and I didn't emerge until Katka's headlights glowed through the window. Daniela stood in the doorway of her room. She had changed into corduroys and a sweater, and when her mother walked inside, she seemed to express everything that had happened just by blinking. It was deeply uncomfortable watching my daughter wordlessly tattle on me. I'd only ever seen that kind of unspoken closeness once before, between my father and the other men out in the dairy in Moravia. They'd survived ice storms and village raids together, and though they rarely said a word to each other, even as a boy I knew an understanding existed between them that I would always be excluded from.

"Give us a couple minutes, Daniela," Katka said, flicking on the television for her and following me into the kitchen. Usually during these Sunday night pickups I'd turn on the kettle and Katka would drag a chair to the table and fill me in on Daniela's friends and parent-teacher meetings and any news she heard from her family in Prague. She always had good stories from the brownstones she cleaned, about the arguments she overheard and the untouched cartons of yogurt and juice those rich people let rot in their refrigerators. We'd laugh as though we were above them in some way, and sometimes, sitting together long after our tea mugs were empty, it would feel as though Katka weren't talking with me simply for our daughter but because she truly enjoyed my company.

This time Katka stood against the refrigerator with her arms across her chest, and before I even opened my mouth I knew anything I'd say, even "You want something to drink?" would sound loud and defensive.

"Daniela's not staying here again," she said.

"You don't even know what happened." I went into the study and came back with Daniela's scrawlings all over my introduction. I fanned the evidence across the table. "Tell me you wouldn't have yelled."

Katka began to gather Daniela's things from the floor—her backpack, her schoolbooks, her socks, balled beneath the table—saying that from now on I could come to New York to see our daughter. "Do you have any idea how much Daniela looks forward to these weekends?" she said. "All her friends have birthday parties and softball games back home and she never cares about missing them when she's coming here. I've always known you saw her as a burden, but you had to let her know that, too?"

And when I said that was ridiculous, Katka looked around, at the coffee grounds on the table; at the dishes, sticky with food and littering the counter; then back at me, as if I were just one more thing preventing this small, dirty apartment from being childproofed, and started using words like "selfishness" and "neglect" with the same force that had drawn people from all over the city into Wenceslas Square.

❋   ❋   ❋

HARPSWICK WAS small, just under a thousand excluding the students, and I felt its size even more now with Daniela beside me. We'd exhaust my entire afternoon of activities in under an hour, once we made our way down the two blocks of shops, circled the tiny college, and there was nothing to do but look at the bay. I walked slowly and feigned interest in the window display of a bookshop. "Pretty lamp," Daniela said, and I followed her in.

It was one of those stores designed to rip off weekenders, with more overpriced nautical picture books than novels and Tiffany lamps like the one Daniela had pointed out. I watched her scan the bestsellers, then poke through the tiny classics section. As she made her way to the even smaller political science shelf, I watched her eyes move through the *N*'s. I always reflexively looked for my books, too, though they'd gone out of print fifteen years ago and I had trouble even special-ordering them online. It touched me to think that every time Daniela walked into a bookstore she thought of my essays, but it also struck me as pathetic that she'd probably never once found them, and I flushed at her witnessing another of my failures. Suddenly I wanted to be anywhere but in the *N* section where my books were not. I lifted the Tiffany lamp out of the display window and brought it to the counter. "We'll take this."

"You don't need to buy that," Daniela said.

"It's a gift."

"How am I supposed to get it on the plane?"

"We'll figure it out," I said. "You see anything else?" I tried to remember the setup of her apartment.

"I don't want any of this stuff."

"You said the lamp was pretty."

"Would you just put it back?"

But I couldn't stop. I pulled a mug off the shelf. I grabbed a globe. What a perfect, fitting end to the play: the aging man darting around this store while his daughter slunk back, embarrassed and ashamed. I wanted to buy Daniela the lamp and a stack of books and the plastic reading glasses dangling near the register and anything else if she would only stop writing this play, and as I watched her move through the shop, putting things back where they belonged, I felt myself starting to spin and finally I blurted, "Do you really have to do this?"

"What?"

"Write about our family."

She stared at me. "Amazing," she said, "that you of all people would tell me what to write."

She swung the door open and headed toward the water. She was walking swiftly, purse thumping her hip, her long dark hair ribboning out behind her. I caught up with her at the dock. She sat on a bench and put her face in her hands. She was right. I had asked her to do the one thing that went against everything I knew about myself, and yet I still wanted to destroy every copy of her play.

"Listen," I said, "I know what you wrote."

"How could you?"

"Your mom."

"She doesn't know."

"She told me everything," I said, and it was only when the words were out that I understood what I was doing. "So you might as well come clean."

"But she doesn't know," Daniela said. "You're lying," she said slowly, almost like a question.

"She told me all about it," I said. "Last night on the phone."

And right then I remembered how I'd felt in that hard-backed chair in the interrogation room, when the StB agent sat behind his desk and told me things I never would have believed about the people I was closest to, that my friend Ivan from the *Chronicle* was the one who had linked me to the type-writer, that the rest of the group was quick to name me the ringleader. So much of me had known to trust my instincts, but the betrayal had felt so real in that bright, windowless room. "We had a good long talk after you went to bed."

"But she never read it."

"Maybe you left a copy lying around her house. Maybe she found it on your computer." I met her eyes. "Or maybe she went into your apartment when you were at work one day, just to have a look around. She has a key, right?"

When Daniela nodded, I said, "Then that's probably it. Mothers have their ways. *Your* mother certainly does."

Daniela was gazing down at the row of shops, then behind us at the water, as if searching for a way out of this, and I said, "So tell me."

"There's nothing to tell."

"Say it, Daniela," I said. "The play isn't about our family. It's just about me, isn't it?"

And that was when her eyes filled up, and there she was, the Daniela I'd always known, whimpering and vulnerable and small. "Just tell me," I said, and when she didn't respond, I said it over and over, until finally her voice broke and she said, "Yes."

I watched a fisherman sift through his bait bucket and pull out a frozen minnow. The air was salty and humid and behind us boats bobbed silently in the harbor.

"Daniela," I said.

But she wouldn't look at me, and I couldn't blame her—I didn't want to look at myself then, either. Suddenly I had no idea what to say next. Part of me was saddened that my daughter was the kind of person who would crack so quickly, that the wall she'd built around herself could be so easily kicked down, but a bigger part just needed to know how the play would begin. Would it start with the time I forgot to pick her up in Queens, or when I missed her birthday because I was giving a talk in Hartford? Would it start with that last visit to Albany?

Daniela turned to me then and said, "It's called *The Quietest Man*. It's set during your last year in Prague, and how when you were brought in for questioning, you were too fearless to name names."

I was so stunned I just kept standing there, wondering if I'd heard her correctly. Finally I sat beside her on the bench and said, "I'm floored, Daniela."

Her face relaxed and I thought I saw something real coming to the surface. "I've been so nervous all weekend. I thought you'd think it was stupid that I was writing about something I'd never lived through. That you'd see it onstage and think, *She got my life all wrong.* I kept trying to imagine what it was like for you."

"It was nothing."

"It wasn't nothing," she said. "They starved you. They kept you awake for days. You could have died."

I decided not to mention the beef and gravy they fed me every day of the interrogation. The guard who pushed an extra chair under my legs so I could sleep a couple hours that first night. Relief was slowly settling in, and what I really wanted was to lie down, right here on this rusted iron bench, and close my eyes for a very long time.

"I've been wanting to ask you about it all weekend," she said.

"The hardest thing to get right is the meetings. When you put together the *Chronicle*."

I thought back to those days. This I could help her with. This was the one thing I wanted to remember. Daniela was staring up at me, a more captive audience than anyone at my readings had ever been, than all of Saul Sandalowski's guests combined. I leaned back and started to talk.

We always gathered at Ivan's after lunch on Sundays to work on the journal, I told her—his was the one flat we were convinced wasn't bugged—and as Katka and I rounded the corner to Táboritská Street we'd grow quiet and glance behind us. I told Daniela about the stray cats that darted up Ivan's dim stairwell, and how once inside we'd slip off our shoes and close the curtains and work silently in his kitchen, all five of us cramped around the rickety wood table. We had to be completely silent, I told her, just in case we were wrong about his place being tapped—so much that when I needed to use the toilet I poured water into the bowl very slowly instead of flushing.

"We'd stay at that table for hours," I continued, "until it got too dark to see." I told her we wrote by hand, on thin sheets of paper I'd gather at the end of the evening to transcribe at the university, and the more I talked, the farther I felt from the bench where we were sitting. Far from Harpswick and all the other towns on this side of the Atlantic that I had tried so unsuccessfully to make my home, unpacking and repacking my books and dishes so often I finally started flattening my moving boxes and storing them in the garage. As I talked, these places started to look like nothing more than spots on a map I had marked with pushpins, and my memories of those afternoons in Ivan's flat felt so clear it was almost as if I were back inside, the linoleum floor cool beneath my bare feet, involved in the single most important project of my life.

I was taken the year we were covering the trial of Jiří Vondráček, a colleague of ours accused of crafting his syllabus from banned books. The government hadn't allowed any journalists into the courthouse and none of it was being reported in *Rudé právo*, so we gathered as much information as we could from Jiří's wife and mother, and every Sunday at Ivan's we'd write up what we had learned. I remembered Katka beside me at the table, her forehead wrinkled like linen as she worked. I'd never been a quick writer—with the luxury of time I could spend half a day piecing together a sentence—but Katka thought in full paragraphs, and sometimes we'd all stop and watch her small white hand move briskly across the page, rarely crossing out lines. All of us assumed she'd be the writer our children and grandchildren associated with the movement, and that was the thing, I told Daniela—everything she'd probably heard about that time was about surveillance and poverty and fear, and that was all true. But there was also something beautiful about those silent afternoons as long stripes of light came in through the corners of the curtains.

"You could hear the whole city downstairs," I said, "but it was like nothing outside that kitchen mattered."

Daniela's knees were tucked beneath her and her hands were clasped. She looked like a girl then, pale and a little eager. "Was I there, too?"

She wasn't. Bringing a crying baby into Ivan's flat would have been too risky, and the most annoying part of those mornings was trying to figure out what to do with her when the downstairs neighbors weren't around to babysit. But I saw how much

Daniela wanted to hear that she'd been there. And if not in Ivan's flat then at least somewhere in the story I was telling—and I deeply wished I could say that she was. I wished I could say I thought about her during those meetings—as much as I wished I could say I remembered birthday parties and pickup times and to stock my house with juice boxes and string cheese before her visits. That I found it endearing that she built imaginary cities and wrote her way into preexisting books, that I had flown her up this weekend not out of fear but from the selfless and uncomplicated pride her mother seemed to feel so effortlessly. I wished I could say I was the kind of person who turned to Daniela then and told her it was her mother's story as much as it was mine—that it was Katka who deserved the attention, rather than being forced to sit in the audience, yet again, while I took center stage. But I wasn't, and I didn't. Because I knew that with her play, Daniela was giving me the chance to feel relevant in the world again, and all she seemed to want in return was to hear she'd once been relevant in mine.

So I lied.

"Every Sunday afternoon, I'd bundle you up in a knit blanket and wheel you down Táboritská Street. I'd park your stroller outside Ivan's flat and stare at you, completely flummoxed. The first time you opened your eyes and focused: it was on me." The warm afternoon was all around us; in the distance I could hear the calls of the gulls. "Inside Ivan's kitchen we'd all take turns passing you around. But I loved it when you came back to me. You were so good—you never made a sound. It was like you knew how dangerous a cry could be in that room. I'd put down my pen and whisper the same song my mother did when

I was a baby. Tichá Malá Panenka. And you were. You were my silent little doll."

I knew the second Katka saw any of this onstage it would all be over, but I couldn't think about that now. Because for this moment Daniela looked as if she believed every word. Or probably just wanted to badly enough. Her gaze was fixed and wide, as if she were watching television. I couldn't tell which of us had scooted closer or if we'd done it simultaneously. But she was so near our elbows were almost touching, and as I continued to talk, I wondered if any of what I was saying would begin to feel like the truth. It didn't yet, but I was just getting started.

Duck and Cover

The day outside is hazy and gray; the fan on the counter blows dust. Jell-O spins slowly in a glass case. The radio, always a notch too loud for my taste, is turned up even higher for news hour. British troops have left Egypt, the Army-McCarthy Hearings are in full swing and the man who invented the zipper has dropped dead.

"Can't you see table six flagging you down?" Alan asks. "You think people like cold coffee?" Alan Mandlebaum. Always behind me ever since we were kids, always watching.

I pick up the coffeepot and move down the aisle of customers. The regulars are at the counter, talking about Roger Maris, as if they'd been the ones up to bat—as if they'd never left the Bronx for Los Angeles. Beside them are their wives: distracted, knitting, fat leather pocketbooks on their laps. And there's my father, in a red vinyl booth near the back. His head is bent over his lunch, so all I can see are newspaper-stained fingers gripping a turkey melt, even though it's Tuesday afternoon and he's promised to go out and look for a job.

❊   ❊   ❊

HOME IS a pale green duplex dropped onto a patch of dry lawn. My father and the guys are inside, squeezed into our tiny living room and scooping up fistfuls of pistachios from a bowl on the table.

"You heard about Murray Hirsch?" My father's voice is low, but the way he speaks makes every word sound absolute. "They got him this morning, right in his own yard. Didn't even let his wife take the kids inside." The guys groan, setting empty beers on the table. My father eyes the bottles, my cue to bring in fresh ones from the icebox. If I stall a minute he'll start to fidget and look around the room, so I'm in the kitchen before he can start.

On our kitchen table is a seashell-pink cloth, dotted with daisies. My mother made it years ago, before she got sick. I was five when she died, and a few years later I had the brains to fold up the tablecloth and stick it in a closet: it makes no sense to stare at another person's things if they're never going to come back. But when I removed the cloth it was somehow still there, and you could tell how old the table was without it, so I put it back on again.

"Judy," Lou Mandlebaum says now, leaning in the doorway. "Hope all this business with Murray doesn't make you nervous." He winks. I've got a feeling Alan will look just like his father later in life, eyes round as fishbowls, elbows and knuckles overshadowing the rest of him. Lou and my father met years ago, before Lou took over Menick's restaurant, even before we all moved out west. Both jailed for organizing cells at the textile plant where they worked, they were best friends by the time bail came through. My father and Lou love to moon over what a match Alan and I will make (In the same tenth-grade class! From the same ilk!); we've practically been engaged since birth. But you want to know what *I* see in a future with Alan? I see decade after decade living under Menick's yellow lights in a housedress, flowered or checked, with rickrack along the hem, serving soup and saltines to old-timers still complaining about their backs and the heat and the lies of the press.

"We're parched in here!" my father calls from the living room.

I pull the bottles from the icebox and hand them to Lou. "You hear that?" I say. "The king has spoken."

❊   ❊   ❊

THAT NIGHT, after the guys have gone home and the dinner dishes are washed and drying on the counter, the two men arrive. Their visits have become the most predictable thing in my life. Always outside on the concrete steps, wearing stiff brown suits. My father in the doorway, yelling that this is *his* house and they're invading his privacy. Don't they understand he has rights? He can cite them, do they want to hear? Then the whack of the front door and my father joins them on the lawn. The low hum of the men's voices, my father's rising higher, but still not loud enough for me to make out actual words. I can see it all through the bathroom window from where I stand tiptoed on the edge of the tub. Moonlight shines on the lawn, giving my father a bluish satiny glow that makes him look almost heroic.

My father joined the Party during the Depression, just another unemployed factory worker looking, as he's told me a million times, for "a model that actually worked." He's been deep inside it since I was so young I can't tell now what's a real memory and what I've invented by staring at photographs too long, trying to fill in the parts the camera didn't catch. Here's what I do remember, real or imagined: Our apartment in the Bronx, always loud and always crowded, the other families from the building coming in and out so often I never knew who had a key. Snow-caked boots by our front door and our broken fireplace, its mantel cluttered with portraits of black-bearded, stern-eyed ancestors my father never talked about. Summer weekends upstate at the bungalow colony, Alan whining about the sun and the bugs and the lumpy mattresses, too afraid of the dock spiders to ever swim out past his knees. I remember women from the Party caring for my mother for years, coming in with baskets of clean laundry and empty cereal boxes for me to use as blocks. My father—no joke—patiently following Party women's instructions: heating up a casserole in the oven, softly rapping on my mother's door with a jelly jar of water. My mother in bed the entire time I knew her, long slim fingers like she should have played piano, her light hair spinning out elegantly against the bleached sheets.

The war ended when I was six and everyone I knew moved to California, replicating our east coast shtetl in stucco duplexes painted optimistic pastels, fenced in by manzanita bushes and baby palms. "Remember the Bronx?" my father loves to say to anyone who will listen. "Men shuffling from home to work and back to their dark, tiny apartments. So poor everyone used towels for curtains. And the winters!" Then he always laughs, crossing his suntanned arms with satisfaction.

Here's how it's been since we came out west: my father gets work, the FBI visits his job and leans on his boss, I walk home from school and find my father on the sofa in his undershirt and slippers in the middle of the day with the radio wailing through the walls, and all over again. I'm the only one working this summer, my tips and paychecks barely keeping us afloat. I know my father will get a job when school starts up again for me in the fall—*finding* one has never been the problem— but he's spent the entire summer lazing around Menick's or in meetings with the guys. He does everything but actually look for employment, though he's always lecturing me on the importance of honest work and how much pride I should take in being blue-collar, especially with Trumbo and all the others still being talked about, as if he's afraid everyone will think all the communists in L.A. have mansions and glossy cars and swimming cabanas. Whenever I ask why he cares what people think, he gets a funny look in his eyes and stands up straighter, like he's about to deliver a speech, and says it sends the world the wrong message. But personally I think his rivalry with the Hollywood liberals is one-sided, the skinny schoolboy waging a silent war against the homecoming king who has no idea the kid exists, and sometimes after a double shift at Menick's, I want to fling one of those laminated menus right at him and tell him I for one don't need a lecture on the value of hard work.

My father's forever telling me not to worry about his activities, that he and Lou have perfected the craft of organizing since their run-in with the cops so long ago, and I try my hardest to believe him. But lately our house has felt cramped with secrets, as though his politics will seep out the windows if we aren't careful. He and Lou have been worried that someone's setting them up. They go quiet when I'm around, but I know what they're talking about: on the last two worker walkouts they organized, someone broke windows at the plant and destroyed the equipment. They're certain there isn't a fink in the group—they've known each other forever—but anyone who hates their politics could be vandalizing the property, then trying to pin the crime on them. My father thinks he's so good at keeping things from me, but I can hear them murmuring and want to tell them not to worry—I know not to leak. The rules have been drilled into me since I was a girl: Never tell a soul what goes on in the living room meetings. Don't forget that everyone can hear what you say on the party line, and that the phone is definitely tapped. Stay away from people, from boys, who aren't involved in the movement—they can't be trusted.

Before school let out for summer, the air-raid drills began in homeroom. If we saw a flash, my teacher said, and then the sky went blank and we heard a terrible noise, we were to crouch under our desks until we were told it was safe to come out. Then duck and cover, he said, sliding his chalky fingers into his pockets. Remember those words.

"What a load of malarkey," was what my father said when I told him about the drills. He was always telling me the Russians were Ike's enemy, not ours, and the authority in his voice made me know he was right.

What I didn't tell him was that the drills had quickly become the part of school I liked most: the hushed, cramped feeling of crouching under my desk, the clack of my teacher's wingtips as he paced the classroom, giving instructions. Now shut your eyes, he said, and keep your hands over your ears at all times. When I closed my eyes, I saw clots of light shaped like cherry pits and plums. After a minute my eyes settled into the darkness and I saw nothing at all.

❋ ❋ ❋

THE MORNING after the FBI guys visit, I'm outside Menick's when I see a boy leaving the hardware store next door, balancing boxes in one arm and paper sacks in the other. He must be my age, though he's almost as tall as my father, his light brown hair slicked back and clean. When he steps onto the sidewalk, the top box falls from his arms. Nails plink on the concrete and roll into the gutter.

"Here," I say, bending down beside him. "Let me give you a hand."

"Thanks," he says. I scoop up the nails and spill them into his open palms. For just a moment, the boy's gaze wanders down to my legs, skirt sliding above my bare knees as I squat on the hot pavement. Our eyes meet. He blushes. I smile, making no attempt to pull the skirt over my thighs. I don't know where that flash of boldness came from, but I can tell he likes it. He stands up and continues down the street. At the corner he turns around and looks at me once more, and at that second I can sense a tiny bit of my life beginning to happen.

❋ ❋ ❋

THERE'S A NEW woman tossing her amber curls around my father's booth, brushing herself up against the Formica, overwhelming the table with the carnationy smell of a beauty parlor. I cough, uncapping my pen to take their order.

"You know what I want." My father's voice has a dreamy edge. "And she'll have the meatloaf and a Coca-Cola."

"Light on the ice," the woman calls out after I've almost reached the kitchen. I turn around and see her cross her legs, stretching out forever like the boulevards downtown. She is wearing, of all things, pants.

"She's sweet," she whispers to my father, loud enough for all of Menick's to hear.

"What's her story?" I ask Alan, soon as I'm out of earshot.

"Gladys?"

"No, the other woman in my father's booth. Yeah, Gladys."

"My pop says she was a big deal organizer back east but that she moved here after her divorce." Alan says the word *divorce* the same way we talk about the black neighborhoods below Robertson: reverentially, excitedly, but a place we wouldn't dare wander after dinner. "But more important, he says she's a nice lady, that she's . . ." He pauses, eyes flicking nervously around the restaurant, then whispers, like a complete dramatic, "That she's committed to the cause."

✻   ✻   ✻

A WEEK PASSES and nothing changes. Gladys continues to sit in my father's booth, inching closer to him, ordering plates of meatloaf. I've never seen a woman like her: wearing pants like it's no one's business but her own, but with enough rouge smeared on her cheeks to remind us all she's female. "You've been spacey lately," Alan says today, moving a rag across the counter in quick strokes. "What's with you?" He looks up at me, waiting for me to lift my arms so he can wipe that spot as well. I don't. Gladys catches my eye from across the room and smiles, but I look away. I raise one hand off the counter and the print of lines looks almost permanent, but then Alan pushes the rag right over it. The remnant of my handprint blurs into the wetness and then slowly disappears. The fan still blows dust.

I'm serving up a short stack when the boy walks past the windows. I take off my apron, grab my purse and run outside. "Hey," I call.

He turns around. His arms are filled with more paper sacks from the hardware store.

"You don't go to Marshall High with me, do you?" I ask.

He shakes his head. "Hoover."

I should have guessed, with his seersucker shirt and Bass Weejuns. I wonder if he'll excuse himself—everyone knows half the Marshall kids' parents are in the Party, and this past winter three Hoover boys chased Alan home after school, shouting *Pink-o Jew, Pink-o Jew*, then beat him to the ground and stuffed fistfuls of dirt in his mouth, right from his own garden. He wouldn't go to school for a week after that. I had to bring his homework every afternoon, and a tray of juice and toast, as if he were sick, rather than simply terrified of whatever was hovering outside. But this boy continues to stand here, like he has no intention of walking away. "Don't you have a hardware store over by you?"

"I like it here better." He looks down the avenue at Leo the druggist locking up for lunch; the cluster of wives outside the bakery, staring up at the clouds and clutching their hats in the breeze.

"Listen," I say. "I've got my own opinion, but like what you like." I eye the sacks. "What are you building?"

"You really want to know?"

I cock my hip. "I asked, didn't I?"

"A fallout shelter."

"No kidding," I say. "Can I take a look?" And in the exact moment it takes him to shift the bags from one hand and back to the other, as if considering every one of my words, I'm already leading him down the street, as if I know the way. After a few blocks, the lawns and houses begin to expand. Wooden fences appear, protecting swing sets and rosebushes. Even the smell here is different: like newly mown lawn, laced with honeysuckle. The boy's house is at the end of a cul-de-sac and has a red fence, dark red like the booths at Menick's. He unlatches it and leads me into the backyard.

Nearly the entire yard has been consumed by a hole in the ground. "Some guys with a backhoe came last month to make the hole," the boy says, "and then me and my dad got to work. Every day we've been mixing mortar and setting the cinderblocks, and yesterday we bought the floorboards." He lights a lantern and we climb down a ladder. Inside it's empty except for pipes and sheets of metal leaning against the blocks, and it doesn't smell musty like I would have thought, but dank and earthy. "I know it doesn't look like much," the boy says. "But when we're done building the inside, we'll put in fold-up bunks and paint the walls some color my mother picks out."

"Won't it be creepy staying here for days, not even seeing the sun?" I ask.

"Well," the boy says, "it's better than dying."

"You in there?" calls a voice from above.

I look up at the sky and see a dark cutout shape of a woman peering down at us.

"Thank God you got more supplies," the woman says as I follow the boy up the ladder. Her voice has a perkiness that makes me nervous. She's wearing a pale blue sweater set and her hair is cut into a harsh pageboy, clipped right below the ears. "Aren't you going to introduce me to your friend?"

I realize I never told the boy my name, and have no idea who he is. "I'm Judy," I say, sticking out my hand.

"Glad you came for a visit," she says, but her stiff smile makes me want to run home and iron all my clothes. "I wish you were seeing the shelter when it's finished, though, I know now it looks just like a gaping hole. I'll be honest, the best thing about it is more storage space. You know Hal can't throw anything out? He still has board games he never plays, swim trunks that no longer fit—"

"*Mother.*"

"So I say to Hal, fine, take all those things out here so my house stops looking like a junk shop," and before she can say anything else, Hal leads me out to the sidewalk. No one's ever accused me of shyness, but with this boy, I can't put a sentence together. Hal looks happy and confused and a little afraid of me, as if he isn't sure how, or even when, I appeared.

"Hal?" his mother calls from inside.

"I should go." I can already predict what his mother thinks of me, a girl willing to crawl into the unfinished shelter of a boy she barely knows.

"Let me walk you home," he says, and I reach for his arm.

I imagine us strolling through the streets as the lawns shrink and fade, up the steps of my duplex where the FBI men may be lurking, my father's voice echoing down the block. "No," I say, and it's only when I let go of Hal that I see the pale dots my fingers made against his sunburned skin. "But don't worry, I'll see you soon enough."

❊   ❊   ❊

I UNLOCK THE door to a dark, silent house. On the kitchen table are a bowl of pistachio shells and an ashtray of stubbed-out cigars: no note from my father about where he went, nothing. For a moment I wonder if he's in more trouble than he's letting on, and I have no idea what to do. Then he walks inside with the newspaper tucked under his arm.

"Where were you?" I say.

"I should ask you the same thing, cutting out of work today." He flicks on the radio and sits down. "Any uninvited guests tonight?"

"I didn't see them."

"Not even across the street?"

I glance at my father to see if I should be nervous, but his eyes are on the paper. "Should I be worried or are you just talking?"

"Worry about those fools?" He taps the sofa. "Relax a minute."

I take a seat, watching my father's eyes dart across the page. The radio, for once, is comforting: loud enough to absorb our silence but too quiet for my father to make out actual words and yell back at the news, wagging a finger in the air. Then he sets down the paper and walks into the kitchen. I hear the icebox open and close, and when he reappears he just stands in the doorway, cradling his beer, turning it around in his hands like he's forgotten what to do with it. Then he says softly, "You've been acting funny. This about Gladys?"

This is so unlike him that I know Gladys is on the sidelines, nudging him to ask, and I can't help it: I wonder if a new woman could be good for us. How comforting to have things back in order like when my mother was sick and the Party women took charge: dinner foil-wrapped and ready to slide into the oven, the sounds of a bridge game and neighborhood gossip rising and falling in the background as I drifted to sleep.

"Do you love her?" I blurt.

"No," he says. "But I like her."

"But do you think you *could*? Someday, I mean."

He stares at me, as if genuinely registering my presence for the first time. "You want to know the truth?"

I nod and he sits back down and says, "Sometimes we'll be out together, eating a meal or something, and I'll be watching her mouth move and hear nothing she's saying and feel like the saddest man in the restaurant. Sometimes I wonder if I was wired to love only your mother. But then I keep thinking, okay. Now's the time for me to be back in my life."

I've never heard him talk this way to anyone—certainly not to me—and part of me knows to let everything fall silent before the mood turns dangerously dark. I can already tell I'm wandering into mapless territory, where I can so easily step over some invisible border and start a whole new war, just like that. But I have too many questions. "Was Mom your first?" I say. "Love, I mean."

He shakes his head. "But after her, the others seemed like rehearsals."

"She was pretty, wasn't she?"

He looks up, startled. "You don't remember?"

I've spent my whole life trying to remember, I want to say.

Instead I say: "I was five."

"You were five," he says, as if it's only now occurring to him.

"No," he says, slowly. "She wasn't very pretty. Sometimes, at certain angles, she looked a little crazy. Like all her features, her long nose and pointy chin, had no business being together on one face. But then she'd look at you head-on and dazzle you." He smiles, as if he can see something on the wall beyond me, some bright and endless reel of images, that will always— always—be invisible to me. "She had such a presence at the meetings. She knew how to be the most powerful person in the group by saying so little. You'd be talking to a room packed with people and she'd just stare at you, and all at once you'd feel drunk and oafish and full of hot air, even when you'd had nothing to drink."

And then the question that's been knocking around inside me for years comes tumbling out: "Do you ever think it isn't worth it?"

"What?"

We've been talking so openly, but suddenly even saying the question feels too risky, as if someone might really be listening. "You know," I say. "Have you ever thought, for just a second, of giving all this up and being—like everybody else?"

"We *are* like everybody else," my father says quickly. "Everyone who matters."

For a moment he doesn't say anything. "You have to understand," he says. "The Party was our life, your mother's and mine. And after she died, the idea of getting out of bed and making coffee and going on with my day seemed . . . impossible. But everyone, they stepped in. The Party women caring for you, Lou and Alan coming by every single day, taking you to school, to the park on weekends. Everybody, all of them, they helped you with your homework, they taught you to read.

I couldn't do any of that myself." He takes a slow sip of beer. "You can't question the Party," he says. "The moment you do— you fall apart."

He's sitting there, his feet tapping the floor to a sharp, even beat and his head squished against the cushions. I have this eerie and comforting feeling of seeing him at ten, twenty, thirty, shifting nervously on all the sofas in every apartment he's lived in. All at once I feel his pain, his life, lean against my heart.

He clears his throat. "It's probably past your bedtime."

"Pop," I say. "I don't *have* a bedtime."

But we both stand up and he puts his hands on my shoulders, steering me down the hall. "Let's you and me pretend, just for tonight," he says, "that I remembered to give you one. Okay?"

"Okay," I whisper. And there's a moment before I go into my room that his hands stay on my shoulders, just resting there: the heaviest, warmest coat.

❁　❁　❁

I'M WIPING down tables the next morning when my father and Lou saunter through the restaurant doors. They seem all business, snagging their booth in the back without stopping to chat with the guys at the counter. "Hey," I say.

My father doesn't look up. So I walk over and say, "The usual?"

"Sure," he says. "Whatever."

And then he waves me away and turns back to Lou. They're so focused on each other that it's like I really am just a waitress to him, some flimsy, forgettable girl in a grease-stained apron with a too-hot pot of coffee. They just keep leaning in and whispering, and suddenly I'm so hurt I can taste it. I'm standing there, feeling like a bigger fool by the second for believing one real talk with my father means another will follow—and then I set the pot down right on their table, untie my apron and push through the glass doors.

"Running out again?" Alan's behind me on the street, so close I can see a rim of sweat above his lip. In the sunlight he looks athletic, like the sweat came from a tennis match rather than working in a restaurant with a broken fan. But I'm already walking down the avenue too fast to answer, past the hardware store and the druggist and the bakery, my sandals loud on the pocked sidewalk. I know the last thing my father will do is tie on that apron, and yes, I *know* it's wrong to make Alan take over my shift, but I keep walking. I turn up one block and the next, smelling everything at once: charcoal and hamburgers, eucalyptus trees, exhaust wafting out from the mechanic's. I cross a boulevard, toward the larger houses set away from the road. Then down a side street, up another and past an intersection, until I'm standing in front of his door.

"Hey," Hal says, opening it after my first knock. His face is pink, like he just scrubbed it. Behind him there's a television flashing and a brown plaid recliner. I can't make out the person in it, just a man's arm, Hal's father's arm, reaching for a sandwich on the tray beside him. There's a western on the screen, and beyond that, lemon-colored walls and thick carpet and the distant sound of a vacuum, humming away in a room I can't see.

Then Hal steps toward me and closes the door on everything. "It's good to see you," he says, leading me out back. "You've got to see what we've done." He lights the lantern and we climb inside.

The rest of the cinderblocks have been set along the sides of the shelter and the boards have been hammered down to create a floor. Canned food, candles and jugs of water rest against the wall. "We did a lot in a day, didn't we?" Hal says, a hint of pride in his voice. "It'll be finished by the weekend."

"What's the rush?" I say. "You're really that worried?"

He pokes a finger through the buttonhole in his shirt. "My mom wants it done. She and my dad have been fighting and I heard him say he'd prefer to sleep in here. That was what he said, *prefer.* Like he was throwing her words right back at her."

He looks up, and I'm afraid he might cry. He's still going on about his parents, about their fights carrying all the way down the hall to his bedroom and how lately he's been wanting to store his dishes in there so he can eat under the covers rather than facing the two of them together in the kitchen, and suddenly it's like everything once fuzzy and glorious is coming glaringly into focus and there Hal is: some regular kid with regular problems, a goofy boy with a peeling nose and mayonnaise on his breath and half-moons of dirt beneath his nails. Even the shelter's losing its luster, and I can see now what shoddy work they've been doing, the floorboards raised and uneven, the paint his mother chose a harsh and terrible green, like overripe avocados. I know that if I let him keep talking, this whole fantasy will topple over before it's even had a chance to rise. So I rest a hand on his knee and feel the thick fabric of his shorts. "I'm glad I stopped by," I say.

And then we're kissing, hands snaking up his polo and my blouse, roaming across shoulders and backs and hip bones. Our shirts peel off effortlessly, as if more experienced people have entered the shelter and are doing all the work. Hal is bony and muscled, with faint freckles scattered across his chest. The lantern goes off and darkness fills the shelter. When the lights come back on again, his lips are even closer to mine.

"What do you want me to do?" he asks.

"I don't know. I've never done this before."

"Oh God," he says. "Neither have I."

"Well," I say, not having a clue, "I think we're supposed to start like this." I pull him onto the floorboards and reach for his zipper. Hal rolls on top of me, pushes up my skirt. I stare at the food stacked beside me: tomato soup, tuna fish, cans and cans of Spam. I know what I'm about to do could taint me forever, and yes, I know I'm supposed to wait until I'm married and much, much older, but I can't think of a single real reason to stop.

He touches my face, looks at me. "We don't have to do this if it's going to hurt so much."

"I don't feel anything," I say. "I don't even think you're in there." I tell myself to focus entirely on the Spam. "Try again," I whisper.

He does, but before he even gets the smallest bit inside, his whole body shudders. He closes his eyes, and a second later he opens them so wide I can't help but think of Alan Mandlebaum. "Oh," he says, the word rolling off his tongue in three long syllables. And then I guess we're done.

"Jeez," he says, leaning back on the boards. He reaches for my hand, and for a minute we lie there silently. Then he sits up. "My dad could come out here any second," he says. "Let's go somewhere. Anywhere. My treat."

I look around the shelter, taking in the wood floor, the lantern and piles of food. I'm thinking I could stay here a very long

time, hidden and protected from the world. I could help Hal
and his father repaint the walls an orange so bright and beautiful they'd forget about the dark. Hal and I could play board
games and flip through the photographs in *Life* magazine, and
when his father went into the house for more jugs of water, we
could take off our clothes and try again so maybe the next time
I'd feel something. But Hal has already zipped up his pants
and is wiping the wet spot off my skirt with his hankie, and I
think of my father inside Menick's and know what I have to do.

"Alright," I say. "I know a nice place."

※   ※   ※

HAL'S MESMERIZED the moment we step inside, the way
I must have looked the first time I saw television. Everything
seems to fascinate him: the regulars at the counter, still talking
about baseball; jar after jar of olives; even the glass dish of
mints on the counter, chalky and dry as detergent.

"It's just the two of us," I tell Alan at the counter. "And I
want a booth." Alan leads us to one in the back. He slaps down
two menus, avoiding my gaze. But I notice his hands are quiv-
ering. "Two Coke floats," I say as he shuffles off.

From my father's booth I hear Gladys' deep laugh, the clink
of ice in an empty glass. I wait for my father to look up and see
me with Hal. He'll pause for a moment: forkful of pie held mid-
air, newspaper lowered and eyebrows raised. Then he'll walk
over to my booth, rest his hands on the table and before he
can say a word he'll take one look at me and know it's too late:
the doors of my life have already swung wide open, and there's
nothing he can do to kick them closed.

My father stands up and makes his way down the row of

tables and booths in my direction. He's walking swiftly, shoes squeaking against the linoleum, his shoulders erect and proud. In his fist is his crumpled napkin. When he reaches my booth, he moves right past, not even shooting me a sideways look. He stops at Lou Mandlebaum's table, where he whispers something into Lou's ear. Lou mumbles something back as they walk outside, and it's then I see the cops waiting under the blinking Menick's sign.

Right away the two officers approach my father and Lou. I can't hear a word anyone's saying, but it's obvious my father's yelling the loudest. He's waving his hands in the air as if he's capable of pushing things around in the sky, while the cops keep their hands at their sides. At first glance the officers look alike, but then I notice one is almost handsome with a black crew cut; the other less handsome but kinder-looking, with a mustache and shiny pink lips like a woman's. I wonder if either man has a daughter and a duplex and a restaurant they eat at every afternoon. The man with the crew cut walks over to a squad car parked out front. He fishes for keys inside his pants pockets and unlocks the backseat. The man with the nice lips takes my father and Lou by the elbow and leads them to the car, but they whip their arms out of his grip. The man leans so close to them that his breath must be hot on their faces, and whatever he says makes my father stop talking altogether. The cop handcuffs them both and pushes them into the backseat.

The car pulls away from the curb, and here I am, same girl as always, except for the boy I barely know beside me. Hal is fiddling with the saltshaker, asking me what in the world is happening outside, as if I have any control. There is the squad car, making its way down the wide gray avenue. I try to picture

my father in the back but it's impossible: all I know for certain
is that the last thing on his mind is what I've been doing with
the boy in my booth. The car stops, makes a right at the light
and then it is gone. There is Gladys, rallying everyone around
the booth that is now hers. There is Alan, setting the half-
made Coke floats on the counter. He's walking toward Gladys,
motioning for me to join him so we can make a plan for what
to do next. It occurs to me that Alan's the only other person
who understands exactly how it feels to watch his father get
cuffed and thrown into the back of a squad car, the only other
person who will be waiting for a call from jail tonight. I know
I have no choice but to leave Hal in the booth and join Alan:
some choices are made for you and that's that. I wish I could
say Alan looks different to me at this moment, but he looks the
way I've always seen him, the way I know I always will: nervous and sweaty, bewildered and pale. There is the glass case
of Jell-O, going around in circles, like not a thing has changed.
There is the radio, turned up for news hour. The Eisenhowers
had the White House staff up to their country house today,
and Fantastique, a tricot fabric made of DuPont polyester yarn,
has just hit department stores nationwide. It's fast-drying and
wrinkle-resistant, the radio announcer says, so forget about the
laundry and enjoy your day outside.

A Difficult Phase

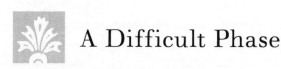

Talia was in line at Café Noah when she noticed a man watching her. He was at the group table by the window, handsome in a nerdy, chaotic way, wearing a rumpled orange t-shirt and metallic glasses a shade lighter than his hair. He smiled. She smiled back. He smiled again, and Talia, interested more in the light buzz of flirtation than an actual conversation, gave him one last look, then tossed her change in the tip jar.

Out on Ahad Ha'am Street, people were clustered around little tables lining the sidewalk, sipping coffee and smoking leisurely though it was noon on a Wednesday. The sun was out after an entire April of rain, and as Talia rounded the corner, she wondered if she was the only person in all of Tel Aviv rushing back to eat at her desk, the only person who would have left the café so quickly when one day, she knew, these situations could magically stop presenting themselves. So she turned back—and saw the man in the orange t-shirt barreling toward her.

"Did I forget something?" she asked him.

"What?"

"In the café."

"No," he said. "You look familiar—Hebrew University?" and when she shook her head he said, "Maybe from the neighborhood?" Before Talia could think of an answer, before she could tilt her head and say "possibly" in an alluring and noncommittal way, rather than the truth, which was that, at twenty-nine, her career was shot, she'd moved back home with her parents in Rehovot, a half-hour south of the city, and the only reason she was even *in* the neighborhood was because she'd picked up fact-checking work nearby at the local paper they left out for free on trains and in Laundromats, Mr. Orange T-shirt blinked a couple times, then said, "Oh, fuck it. You were flirting with me in there, right?"

She *had* been flirting, and the realization made her feel better—at least it was interesting. Better than going back to her office, where a deadline and a morning's worth of unopened emails loomed. The man looked about forty, with large blue eyes and pale, stubbled skin. Though they were standing still, he was out of breath, and his sense of personal space was off by a centimeter or two. She did a quick ring check and pegged him as recently divorced, the type who patrolled cafés for love during his lunch hour.

"It's hard to tell," he continued. "Maybe you were just being nice."

"No," Talia conceded, "I was flirting." She'd said a lot of bold things in her life but never something so direct to a person she didn't know, and it threw her so off-balance that when he started to walk, Talia fell into step with him. She was aware they were heading away from the paper, but she could feel

the day breaking open. She liked that neither of them seemed
to have a particular destination, that they were just ambling
around, something she only did on vacation. They turned down
a narrow street, and she watched two girls, quick and earnest,
chase each other through a courtyard while an older man, several stories above, watered his plants. Everything felt squint-
ingly bright and a little too in focus, as if she'd just stumbled
into the daylight after a heavy night of drinking: the cloudless
sky, the sparkly asphalt road, the squares of silver foil covering
a woman's hair in a salon window. At the corner Talia and the
man made a right, then crossed a boulevard and walked up
another road until they were standing in front of a junior high
school. "I have to go," he said, and Talia realized that on her
supposedly aimless, carefree walk she'd actually followed this
man back to work.

"You're a teacher?" She felt so exposed. What had she
expected—to run off to some hotel room together; that an
hour with a stranger, something she only right then realized
she'd even been contemplating, was going to fix everything?

"I have a meeting with the principal. My daughter's been
cutting class."

"I was terrible in school," Talia said, to say something. "I
cheated on all my tests."

"I'm late," he said, "but can I call you?"

Talia hesitated. But she liked his messy hair and light eyes and
the open and slightly injured way he stared at her, so she gave
him her work number. "Thanks," he said, buoyant with approval.

He waved and sprinted across the street. At the sidewalk he
turned around. "I'm Tomer," he yelled.

"Talia," she called back.

"Ah," he yelled. "Dahlia. What a beautiful name," and then dashed up the steps of the school, disappearing into the crowd of teenagers being beckoned inside.

✣   ✣   ✣

SHE WAS surprised to discover how giddy she felt when Tomer didn't wait the requisite three days to phone but did so that afternoon, when she was still at her desk, waiting for a callback on a story.

"Do you like food?" he said when she picked up.

"Only when I'm hungry."

"*Indian* food," he said, as if it were her problem for not inferring that in his question. "There's a new place on Rothschild that has the best curry, made by guys from Goa. They cook it different there."

"I know," she said. "I've been."

"What are the chances?"

"I'd say they're pretty high," she said. Asking a Tel Avivian if they'd been to Goa was like asking if they'd been to Jerusalem, and in fact the main reason Talia lasted only a month in India was that it had felt like an extension of college, the army, her old neighborhood in Rehovot. She'd left Israel to meet new people, not to run into her neighbor on a trek through Netravali or her father's cousin Rivka at a full-moon beach party. And so, when a job finally opened in Kiev, Talia had taken off immediately. When are you coming back? her parents would ask during their weekly calls—they thought she was insane for wanting to report on the very city her grandparents had worked so hard to leave. The moment Talia heard their voices, she felt as if she'd been yanked across the Mediterranean and transported back home, her father on the porch listening to the radio, her mother always beside him, shelling fava beans or peeling beets, her two sisters chasing after their toddlers while their husbands relaxed on the lawn.

"Things are working out here," Talia would tell them, wondering how just having them on the end of the line could make her feel as defensive as she'd been at sixteen. Though they never said it outright, she could hear the question that always lurked beneath: when was she going to get this silly rebelliousness out of her system and move home to start a family? But the truth was that things *had* been working out. Talia had wanted to be a reporter since she could remember, and it had stunned her, sitting in her cubicle in Kiev, that her life was actually unfolding the way she had fantasized. She'd started at the Jerusalem bureau of an American paper right out of college, doing whatever grunt work was needed: filing, fact-checking, going on coffee runs when the intern was busy. But her English was near-fluent, and after years of begging and badgering the bureau chief, he finally started giving her work, as if the very behavior that had gotten her sent to the corner as a child was the thing that garnered his respect.

It was true, he had said, that she was living in one of the hardest countries to find staff jobs: no one ever left their positions at the Israeli papers, and reporters from all over the world competed for work at the foreign ones. But with her language skills—she also had Ukrainian from her grandparents and Russian from college, probably the one time her Slavic literature degree made her *more* employable—he'd lobby the higher-ups in Chicago to send her to Kiev if things got bad enough to need someone on the ground. That was four years ago, in the fall of 2004, and Talia remembered sitting in the flickering, fluorescent-lit conference room of the Jerusalem bureau, watching it all unfold on TV—the election fraud allegations, Yushchenko's terrifying, ever-changing face—and holding on to a shameful, selfish hope for things to keep spiraling.

She'd always felt so envious of the other reporters at her paper in Jerusalem, none of them Israeli, all of them cabbing over to the bar at the American Colony Hotel every night after work, as if living out some vintage fantasy. They were all smart, they all spoke the language, many had relatives there and knew the country even before they were hired. But there was something so romantic about the way they saw their jobs, sinking into chairs in the garden bar, press passes still dangling from their necks, immediately launching into thrilling tales of how they were *this* close to danger that day, before pausing and taking a handful of the free cashews on the table. Even her bureau chief, whom Talia genuinely admired, still acted as though he was playing the part of the daredevil reporter, always driving himself into the territories, traveling with a separate passport through Lebanon and Syria, as if relentlessly performing for a rapt, imaginary audience back home in Chicago. It had always bothered Talia, listening to them debate her country's politics, when it was implicitly understood that the moment their brushes with danger went from being *this close* to *way too fucking close*, they could leave. But then she was given the same opportunity, to be lifted from her life and plunked down in a place to which she had an even flimsier connection than many of her coworkers had to Israel, and she'd found herself guilty of that same excitement. Anyone would have felt it covering the demonstrations, of course. But she'd been just as amped in the months that followed, sitting in the stuffy, windowless media room in the district courthouse, or transcribing at her desk for hours, eating meal after meal of crackers with chocolate spread, as if everything took on a significance she'd never felt back home: the thrill of living on the other side of the glass.

Even the things in Kiev that should have frustrated her—the weather, the drunks who catcalled her on her way to work, the horrible bureaucracy that made even cashing her paycheck feel like that nightmare where she was walking down a long hallway and every door led to yet another endless hallway of doors—seemed funny and removed, as if they were simply anecdotes in an elaborate story she'd tell one day to her *own* imaginary audience back home. Her office building in Kiev housed foreign correspondents from all over the world, and she loved how easily they buffered the loneliness of living in a new place, heading down to Baraban, which had quickly become their default bar, every evening after work. Those nights, squeezed into a booth with her office mates and a roving crew of aid workers and NGO groupies, even her life in Israel seemed a little lighter, a little more entertaining, than it had actually been—as if she weren't even describing her own neighborhood, her own family, but a cast of pushy and lovable characters on some wacky sitcom.

Then came the financial crash and her bureau chief called from Jerusalem with the news that the Chicago paper was closing some of its foreign desks, Kiev among them. It had nothing to do with her work, he said—they just couldn't afford to keep her when they could get copy from the AP. "Try not to panic," he said. "What's that saying about things going to shit right before they're good again?" He laughed, but it came out as more of a hiccup. Then he cleared his throat and suggested she go freelance. Which Talia did, though soon even that became difficult and she had to cut her rates by half, and one night she walked over to Baraban for a much-needed drink and found the place full of twentysomething American bloggers. A few months before she'd had a bad and wholly forgettable night with one of them—Ethan from Michigan—and had prayed he'd gone back to the States once jobs became scarce. But instead it appeared he'd invited all his friends from college to set up shop there, a cluster of them laughing and yelling in English, the other patrons forced to weave around their power cords, as if the Americans and their laptops had become as essential to the bar as its wobbly chairs and shelves of bottles that lined the wall.

"You're lucky," one of her old office mates said. He seemed to have implanted himself at the bar since his own layoff, and had the sallow pallor of a man who'd spent too many consecutive days drinking indoors. "You can go home and some war will start up again." He was Danish, and Talia detected a spark of envy in his gaze. "Go back and wait," he said. So Talia wrote to every contact she had in Israel, including her former boss at the American paper, who said he'd gotten word that they were now closing all the foreign desks and reshuffling the staff back home, and that he could tell her exactly what the job market was like, because after thirty-three years he was back in it, groveling for positions at wires he'd been over-qualified for two decades ago. The one place where he could put in a call for her, he said, was at *Boker Yisraeli*. It was the free city paper the two of them used to mock, singsonging the glowing profiles of the wealthy businessmen who clearly funded it and their Judaica artist wives. But Talia knew she had no choice but to gratefully accept the offer. And though it was even worse than the first job she'd taken out of college, and though the pay was so low she'd had to move back in with her parents, back into her childhood bedroom, which was no longer her bedroom but her mother's extended storage closet, the key, she told Tomer later that week at the Indian place, was to view her time home as a disappointing but brief blip in her real life abroad. "I've been home two months and I'll stay through the summer," she said. "The only way to get back into reporting is to be a one-man band, and the second I've saved enough for a video camera, editing software and sound equipment, I'm leaving again. But for now I'm here, fact-checking the features."

"I know," Tomer said, spearing a chickpea. "I Googled you."

Talia frowned. "You're not supposed to *say* that."

"I found a couple stories you wrote on Yushchenko."

"Oh," she said, trying to sound offended, though the idea of him searching for her online was oddly flattering: she couldn't even get her own family to feign interest. Tomer had seemed so nervous and overeager outside Café Noah, but here, signaling the waiter for another order of naan, he was surprisingly at ease. Or, rather, at ease with his overeagerness, as if he knew it afforded him an accessible charm. He was more attractive than she remembered, a large, hairy man with the harmless and comforting quality of a stuffed bear. The entire time she'd been talking he'd sat there smiling, as if experiencing a certain delight just being across the table from her. There was something so reassuring in that—for all the stress and disappointment she'd been feeling the past few months, all she had to do was share a meal with this man to get him to light up.

"And that piece on Gongadze," he said. "Do you have a boyfriend back in Kiev?"

"We broke up. When did you get divorced?"

"How do you know I'm divorced?"

"You have that look about you," Talia said. "Like you just ran out of a burning building."

"Well," he said, "we're not divorced. She died."

Talia twisted the napkin in her lap. Tomer picked up his fork, as if all he could focus on was his curry, and she wished the waiter would appear with a water refill or a dessert menu, anything to break the silence. "When?" she said, finally. "That's horrible."

"Sixteen months next week." Then he stopped. "I'm making you uncomfortable. What's this one-man band—you'd do all the reporting and filming yourself?"

"Yes," Talia said, more quickly than she intended. Then she said, "It's okay. You should talk about it," but when he started to, his gaze shifted right past her, as if he were staring at some indeterminate spot on the wall. He'd met Efrat after the army, he said, through a friend of a friend here in Tel Aviv. They'd spent their twenties breaking up and getting back together, filling their lives with the unnecessary drama kids always do, Tomer said, as if he'd forgotten, or hadn't noticed to begin with, that Talia was still muddling through the tail end of that decade, the graduating senior showing up at all the high school parties. "We married at thirty and had our daughter Gali a year later. We kept telling ourselves we wanted to wait until we had everything figured out," Tomer said. "First we had no money, then Efrat was getting her catering business off the ground, and then *my* job started taking over—I'm a contractor, mostly vacation homes in Herzliya," he said, almost as an afterthought, as if he'd only now remembered he was on a first date. Talia already knew that (she'd Googled him, too), so she said, "And then?"

"And then we went skiing in France. Our splurge every couple years. I was with Gali in the lodge and Efrat went on one more run. She came back looking dazed and said she'd fallen and hit her head. She said it hurt but that it wasn't a big deal. But that's what Efrat said about everything. So I took her to our room to rest. And she seemed fine. The next morning she still had a headache and wanted to stay in and nap. She told Gali and me not to waste a day hanging around inside when we could be skiing. So we left. While we were gone she went out for some air, and on her way back into the lodge she dropped to her knees and started vomiting. And then she just tipped over. Right on the deck and everyone ran out, and when Gali and I got the news we were on top of a mountain. No one knew it was a brain injury, at first they thought she was drunk. And everyone kept saying how lucky we were that Gali was with me, that she didn't see it. They kept saying we were lucky." Tomer was speaking quickly, his eyes darting around the restaurant as if he couldn't quite believe what he was saying was actually real, let alone that he was divulging it to a near stranger, and he kept lifting his glass and setting it down, as if he could no longer remember its use.

He pushed his plate away and stared at his lap. His hands were wrapped so tightly Talia could see the crescents his nails made in his skin, and she had never, in her entire life, felt so bad for another person. She'd interviewed people who had lost loved ones in fires, bus accidents, a massive train wreck outside Kharkiv that killed forty-three people, but this—being alone with a man so openly grieving—was even harder to watch. A waiter cleared their dishes, and as Tomer continued to talk, about his therapy sessions and his daughter who, he said, was essentially a good girl but, at fourteen, going through what one of her teachers called a "very understandably difficult phase," something strange happened, something Talia wouldn't want to admit to anyone: She realized she was enjoying herself. That she hadn't, if she was going to be completely honest, had such a good time in months. Getting Tomer to sidestep the terrible first-date small talk and move straight to the core of things was making Talia feel, for the first time since she'd lost her job, like a journalist. *This* was what she was good at: being the blank, understanding face across the table; putting people so at ease they revealed the things they didn't want to share with anyone, the things they wished didn't exist at all.

"I'm sorry," Tomer said, reaching for the check. "You're the first person I've been to dinner with and I probably shouldn't be let out of the house."

And though Talia knew he was right, and though she knew there probably wasn't a man less ready to date in all of Tel Aviv, possibly the entire Middle East, somehow that was making him all the more appealing. Since coming home she'd felt it impossible to hold on to the spontaneity she'd embraced so effortlessly in Kiev, as if it had been confiscated with her liquids when she passed through airport security. The past couple weeks she'd found herself waking in the middle of the night, startled and breathless, the top and bottom sheets untucked and twisted around her, her feet hanging off the edge of her narrow bed. It occurred to her now that she might as well enjoy herself while she was stuck back here, and that if there was one person even less equipped for anything substantial, it was the man across from her. And so as she watched him sift through his wallet for his credit card, such a jumbled mess of shekels and receipts it more resembled her mother's kitchen junk drawer than something he could actually slip back into the pocket of his jeans, Talia said, "I'm not looking for anything serious, but I'm guessing you haven't had sex in a while—"

"Sixteen months," Tomer seemed to shout. He stood up and sat beside her, and then he pounced on her, like a squirrel spotting a nut in the distance. He smelled more boyish than she would have imagined, and he was a desperate, handsy kisser who used his tongue right away. There was something about being pushed against the leather booth right there in the restaurant that made her feel as if she were shrinking in a weirdly pleasurable way, as if she were becoming half a woman, no longer the Talia with her name in print, who always needed to be working, traveling, writing—all of that was gone now and there she was, a pared-down version of herself, perfectly balanced beneath this man.

"Ilivesixblocksaway," Tomer said all in one breath.

"But your daughter."

"She's staying at a friend's," he said, taking her hand and leading her out. He lived in Neve Tzedek, one of the prettiest parts of the city, with its cracked brick roads and squat stucco houses, orange and white and pink as the bougainvillea that snaked through fences and blanketed the roofs. Tucked between the beach and the high-rises that blinked and hovered overhead, the neighborhood always made Talia wish she'd been an adult here in the nineties, before all the wine bars and gelato shops and French millionaires moved in—a time when, Tomer said, unlatching his gate, he and Efrat had been smart enough to buy. A rusty bicycle was parked outside and all the plants in the terra-cotta pots hissed dryly in the wind. He unlocked the door and ushered her inside, where the lights were on and the stereo was up at full blast, some bass-heavy electronica that Talia didn't recognize.

"Gali!" Tomer yelled, and when his daughter emerged from her bedroom, the telltale sign of too much air freshener wafted out with her. "Seriously?" he said, flicking off the music.

"I don't know what you're talking about," Gali said.

"I thought you were sleeping at Dana's."

"I thought you were on a date."

"So you threw a party?"

"It wasn't a party. No one's here."

Tomer looked at Talia—for alliance, support, she didn't know what. Gali, for her part, seemed to have had the foresight to use eyedrops before they came home, but the way she kept tugging on her ponytail let Talia know she was high. She was pretty, Talia thought, with full cheeks and brown eyes and thick blond curls, but obviously still learning to apply makeup: her concealer a shade off, her black eyeliner heavy and frightening. Plus she had on so many plastic necklaces and bangles that the whole effect was dizzying and distracting, and Talia wondered why no one had told her she was overdoing it. Certainly not her father, whose idea of fashion seemed to be to pull the top shirt and pair of pants from his dresser, which meant that one day Tomer could look haphazardly artsy, like that first time in

Café Noah, and another, like tonight, as if he'd gotten dressed in the dark.

"Yes?" Gali said then, and Talia realized she'd been staring.

"I'm Talia," she stammered. Gali nodded, then put her hands on her hips and shot a look that sent her straight back to junior high, and Talia wondered why she was still standing there. She took a step back and Tomer whispered, "Please don't leave," so she slipped into what looked like his room and closed the door behind her. It was tidy and small, with turquoise walls and furniture Tomer and Efrat must have hauled in off the street and stripped and repainted themselves. This was exactly the kind of place Talia would have picked out—not just the apartment but the way they'd decorated it, everything mismatched but so carefully chosen. Tucked into the dresser mirror were photos of the three of them through the years: on the tiled apartment steps Talia had just walked up; in a restaurant; in a park at what looked like Gali's first birthday, sitting on Efrat's lap. Efrat was attractive in the sort of way women noticed as much as men: laughing at whoever was holding the camera, her long blond hair in a frazzled knot, holding her daughter by the shoulders as if they were both about to tip over. Tomer was squatted beside them, his mouth open and eyes wide, as though he were making silly faces to get baby Gali to coo.

Talia sat on the bed and listened. She knew she should leave—it seemed only sensible—but couldn't find the will. Gali's story was growing increasingly elaborate and Tomer was caving, and Talia could see when he walked in now, wearing the tired and gentle look of defeat, that his daughter had won this round.

"Didn't she know you'd be back tonight?" Talia said.

Tomer took off his glasses and nodded. "And now," he said, lowering his voice, as if Gali could hear anything above the music she'd flung back on, "I look like a pushover."

"True." Talia regretted the word even before it had left her mouth—it couldn't be fun bringing a date home to witness this. But Tomer just flopped beside her on his stomach and said, "I can't believe I got caught with a woman. I guess we'll have to get married now."

He had to be joking. But something in his voice, low and tender, made Talia wonder if a nugget of truth existed within those words—if he just might not be wired for a one-night thing. She stood up.

"I was kidding," Tomer said. He reached for her, but she intercepted his hand. "I'm sorry," she said.

He looked hurt, in a puppyish and confused way, as if he didn't completely get it. He rolled onto his back. "Okay," he said, sighing. "I'll call you."

On her way out, she passed his daughter's door, cracked halfway open. "Nice to meet you too," Gali called out, as if Talia were the rude one, so she poked her head in. Papers and makeup littered the carpet in messy but distinct piles, as if a complex order existed that only Gali understood, and the entire room smelled of burnt hair and nail polish. She was lying on her unmade bed with her hands behind her head. "You're leaving?" she said.

"It's late," Talia said, though she had no idea what time it was. "I work early."

Gali squinted at her suspiciously. "What do you do?"

"I'm a reporter," Talia said, and when Gali said, "That's cool," Talia felt as if she were letting them both down when she admitted, "I'm actually between jobs. Right now I'm fact-checking for *Boker Yisraeli*, the free paper? I kind of hate it."

"Sucks."

"It *does* suck." The music was so loud that Talia's cheeks throbbed, but at least she felt a little hipper for recognizing the song that came on. "I love Kaveret," she said. "They were my first concert."

"My dad likes them, too," Gali said. "My mom was kind of a music snob and this was one of the things we could all agree on, in the car and stuff." She said it so matter-of-factly, and Talia wondered if this was casual conversation or if Gali, for whatever reason—the pot, perhaps?—was opening up.

"I've got a bunch of Yitzhak Klepter's solo stuff on vinyl you can borrow. Come over sometime," Talia said, immediately wishing she could retract it. She had a habit of over-offering when she was nervous and wanted people to like her, but why did it matter what this fourteen-year-old thought?

"Thanks." Then Gali lay against her pillows and looked up at the ceiling, and Talia stood there, not knowing whether the girl wanted her to leave or stay, or why she even cared. "See you," Gali said finally, and when Talia backed into the hall, Gali lifted her leg, and with one bare, red toenailed foot, kicked the door shut.

❋   ❋   ❋

"I ADMIT THAT didn't go perfectly," Tomer said when he called her at work the following morning, so early Talia was still blowing on her to-go cup of coffee. "We just need to try again."

"It's a bad idea," Talia said, clicking through her email. She was determined not to give him her full attention. "And," she said, emboldened, suddenly, by the distance between her office and wherever Tomer was calling from, "maybe think twice before bringing someone else home to your daughter."

"I made a mistake," he said. "I'm a human being."

"I'm sorry."

"She's gone this weekend. On a class trip to the Golan."

"I'm hanging up now."

"Let me make you dinner this weekend. My famous baked chicken."

"Tomer," Talia said, "this is nonnegotiable." There was no point in making her life this cluttered. Not when she was leaving, not when these weren't her problems. Not when the last thing his daughter needed was a new woman around. (Or was it what she needed most, and wasn't that an even bigger reason to stay away?) That was what she told herself after she hung up and immersed herself in the details of a story so dull she wanted to bang her head against the desk, calling the kosher certification board to hear their latest verdict on swordfish, and whether a restaurant open on Shabbat could even *claim* the fish was kosher if the board deemed it so, and at lunchtime she went around the corner to the falafel place on the off chance that Tomer was at Café Noah. That was what she told herself all through dinner with her family and the following day at work, and even as she passed her bus stop home and strode into a market in Neve Tzedek, where she walked right up to the grocer and asked which wine he thought went best with baked chicken.

She'd imagined sex with Tomer would be primitive and charged, that they'd have ripped off each other's skin if they could. But he was slow and nervous and kept his eyes open the whole time. At one point, he stroked her cheek in a way that felt so stagey and cinematic she wondered if he was going through the moves Efrat had liked, if she was a stand-in for his wife. But then he turned to her, and the expression on his face seemed to be only for Talia: filled with desire and gratitude and something close to joy.

Afterward they lay around for hours. Talia had forgotten how much she liked that time, when everything—the rough folds of Tomer's elbows, the coin-sized scar on the back of his thigh, from when he'd fallen off his bike as a kid—was new and interesting and had a story. She liked how purely herself she could be around him, initiating sex when she wanted it, clicking on the stereo without asking, sifting through his dresser for an undershirt. She liked how, when she woke the following morning in that tiny turquoise room, the kettle was hissing and milk was on the counter, and when they walked out to the terrace off the kitchen, the rest of the city was going about their day. She'd forgotten about them. About everyone—and yet there they were, still functioning as though nothing had changed: a line of people outside Tazza d'Oro, a woman leaning against a Vespa and laughing into her cell phone, a black dog barking on a roof.

She couldn't remember falling for someone so quickly and kept waiting for a gust of reality to swoop in and slap her out of her daze. For an awkward silence in which they realized how little they actually knew each other, or a moment when she'd step unwittingly onto some emotional land mine. Or simply for boredom to settle in, because as much as Talia liked hearing other people's stories, the excitement of sharing her own, of pulling down the sheet to reveal her own scar from falling off her bike as a girl, then the one, higher up her thigh, where she'd sat on a rusty nail, felt, with every new relationship, more and more perfunctory. It was like a monologue she'd developed sometime between the army and college, which she updated periodically with new noteworthy events, putting less and less effort into every subsequent performance. But it was easier with Tomer. His questions were so thoughtful, so careful, that they immediately pulled her out of her routine, wanting to know names, places, unpacking even the tiniest anecdotes, as if learning about her was a serious task that demanded his concentration. She couldn't tell if he'd always been this way with women, or if it had to do with being married so long—that perhaps dating a man who had so fully loved and admired and accepted another person allowed Talia to cross a threshold so effortlessly she hadn't even realized she'd done it until she was safely on the other side.

On the second morning, she dressed and found Tomer in the living room with a tray of omelets and toast and coffee on the rug beside him. Talia was touched that while she was sleeping, he'd been quietly setting this up. He kissed her and handed her the paper, and she reflexively scanned the international pages for the bylines. There in Moscow, covering Medvedev's swearing-in ceremony, was Ethan, that American blogger. Talia's chest ached, wondering how she'd ended up fact-checking the swordfish kosher debate while this guy got to break one of the biggest stories of the year, for an international wire no less. He'd barely even known enough Russian or Ukrainian to order a beer—something Talia had discovered that night she'd first met him at Baraban, that night she'd

ordered a few too many herself before taking him home. But
now there he was, parachuting around Europe, building up
clips. That night at the bar, he'd struck her as overconfident
and young, one of those reporters whose interest in Ukraine
only sparked once the protests began, and who expressed no
qualms about leaving the country the moment a hotter story
appeared. But he was cute and she was drunk and figured she
was abroad so why not. The sex had been clumsy and fast and
had sobered her up immediately, and afterward she'd looked
at his hairless arm, flung across his eyes, at his cargo pants and
suede Adidas sneakers strewn on her apartment floor, and told
herself to ignore the regret that was already swelling into her
throat—it was nothing but a silly, onetime mistake with a guy
she'd eventually never have to see, or even think about, again.

But there he was, in Tomer's living room, his byline taunting her about all the things she was missing. Then she felt
ashamed—what kind of journalist had she become, so jealous
she hadn't written the article that she wasn't the least bit interested the inauguration was even happening?—especially when
the story was admittedly pretty good. That was when Tomer
looked up from the food section, alarmed, and said, "Gali said
she'd call from the Golan. She said she would and she hasn't."

"Call her," Talia said, and Tomer said, "You're right. Of
course you're right." But when his daughter picked up, he
shushed Talia, though she hadn't said a word. "How's it *going*?"
he said, his voice suddenly a full octave higher. He sprang from
the carpet and began to nervously pace the room, as if he were
on a conference call with the prime minister and the national
security advisor and the entire defense cabinet. It bothered
Talia that he was so afraid of his daughter, though she'd herself

felt too timid to open Gali's door all weekend, as if there were a hidden camera lurking in that den of makeup and curling irons and stashed bags of marijuana. Plus hearing Tomer on the phone was nagging Talia to call her own parents, whom she hadn't spoken to since she'd checked in to say she'd be gone all weekend. And though they were easygoing about it, the fact that they didn't grill her just made Talia certain the third degree would be waiting when she got home. Which was just so frustrating, she told Tomer after he hung up, when she was almost thirty years old.

"Why do they get to you so much?" he said, and she was about to say they didn't, that she was just being dramatic, when it occurred to her he genuinely wanted to know. So she told him she loved her parents, that they were warm and dependable and unbelievably generous to let her come crawling back home, but that they were just so judgmental and involved. Even thinking about them now made Talia feel tired: everyone gathered together in the loud, messy house on a hill not far from the airport, where her father and brothers-in-law all worked as mechanics.

"It doesn't sound bad," Tomer said. "Having so many people around."

"It *wasn't* bad," she said. "Growing up." In fact, there were parts she had loved. Living in a neighborhood where everyone knew each other, her summers a blurry series of days sprinting through the backyards of all her friends. She loved the sea, the heat, sleeping with her windows open much of the year. She loved the expansiveness of her parents' property, hills on one side, a kibbutz on the other. When she and her sisters were younger, they used to sneak onto the kibbutz at night and hang out in the date palms, careful to avoid the toxic thorns that covered the trunks. Talia had been spiked dozens of times, but even then she had wanted to be close to dangerous, exciting things. The pricklers would pierce her skin—a strange, numbing wound that always made her sisters cry but that Talia would give herself over to. They had a pact: whatever was said up there wouldn't leave the kibbutz, and there was something so simple, so clarifying, about those nights—everything in her life seemed solvable among those trees. She even loved the walk back home, the highway desolate, the road so dark she couldn't distinguish where the hills ended and the sky began.

She could go on, she told Tomer—there were a million things she'd missed about home. But there was no denying how painful it was to be in a family that had always seemed so confused by her for stubbornly studying the languages of all the places they'd never go, as if it were some geeky form of rebellion, rather than what learning them had always been to her, a shield against loneliness. They'd never said outright that they didn't respect her work, but they never read her stories either—whereas at even the hint of a boyfriend they couldn't stop talking.

"I think in their hearts they won't think I'm safe until I'm married with kids," she said. "And living down the street from them."

"Well, I'm glad I met you," Tomer said. "Even if you hate being back."

Talia looked at him. "It's not that simple."

"I get it. You went to bed a journalist and woke up a fact-checker."

"It's more than that," she said. "You don't know what it's

like—to have invested your whole life in something that doesn't exist anymore."

"I do know," he said, with such emphasis that it came to her all at once. Of course he knew.

She wasn't sure whether she should lean over and kiss him, or simply hold him close, or something else entirely. Then Talia saw his blank, distant gaze and knew she wasn't expected to do anything. She wasn't even sure Tomer was aware she was still in the room. It was as if he'd opened his mouth and tumbled directly into some dark, private tunnel whose entrance Talia couldn't see. He couldn't even sit through a moment like this, reading the paper on the floor while long rectangles of light came in through the window, Talia thought, because it was still incomprehensible that this was now his life. She looked around this adult apartment, with its coffee-table books and actual art on the walls, at the care Tomer and Efrat must have put into every detail, following their own private manual of what a beautiful marriage should look like. And now here was Tomer, hunched on the floor, pain shooting past his eyes. This was all so scarily mature, Talia thought. She knew she was doing nothing good for him by being there. She was still sipping her juice and flipping through the paper, but all the while her mind churned for a way out of this. She'd never been good at breakups—and in fact had ended things with a boyfriend in Kiev in such a passive, roundabout way that he'd sat around Baraban telling all their friends he'd broken up with *her*. Here she knew to do it quickly, a needle in the arm before the nurse counted to three. She scooted beside him, conjuring up the least hurtful way to phrase it, when Tomer said, "This is happening too fast, isn't it?"

"I'm just not ready to be part of—this," she said, gesturing clumsily around her. "I'm sorry."

"*I'm* sorry," he said. "I've felt better with you than I have all year. But it's like I forgot how to enjoy myself."

"You will again." Talia wished she could say it with certainty.

"I used to be the kind of person who could eat a really good sandwich and that would be enough," Tomer said. "And now I walk around and see people laughing, at the movies or wherever, and it's like I'm a separate species."

"But with me you feel better?"

"Definitely better than before."

"Did your therapist teach you to talk that way?"

"Gali and I go to him together. He's good. But you want to know the truth? All the stuff I'm supposed to do with you in the beginning, all the not saying what's on my mind . . . it just feels exhausting. It's like I'm learning how to put sentences together again."

Talia's heart jogged, thinking about him struggling through every minute.

"But you're leaving," Tomer said. "Let's say that if in five years you're back in the country and I'm less of a mess, we'll try again."

"Deal," she said, wondering how such a self-proclaimed disaster could be this deft at breakups. She kissed him good-bye, and when he kissed her back, she decided not to overthink it as she followed him into the bedroom. They fell back on his mattress, pulling up shirts, kicking off pants, spending so many hours back in bed that when Talia finally looked up, the sun was going down. Tomer propped himself on an elbow and smiled at her. "I forgot how good breakup sex is," he said, and

Talia pushed away her niggling disappointment at the finality of his comment, when it had been just as much her idea. She slipped on her clothes and headed down the block, and when the bus pulled up and Talia took a seat in the back, exhaustion swooped right in. Ending things was so obviously the right idea, she told herself, gazing out the window at the rows of baby palms lining Har Zion Street. A prostitute leaned against one of them, pulling at her nylons, probably beginning her day just as Talia was ending hers.

Then Tomer called. "I found your hair band under my pillow. I miss you."

"I miss you too. But Tomer—"

"I know, we're broken up," he said in singsong. "What are you doing?"

"I'm watching an Orthodox guy pick up a prostitute. He's acting like he's asking for directions."

"Ah," Tomer said dreamily, and Talia said she had to go. The only way to get over this, she knew, was to put him out of her head. And though she thought she was doing a decent job of it, Talia wasn't home fifteen minutes before her mother looked up from the table, which they were setting for dinner, and said, "What's his name?"

"He's just a guy, okay?" Talia said, knowing she sounded more like Gali than she wanted to admit. "I'm sorry," she tried. "It's just weird talking about something that turned out to be nothing." She glanced around the kitchen, at the scratched wood table, stained with decades of art projects and baking disasters; at the stack of bills on the chair; at the new counters Talia's father had promised to install for her mother's fiftieth birthday, still half-finished as he waited for a time they could afford to complete the project. Her parents weren't planning to interrogate her tonight about her love life, Talia thought. It was seven-thirty and her father wasn't even home from work. This was the year he was supposed to retire and instead he'd signed on for two more.

"It's good being back," Talia blurted, but it came out as more of a question. She pulled her mother into a hug. Talia was shocked by how tiny she felt, her shoulders delicate and narrow as a girl's.

✻   ✻   ✻

TALIA WOKE the following morning feeling gratefully, dizzily free of Tomer, as if the whole relationship were a brief and delirious flu she had kicked with aspirin and hot tea and a night back in her own bed. Even coming home from work that evening felt comforting, and she surprised herself by offering to cook dinner while her mother worked in the garden and her father puttered around the garage. She was chopping eggplant when her mother walked in and said a girl outside was looking for her.

Gali was standing in the driveway, the whole dusky sky behind her, wide sweeps of orange and gray. She was panting and her eye makeup was smeared, as if she'd just stopped crying, or was about to start all over again. "You live in the middle of nowhere," she said. "I got lost even from the bus stop."

"How do you know where I live?"

"I looked you up."

"Gali." Talia wished she could be done with the conversation before it even began. "You know your dad and I broke up."

"Yeah, it's obvious. He's pretty much been on his period since I came home last night."

"Then why—" Talia struggled with a tactful way to phrase it, then gave up and said, "are you here?"

Gali was kicking gravel around with her sandal, and for a second she didn't answer. Then she mumbled, "You said we could listen to records?"

Talia stared out at the silhouettes of olive trees on the distant brown hilltops, the city hidden beyond. Winding up the road, so quickly dirt flew out behind, was a silver truck, and as it came closer Talia could see Tomer behind the wheel. He threw the truck in park and hopped out. He looked like he was coming straight from work, in jeans and boots and a button-down, his cell phone clipped to his belt loop. Even before he opened his mouth, Gali stiffened and said, "Where was I *supposed* to go?"

"Nowhere," Tomer said. "Because you're grounded."

"I can't believe you followed me," Gali said.

"I can't believe you stormed out of the house like a three-year-old." Then he turned to Talia. "I'm sorry my daughter's so rude, showing up unannounced."

"And I'm sorry my father's such a two-face," Gali said, "sneaking into my room and going through my stuff."

"And I'm sorry my daughter gives me so many reasons to think I *need* to search her things."

"Talia?" her mother called through the kitchen window, and Talia, never so grateful for an interruption, said, "It's dinner, so—"

"We'd love to," Gali said, and before she knew it they were all walking up the path and squeezing around the table, passing lentils and eggplant and salad as if this were perfectly natural, as if middle-aged men and their sullen teenage daughters frequently showed up looking for Talia.

And yet she seemed to be the only uncomfortable one. Tomer and Gali had calmed down and everyone was acting like such *adults*, so adept at skirting awkwardness with talk of the latest bribery charges against the prime minister and his upcoming talks with Syria. Even Gali seemed nervous and polite and almost docile at that table with people she didn't know, as if, when no longer controlling the joystick to her life, she was actually a good kid. Her voice was so soft she had to repeat herself when asking for seconds. She finished her food and excused herself to make a phone call, slipping down the hall so quietly it was as if she'd been replaced with a better version of herself.

Tomer was an enthusiastic eater, piling thirds onto his plate, praising everything from the lentils to the lemon slices in the water, while Talia's mother beamed, warming under the light of a handsome, younger man. Talia looked around, trying to see what Tomer did. Her father was still in his work shirt, chest hair trellising up the collar, and her mother's face was shiny from weeding the garden. She'd been prettier than Talia, with high cheekbones and a full, easy smile, but Talia had known her parents for too long to have any idea what they actually looked like now.

"This is great," Tomer said, and her mother, in the same prodding voice that had always sent Talia reeling to her room, said, "I just heard a little outside, but it sounds like things have been rough."

"Sixteen months," Tomer said, though her mother had

obviously been referring to Gali. "It feels so unreal." He set down his fork. "I'm sorry."

"No," her mother said. "Please. We *want* to hear," and then Tomer scraped his chair back and put his head in his hands and told the entire story. About the ski trip, about the injury, about everyone assuming she was drunk. "I was on a mountain when I heard the news," Tomer said, and all at once Talia's mother started crying. Her father grunted, his equivalent to tears. Tomer had the same far-off look from that night at the Indian place, and Talia felt weirdly robbed hearing him repeat the story, but also ashamed for turning this back to herself when he was suffering so vividly, and most of all frustrated that she was even a part of this dinner, that this was her life, when she'd worked so hard to be somewhere else entirely.

"I'm sorry," Tomer said again. "I don't know how to talk about it. Is that caesarstone?" he asked, eyeing the counters, and when her father said it was, Tomer nodded approvingly.

"But it's so expensive," her mother said.

"Yeah, but they'll last forever," Tomer said. "You can put pots right on the surface and they won't leave a mark."

"You really think they're better than granite?" her father said, back in his emotional element.

"Five times as strong," Tomer said. "I put them in every house I do. I've got some slabs at work, and some scraps of Moroccan tile that would look good along the backsplash. I can finish it for you in an afternoon, a day tops."

"No kidding," her father said.

"Not a problem," Tomer said.

"Maybe Talia can help out," her mother said. "Get some work experience."

"I *have* a job," Talia said, and when both her parents said "Journalism?" they laughed, as if she was five years old and had just announced that when she grew up she wanted to be a robot, or a dragon. Then they smiled at each other, as if pleased and surprised that thirty-plus years together could inspire them to blurt the same question in unison. Talia stood up, needing to be anywhere but in that kitchen. "It's a joke," her mother called after her, but Talia was already walking into her bedroom. She leaned against the wall and exhaled.

"Hey," Gali said, from the floor. She was sprawled on the rug, texting on her phone.

"Your boyfriend?" Talia asked.

"Yeah." Gali reddened. "I think so."

"What's his name?"

"Nir." Her voice had a candied edge.

"He's in your class?"

"In the army. On leave this week." Then Gali flipped her phone shut. "My dad doesn't know. Promise you won't tell?" and when Talia nodded, Gali said, "I know it was weird showing up like this."

"Why *did* you?"

Gali was quiet, as if searching for an honest answer. "I get so pissed at my dad," she said, "and I just needed to be out of the apartment. To be somewhere else. And the idea of sitting around listening to records with you sounded—nice."

Talia eyed the girl, making a sincerity check, then felt terrible for doing so when Gali seemed so vulnerable. She looked around her room, the place where she'd once made blanket forts and dressed up her stuffed animals. Draped over her closet door was a satiny wrap top, and she impulsively pulled it off. "This would look good on you," she said. "Wear it out with Nir."

"Seriously?"

"Try it on."

"Then close your eyes," Gali said, and Talia was touched that such a sassy girl could still be self-conscious. Talia hopped on the bed and put her face in a pillow, as if they were two girls goofing off at a slumber party, and when she opened her eyes, Gali had the shirt on and Tomer was in the doorway.

"Your wish came true," he said, and Gali grinned a little at her dad's dorky joke. "Sorry to break up the party, ladies," he said, "but it's a school night."

Outside, Talia waved to Gali as she climbed into the truck, and Tomer gathered her into a hug. "You saved me tonight. I don't remember the last time I saw Gali smile—I forgot she had teeth," he said. "Your family's great, Talia. I don't know what you're complaining about."

"Where's *your* family?"

"Haifa," he said. "And my brother's in London. My parents were there for us after Efrat, of course, but after a couple months they went back to their lives. That's how they are. They love me and Gali, but they're not involved like—this."

Tomer tightened his arms around her. "You make everything so easy," he whispered. The automatic porch lights blinked on, catching the gloss in his hair, the stubble on his face. Talia felt a stab of longing and reflexively leaned into him, her cheek remembering just where to rest against his collarbone. She circled her arms around his waist, linking her fingers in his belt loops, before realizing what she was doing.

"Sorry," she said, finding her voice lodged in her throat. "I just forgot for a minute."

"You really think it's for the best?"

She stared at him, suddenly knowing how dangerous it was, even standing this close. That was how people grew to be unhappy, she thought—by not making choices, by just letting what was warm and wonderful in one moment dictate the next, until one day they were living a life completely unsuited to their dreams. She took a big, stumbling step back.

"Okay," Tomer said. "She thinks it's for the best." Then he said it again, as if forcing his own words on himself, and walked to the truck. The porch lights went off and Talia looked out in the distance. The wind picked up and she felt a creeping chill. She waited for a plane to interrupt the silence, or for her parents to come out, but she could see them moving inside the orange glow of the house. Everything around her was still. Then Tomer started the engine and steered down the driveway, and there was Gali at the window, face pressed to the glass, waving goodbye.

✻ ✻ ✻

AFTER TOMER left, after she watched his truck grow smaller in the darkness until it was just two yellow taillights like the creepy eyes of a cat, Talia heard her parents on the phone with one of her sisters, on separate extensions, talking enthusiastically about Tomer. "We're not together!" Talia said when they hung up, turning to her mother in the kitchen, then to her father down the hall, on the phone by the steps. "Anyway, can't you see how unready he is?"

"He's going through a rough time," her father said stiffly, as if she'd insulted his friend, and her mother said that of course the age difference and the daughter situation and the timing in general weren't ideal, but that he was obviously a good person. "I'm not saying it's perfect, but if anything the whole thing shows he knows how to be in a relationship," she said, and Talia stood baffled in the doorway: all this time, had her family seen her as more broken than she saw herself?

She marched into her room and flung herself on the bed. But wallowing was useless, she knew, so she opened her laptop and emailed all her former office mates from Kiev who had kept their jobs to remind them she was alive and still looking for work, and when she saw that one had immediately responded, she applauded herself for being so proactive. And when it turned out to be a vacation autoreply, she spent the next fifteen minutes obsessively refreshing her email. From there she Googled herself, her bureau chief, Ethan the blogger, who was still in Moscow, tweeting live from Putin's address to the Duma. She sat there, feeling like the world's youngest relic, and then pulled the blanket over her head, this ladybug comforter she'd had since elementary school.

She awoke, just before eleven, to her cell phone ringing.

"Talia? It's Gali."

Talia sat up. "Everything okay?"

"I'm fine. I'm with Dana at the movies. Would you let my dad know I'll be staying at her house tonight?"

"Why don't you tell him yourself?"

"He's asleep."

"Gali. We're broken up."

"Listen," Gali said, "I texted him. But if he wakes up and wonders where I am, I don't want him freaking out."

"Fine," Talia said, "I'll let him know." But after she hung up, she felt ashamed for surrendering so easily: if Tomer was this deep in the dark, didn't someone need to make sure Gali was okay? She was certain she'd heard a boy's voice in the background, and even if Gali *was* telling the truth, Talia doubted Tomer would want her staying at a friend's house in the middle of the week. Plus it must have been an effort to find her number in the first place, as if Gali knew going through Talia was the easy route, that she was too big a pushover to say anything but yes. Most of all she felt manipulated, as if any bonding earlier that night had simply been a calculated act on Gali's part to get what she wanted.

She called the number back. It rang and rang until voicemail picked up: *This is Nir, you know what to do.* She pressed redial and got the recording again, and finally, the third time, Nir answered.

"Let me talk to Gali," she said.

"Who is this?"

"You know she's fourteen."

"And?"

"And give her the fucking phone!" Who was this guy, Talia thought, out with a little girl on a school night? She heard the muffled sound of a hand over the receiver, then Gali said, "Talia?"

"Tell me where you are."

"I told you. At Dana's."

"Don't lie to me."

"But I *told* you," Gali said.

"Gali, I won't call your dad, but I just need to know where you went. Tell me right now or I'll—"

"What?"

"I'll tell him you're a liar who's sleeping with a much older boy, and that you've got pot stashed in your room." Talia had no idea about the truth behind any of this, but Gali whispered, "*Fine*. We're at Alma Beach," and Talia pulled her parents' spare keys off the peg near the door. "I'm taking the car," she called out, and her mother yelled, "Tell him hi!"

She backed out of the driveway and sped through Rehovot's silent roads. Even the highway was nearly empty, and within twenty-five minutes she was cruising down Hayarkon Street, searching for parking. It was a pleasant, balmy evening, and as she strode down the beach, she saw people huddled around fires or playing matkot. She walked closer and found Gali and her friends by a bonfire closer to the shore. Most of them were coupled off, nuzzled on each other's laps or making out, and a girl in Bedouin pants and a tank top was playing guitar. Gali's arms were around this Nir's neck, and he looked like a nice-enough kid, skinny and small and in civilian clothes, his dark hair buzzed so close Talia had a feeling he'd only recently been drafted. He didn't even have facial hair, just some optimistic fuzz above his lip, and it occurred to Talia that he probably wasn't all that older than Gali.

The scene was so much more hippie-ish and earnest than Talia would have imagined for a girl like Gali, and she wondered why she'd gotten so upset over one silly lie when the truth was that she didn't want to leave the beach herself, that what she really wanted was to crouch by the fire and just relax. So she walked closer, listening to the breeze and the guitar, when she noticed the entire group was staring. They were looking at her like she was such a *grown-up*: still dressed for the office, her cardigan flapping behind her, her sensible leather flats disappearing into the sand—and it was right then that Talia understood she was no longer young.

Talia stood there, waving her keys like the unwanted chaperone she knew she was, until Gali finally got up, clearly humiliated, and followed her back to the car. Gali hunched in the passenger seat, and as Talia drove away from the curb, she said, "I don't know what your problem is, Talia. This isn't your business."

"It is when you lie to me. I was worried."

Talia pulled onto Tomer's street and up to his apartment, keeping the engine running. Through the window she saw the television flashing and his bare feet on the coffee table. She couldn't see anything past his sweatpanted legs, but she knew he was probably asleep on the couch, unaware that his daughter had gone out, let alone that any of this was happening in her life. Watching him through that window, a gloomy fish in a beautiful aquarium, filled her with such a massive rush of sorrow that when Gali whispered, "Please don't make me go up there—I can't deal with him right now," Talia nodded and put the car in reverse.

She'd planned to take Gali to Rehovot, to set her up in the kitchen with a snack before sneaking off to call Tomer. But as she turned off the highway and up the hill, she saw, in the distance, the kibbutz near her house. She hadn't been there in more than a decade, but when she drove through the gates and parked in the side lot, the familiar sounds swept right in: crickets and owls and the faint chatter of a few kibbutzniks, far away, sitting outside the dining hall.

"I used to come out here all the time," Talia said. She led

Gali down the path she and her sisters had always taken, near the ulpan classrooms where the foreign volunteers lived, people who wouldn't be surprised by unfamiliar faces. But no one was outside the cottages anyway, and they walked past the irrigation equipment factory, the swimming pool and the avocado orchards, until they were standing at the edge of the date palm groves.

And Gali, who hadn't uttered a word on the entire drive to Rehovot, who'd been glumly following Talia through the kibbutz as if this were one more punishment she'd have to endure, stopped and said, "Wow. This is beautiful."

It *was* beautiful. Hundreds of tall palms, planted in perfect grids, surrounded them. Talia hadn't even known if they'd still be producing dates, but everything looked just as she remembered. The ground was blanketed with fallen fronds, and even the smell of donkey manure wasn't so bad when mixed with bark and overripe dates. Parked against one of the trees was a forklift, with clippers and an old, dust-beaten radio resting beside one of the tires.

"My sisters and I spent so many hours up in these trees," she said. "It was like this quiet place where we were safe from whatever was happening." She couldn't remember what she'd found so stressful as a teenager—probably just boys, slipping in math, her parents—but Gali nodded solemnly and followed her up the forklift's ladder. She was quicker and more confident than Talia would have expected, reaching the top of the trunk and testing the fronds until she found one sturdy enough to hold her weight. They sat side by side and gazed out. Until now Talia hadn't even noticed that the moon was almost full, illuminating the tarped-over farmland and the dairy, a couple leaving the dining hall and walking hand in hand down the narrow brick path to their cottage. Beyond, Rehovot stretched out in its entirety, looking just as Talia imagined architects and contractors like Tomer had planned it in miniature: the terra-cotta roofs, the murky gray line of the highway, the tall white apartment complexes jutting up against the hills, so small they were like plastic pieces she could move around on a game board. "We had this deal," Talia said, "that up here we could tell each other whatever we wanted and no one would judge. That it would never leave the trees. So if there's anything—"

"We didn't sleep together," Gali blurted. "Like you accused me of. Though we've done everything but."

Talia eyed her sideways, and Gali continued, "It was kind of bad. I mean, *I* was bad at it."

"Everyone is in the beginning."

"Really?"

"No one knows what they're doing. You know with my first boyfriend I took it literally and actually sucked on—his *thing*? Like a lollipop." She was doing it again, speaking without thinking, but Gali looked so relieved that someone out there had humiliated herself more, that perhaps she would receive the silver medal, rather than the gold, for history's worst blowjob, that Talia would have recited excruciating story after excruciating story if it made the girl feel any better. She remembered what it was like, all that shame and uncertainty, how the room could never be dark enough.

"I've been writing letters," Gali said then. "To my mom. It was my therapist's idea. And he's sort of a tool."

"Your dad likes him."

"My *dad's* a tool," Gali said, and sighed. "I'm supposed to write what's going on with me, at school or whatever. Just to feel like she's still with me," she said. "And sometimes I'll write about Nir. Nothing graphic, obviously, but, you know, just who he is and stuff. You know I don't even know if she had another boyfriend before my dad?"

"Because you were too young to know which questions to ask," Talia said quietly.

"Sometimes I write other things," Gali said. "Like how I wish I'd died first, just so I wouldn't have to miss her this much."

Right then Gali looked so small and confused and lost in the world, her eyes wide, sugary lipstick smeared across her chin. She was playing with the hem of her satiny sleeve, pulling at the delicate threads with her fingers. "Would it be alright if . . . I stayed over tonight?" she asked, and Talia thought about how good it might be if she just said yes. She could see it all unfolding as clearly as if clicking through a series of digital photos: Tomer on her parents' kitchen floor, telling goofy jokes while he scraped off their linoleum, already entrenched in a new fix-it project now that the counters were done. Her sisters over on weekends: a house of mothers so ready to dote on Gali, their toddlers worshipping her and following her from room to room. Her parents, relaxed and smiling at the table, grateful to have their family back together again, Tomer and Gali such an intrinsic, immediate part of it. She thought about Tomer asleep on the sofa in his apartment, how any moment he'd awake in that dark, empty room and start calling his daughter. Maybe she should stop this back and forth with him and just accept how easy it could be with a man who already knew how to be a boyfriend, a husband, a father. Maybe her need to travel, to hear other people's stories, to make a name for herself—maybe it had never been ambition and curiosity that drove her but the plain and simple fear that she wouldn't know how to face real life.

But even sitting there in the tree, even just entertaining the fantasy, made Talia feel restless and slight. As if the brown hills surrounding her just kept rolling out into nothingness, the great unknowns in Kiev and beyond so distant they no longer belonged to her. As if it were someone else's future, some girl Talia had always envied from afar who she bumped into now and again, when everyone was home visiting their parents over Chanukah Break.

"My therapist tells me other things," Gali continued. "I go in and he talks and talks. But I wish he'd stop giving me home-work and just tell me how to be happy again," she said, and Talia wanted nothing more than to give her an answer. For so long, she'd told herself happiness came from finding the thing you loved most and figuring out a way to make it central to your life. But that seemed so unreachable now, some abstract theory, and Talia knew she'd come up here as much for her-self as for Gali, hoping everything might look clearer from this vantage, that she'd be able to reach a decision about what to do next.

"When I'm with you, I feel—not alone," Gali said suddenly.

And then something seemed to kick inside her and before Talia knew it, Gali had scooted so close she could smell the bonfire in her hair. For a moment they sat there awkwardly, breathing silently in the tree, and Talia had a flash of what that night of Everything But must have been like for Nir, graceless and unnatural, Gali's advances clunky and poorly timed. Then

Gali leaned in to hug her. The gesture was so sudden, so jarring, that Talia jerked back—and Gali, arms stretched wide, wobbled on the frond and lost her balance.

"Gali!" Talia yelled, reaching for her. But Gali had already grabbed the trunk to keep from slipping. As the thorns pierced her skin, she let out a cry so loud people might have heard her on the highway. Talia knew she'd be fine—she'd steadied herself in time, was in no danger of falling. But sitting there on the frond, holding tight to the tree, she looked so shocked and afraid that Talia's heart seized. She gathered the girl carefully in her arms, resting Gali's head against her chest, wiping her damp, hot face with the back of her hand. Gali winced, and Talia, left with no real words of comfort, no guarantee things would ever get easier, said the only thing she knew for certain: that any moment the poison would kick in, numbing the places that hurt the most.

The Unknown Soldier

Fridays were busy outside Alameda Point. Women shouldered past Alexi, coiffed and perfumed and in pumps and
pearls and fuzzy sweaters, calling for their children to hurry
up and take their places in the inspection line. For the past
twelve months, Alexi had only known the other side to these
afternoons, the men's collective anticipation of those sacred
hours in the cramped visiting room or, on sunny days, at the
picnic tables in the yard—men who had stopped, at a certain
point, asking Alexi about his own family once it was painfully
clear they were never coming to see him.

Standing at the entrance now, watching his ex-wife and son
pull up to the correctional facility, Alexi felt jumpy and nervous
and a little out of breath. And not just about his release, or the
fact that Katherine was giving him their son for the weekend,
but because she'd agreed to come to begin with. He wondered
what it meant—a move toward forgiveness, maybe nothing at
all. He couldn't even tell if, after a year inside, he looked any
different. Maybe a few pounds thinner but wearing the same

slacks and button-down they'd known him in last, clutching, in a flimsy plastic bag, all his remaining possessions: his wallet, containing a mere twenty-two dollars; house keys that would no longer work; the sports section from the morning he was brought in, August 12, 1950, which felt like a cruel joke, as if flaunting that on top of everything else, he had missed the Yankees' repeat as world champions.

"Benny!" he said, peering into the car. Then, turning to the driver's seat, "Katherine!"

But she wouldn't look at him. She just sat there, checking her watch as if frustrated that she'd never get these seconds of her life back, while Benny crawled into the backseat for his suitcase. It was technically *Alexi's* suitcase, and he had a sudden image of everything else he'd once owned in Los Angeles, before the house was seized earlier that year and Katherine had dragged all of his belongings, his books and clothes and excellent record collection, out to the street on garbage day and moved with Benny to a tiny studio in Palms.

"Drop him at Ellen's Sunday's morning," Katherine said, staring at the dashboard, and Alexi found, with a pang, that she still had a disorienting effect on him: her high cheekbones and light brown eyes and delicate hands gripping the wheel, so small they always made his own in comparison feel massive and clumsy. But he noticed, too, the lines that had begun to deepen across her forehead and how pale she was for summer, as if she'd barely had a chance to go outside.

And then, finally, she met his gaze. All at once everything he'd been planning to tell her, the carefully crafted apologies he'd been working on so much of the year—suddenly all of that was moot, seeing from her such a look of disdain it was clear she wanted him erased from her life. "She's on 28th and Church," she said flatly, scribbling down her sister's address, all their road trips to visit Ellen in San Francisco apparently cast away and forgotten, some other couple's history.

Benny climbed out of the car and ran to him. Alexi stroked his soft hair and breathed in everything at once, gum and sleep and cheese on his breath, wondering, if just through smell and touch, he could determine whether his nine-year-old was okay. "I missed you," Alexi said, and right then something seemed to kick inside Katherine and she bolted out of the driver's seat. She pulled their son toward her, pressing his face to her blouse, and whispered, "Call me at Aunt Ellen's if you need *anything*." And when Benny said, "Jeez, Mom, it's just two days," she reached through the open car window, pulled a five-dollar bill from her pocketbook and thrust it into his hand. "In case of emergency," she said, as if Alexi weren't standing right there, as if Benny weren't going away with his own father but a derelict stranger, hurtling her boy into the wild.

She kissed Benny's head, then got back in the car without even a wave goodbye to Alexi, and he led his son across the lot to the Plymouth he'd arranged to borrow for the weekend, rusty and dilapidated with candy wrappers and cola bottles cluttering the backseat. He slid in beside Benny and drove out of the gates and onto the bridge, where all at once the San Francisco skyline came into view. Flawless, if it weren't for Katherine in the rearview mirror, as if signaling that the three of them would never be together in a car again, the windows down, her cheek on his shoulder, his hand on her calf.

He sank his foot onto the gas and the cluster of cars surrounding him, Katherine's included, quickly disappeared.

Then he glanced sideways at his son. As a baby, Benny had looked so much like him that even the sight of his child, sitting in his high chair or napping in his crib, used to startle Alexi so intensely he'd forget why he entered the room in the first place. He'd read somewhere that there was a biological reason for it, that it afforded fathers the kind of closeness and recognition mothers inherently felt after pregnancy. But over the past year Benny had begun to resemble him less, his curly black hair now wavy and light like Katherine's, his once-olive skin so pale it was like the whole veiny map of his interior was open for public viewing. He'd shot up maybe four inches since they'd seen each other last but hadn't put on any weight—though maybe, Alexi thought, his son could work the gangliness in his favor if he played the smart, serious card with girls. He knew from Katherine that once again Benny had gotten all A's, about which Alexi was deeply proud and had been bragging to everyone inside.

"What's your favorite subject?" he asked his son.

"Science, and probably history."

Alexi nodded. These seemed like solid answers. "Who's your best teacher?"

"It's August," the boy said, looking at him curiously. "I'm on summer vacation."

"Ah," Alexi said. He pulled off at 19th and drove along the park. He'd never liked San Francisco. Its beauty had always felt so showy, with its choppy blue water and steep, craggy hills and all those frilly houses painted candy-egg colors. Alexi was an actor and it had always felt to him, visiting the city, that he was on the set of San Francisco even when in the middle of it, even drinking coffee or eating a sandwich or waiting outside the ferry terminal. His closest friend from inside, Karl Mueller, had set him up with the car, along with a friend-of-a-friend's apartment for the weekend. But the directions were complex and confusing, and as Alexi backed out of a one-way street, then headed down a dead end, he found himself pining for the wide, no-nonsense boulevards of Los Angeles.

"I have it all planned out," Alexi said. "I've got us a great place for the weekend"—if he ever found it, he thought, silently cursing yet another one-way street to nowhere—"and we'll do it up, a steak dinner tonight, pancakes for breakfast."

"Is that what *you* want?" his son said.

"What do you mean?"

"Your first weekend out."

How grown-up of Benny to consider his needs, Alexi thought. He'd always been that way. Alexi remembered picking him up from nursery school years ago, and the teacher telling him that when they were playing musical chairs and the girl left without a seat began to cry, Benny immediately stood up and offered his. He'd relished seeing his son through the teacher's admiring eyes, though lately Alexi had been worrying about the line between generosity and patsiness growing murkier now that Benny had been alone with his mother. He'd sensed, in his calls to Katherine from Alameda Point, the weight that had been thrust on the boy. Usually she'd pass the phone off to Benny the moment she heard Alexi's voice. But the few times she relented, her responses seemed as predictable as the clicking sounds they always heard five minutes in, saying things like "It's been rough, but we're getting through it," or "We're finding ways to brighten up the place in Palms," as if it were perfectly acceptable that their nine-year-old was shouldering half of that "we." And though he was out now, though he'd been offered his friend's pool house in L.A. for a month while he, supposedly, figured out what was next in his life, Alexi knew that having a weekend dad wouldn't save Benny from the year he'd been left without one.

The apartment Karl had set him up with was on a hill at the crest of Buena Vista Park, tidy and bright with a Murphy bed in the living room. On the kitchen table was a note from Karl's friend's friend, wishing them a great weekend and offering whatever was left in the icebox. Alexi was touched that someone he'd never met would be so kind.

Benny walked to the window and Alexi followed him. It offered yet another unobstructed view of the skyline, as if the entire city had been built to brag about the same postcard image. Alexi looked out at the treetops, the low-slung buildings and the water beyond, the light so sharp he wondered whether his eyes were still adjusting after his time indoors or if it was, simply, a truly beautiful day. Even the undershirts fluttering from the clothesline seemed particularly white, the trash bins on the sidewalk a glorious green—and though he had no idea where Ellen's apartment fit within this scene, the fact that she and Katherine were out there somewhere, that they too could be going for steaks tonight and pancakes in the morning but doing everything in their power to avoid running into Alexi, suddenly made him feel queasy and warm, and he backed away from the window, turned to his son and said, "Forget San Francisco. Let's blow it off and head to Napa. That's how I want to spend my first weekend out—to relax somewhere, just the two of us. Who knows, maybe we'll make it up to Oregon."

"Really?" the kid said, sounding more excited than he had

all day, and Alexi, suddenly excited himself, said, "Really." *This* was what it meant to be out in the world again. To change plans on a whim, to speed down that narrow one-way street with his son beside him, leaving the city behind as he steered onto the bridge, the windows down, the possibilities flying everywhere.

✧   ✧   ✧

SOMEWHERE IN Napa, Alexi realized he had no idea where he was. Part of the problem, he knew, was that he'd been there only once, three years ago, and he hadn't been driving. He had been drunk in the back with Julia Wexler, the film's head writer and cause for so much of the trouble in Alexi's marriage to begin with, while the husband-and-wife producer team drove them from winery to winery. Stella and Jack had been going to Napa for the past fifteen years, even before it *was* Napa, when it was just a handful of vintner families scattered across the valley, trying to make a living post-Prohibition, and that entire weekend had felt meandering and glorious, discovery after discovery.

Now he was lost, and it was dark, and the towering oak trees and skinny dirt roads that had once felt so inviting seemed menacing and sinister. For almost an hour he couldn't find a single place to stop. Benny was staring out the window, his cheek against the glass, and Alexi passed orchards and cattle farms and rickety wood houses, feeling more and more hopeless, until finally, in the distance, he saw an inn and pulled over.

"Stay here," he told his son, and jogged inside. It was no-frills but perfectly adequate, with overstuffed leather chairs and dark green walls, like a hunting lodge without the guns or taxidermied animals. Through the glass doors Alexi saw picnic tables, and his mood immediately lifted as he envisioned a decent night's sleep after a year on that stiff, dirty cot and a lovely breakfast on the patio in the morning, coffee and juice, eggs and fresh muffins. The pretty redhead behind the desk was reading a thick paperback she set down then and said, "Welcome to the Pinecone. Just you?"

"One room, two beds," Alexi said. "For me and my son."

The woman smiled at him. Her hair was pulled away from her face and Alexi admired her long, creamy neck, the tiny, almost inconsequential buttons climbing up her blouse. It had been twelve and a half months. There had been a time in his life when it would have felt so easy to lean over the counter and ask this woman when she got off work, then meet her for a drink, or three or four. But her skin, her lips, the sparkly blue stones in her delicate earlobes—all of it gave him a jolt of sadness, just another reminder Katherine wanted nothing to do with him.

"That'll be eighteen dollars," she said, and Alexi cleared his throat. If he paid for this room, he and Benny would be sharing a pack of gum for dinner. He realized he had no idea what things cost in Napa—everything had always been paid for, Stella and Jack opening doors to every inn, winery, restaurant, and all that was ever expected of Alexi was that he glide right in. He was struck by a feeling he hadn't had in so long, a feeling that had thrown him into a crippling panic when he was in his early twenties and first auditioning: of being an imposter, a single step away from being found out. He raked a hand through his hair and looked at the woman. A trio of brass mirrors hung behind her and he could see himself reflected back, dozens of tiny blinking Alexis.

"Just give me a minute. Let me get my wallet from the car," he said, backing out. He let himself into the driver's side and took a long breath. Benny was bobbing along to some radio song that sounded to Alexi like all backup vocals. "It was crummy inside. We'll find something better," he said, and threw the car in reverse.

He sped down another dark, curvy road. He had no idea where to go. Benny didn't seem concerned, though—he perked at the task. "There's one," he said, pointing to a vacancy sign, and when Alexi drove right past he pointed out another, as if they were simply playing car games on a family road trip. He knew his son was trying to help, but he hated the game—*I-Spy Another Inn My Father Can't Afford*—and when Benny pointed out a third, Alexi mumbled, "You don't think I see them too?"

Benny looked as if he'd been struck in the face.

"I'm sorry," Alexi said quickly. "Oh Benny, I'm sorry." But his son had already slunk into his seat, and Alexi stared ahead at the road and wondered how the trip was, so soon, panning out this way. Driving with Benny through the night, possibly being forced to, at a certain point, pull over to the side and sleep in this borrowed shitheap. He'd once, not so long ago, won the starring role as Lev Gorelik, hardscrabble peasant turned war hero. The Russian paratrooper from the tiny, impoverished village of N., who, when forgotten behind enemy lines, finds himself trapped in a collapsed building with seven SS soldiers. Before he'd landed the part, Alexi had been stuck singing hair-care ads for the radio, and he couldn't believe, sitting in the Paramount lot in his Red Army fatigues, that for much of his adult life he'd actually gotten up in the morning to sing jingles like *Wildroot Cream, a little goes a long, long way* without want-

ing to kill himself. *The Unknown Soldier* had been a serious
and character-driven project, following Lev's fateful encounter
with the Germans—a moving film, the publicists promised,
with "drama to touch the heart of every woman, adventure to
stir the blood of every man." It had been, in all possible ways,
the part of a lifetime, and everyone—the casting director, the
producers, Julia Wexler—had believed that he, Alexi Liebman,
a working-class Russian himself, was perfect for the role.

Of course, not one of those people knew that, while Alexi
may have been born in Russia, he had lived in Queens since
he was two. That he hadn't grown up wealthy by any measure
but had been perfectly comfortable; that in fact his parents
had dedicated their lives in the States solely to maintaining
this level of comfort, his father spending his days off from the
bottle factory in their driveway, waxing his beloved Model A,
his mother stashing away every Sears catalog that came in the
mail and combing through them slowly and obsessively in the
evenings, her personal pornography. That communism was the
exact reason they'd escaped when they could, saying it had
only made their lives more miserable, and that, beyond sharing news about relatives still there, they never mentioned Moscow at all. That as a boy, Alexi, in a desperate attempt to seem
like more of an American, had dropped the *i* at the end of his
name, and that, by the time he got a high school scholarship to
Collegiate and had a whole new group of friends in Manhattan,
he was already known by everyone, including his parents, as
Alex. That when he was eighteen and both his parents died of
heart failure the doctor was certain had been brought on by
the stress of their early lives, he found himself barely thinking
at all about Russia, a place he had not a single memory of. That

it was only when he moved to Los Angeles and wasn't even getting callbacks for hair-care ads that it occurred to him his heritage could make him stand out in a good way, could actually give him leverage, when trying to break into an industry run by his own people. And so right away he went back to calling himself Alexi, even paying extra to have all new headshots printed with the name change, fifteen extra dollars just to have that *i* back where it belonged.

Everywhere he went people thought he was foreign. Somehow, being the child of immigrants gave him the look of an immigrant himself: his thick hair, gray since his twenties, made him seem world-weary and somber; his dark, droopy eyes gave him an air of mystery and exhaustion, as if he'd witnessed terrible, unmentionable things, even after a blissful night's sleep and a weekend bodysurfing in Malibu. Even his slight, skinny frame, the one thing he'd never liked about his looks, only added, according to *Variety*, to his "rakish appeal." And it wasn't just *Variety* that believed in him. In the early reviews, *Backstage* had called him "an old soul, by turns mesmerizing and terrifying to watch." The *L.A. Mirror* had called him "a virtuoso capable of embodying both the horrors of war and the optimism of the future."

And he had believed it. Everyone had. Since the day he'd been cast as Lev, Alexi had been aware that he was getting away with something—though, he reasoned, he'd never explicitly lied about anything. He just never told the complete truth. He may have, when asked about his American accent, mentioned the pronunciation workbooks stacked on his family's kitchen table, as if he, and not just his parents, had pored over them nightly. He may have once, a little drunk at a party, pretended to forget the English words for the pigs in a blanket being passed around. He may have, that night and possibly a few others, begun sentences with, *In my country* . . . He may have, when asked by the film's very openly communist director one night over steaks at Musso's what he thought about Truman, parroted back what he'd overheard at the writers' table, that he was narrow-minded and ruthless, his doctrine a farce and an affront to civil liberties. He may have, at Stella and Jack's invitation, attended a number of meetings in their Hancock Park living room, where there may have been some pretty detailed discussions about following their Soviet comrades down whatever path they took. He may have, on one of those evenings, filled out one of the Party membership forms being passed around, simply because everyone else was. He may have lied to Katherine about his whereabouts, inventing a rummy game with the guys. He may have, after those living room meetings, followed Stella and Jack and Julia and all the others to the Polo Lounge for drinks, where there may have been talk about making another, even more politically charged film than *The Unknown Soldier*, a film so important, so heartbreaking, so *stirring*, the director said, that he'd eat his own shoe if it weren't an immediate classic. Alexi may have gotten an erection at the possibility of starring in said film. He may have downed his vodka martini and announced, to every bigwig in the room, that if they weren't considering anyone else, if they hadn't already made a casting decision, that it would be both an honor and a gift to marry his political and artistic passions in such a project, to entwine them so entirely, and they may have, every person in that room, eaten it all up completely.

Not that he'd admit to any of this, even under oath. *Espe-*

cially under oath. Alexi Liebman may have been a lot of things, but one thing he'd never be was a snitch. Anyway, none of that information, he knew, would have made a difference in court. He'd still gone to meetings, starred in a flagrantly political film, been a card-carrying Party member, even if he often was late paying his dues. Right after the cast and crew had been subpoenaed, Stella and Jack had mobilized everyone—there must have been twenty people—in their living room. They brought in the best lawyers they could find, sympathizers themselves, who all said, over and over, that if everyone banded together in court and invoked the Fifth Amendment, they'd not only protect the group but challenge the House Un-American Activities Committee's right to ask such unconstitutional questions in the first place. Anyway, the lawyers said, they were certain of victory. Look how easily Howard Hughes had shouted down the congressional committee. The list went on. If everyone stuck together, the lawyers said, if they all meticulously coordinated their statements—and Alexi remembered how glaring Julia Wexler's absence had been that evening, though they hadn't yet learned that she'd named names, then scrambled to find work script-doctoring another film—they'd get through this relatively unscathed.

Alexi had believed them. He hadn't known, that night at the meeting, that the group's own refusal to give up names would get them cited for contempt of Congress, and that, when their final appeal was denied by the Supreme Court five months later, they'd all be sent to jail. No one—not Stella or Jack or the lawyers—really thought that was a possibility. Their group was one of the first brought in to testify, and at the time not even the lawyers were taking the Committee's threats seriously. The best thing Alexi could do, they told him, both for his career and for his family, was to plead the Fifth; when the inquiry was finished—and they were all convinced it would blow over quickly—he'd want to be seen as loyal and trustworthy to his higher-ups so he could get back to work. Alexi had no choice but to listen. His career, once on the brink of massive success, was suddenly in danger of being orbited into obscurity, black- listed before the world had a chance to know he existed. And so he did what he did to stay in the good graces of the only people who'd ever hired him. He approached the witness chair that day in Washington and handed the Committee a short statement the group had scripted: that in America there was a secret ballot, and he didn't believe the government had any more right to inquire into his political affiliations than an elec- tion official had to walk into a voting booth and examine a bal- lot marked by the voter.

But as the chairman glanced at the statement, so quickly it was impossible he'd gleaned anything from it at all, Alexi had looked out at the packed caucus room, every seat filled, every newsreel camera and microphone aimed at him, and had been filled with a rush of disappointment. Because while he'd prepared himself for the spectacle—everyone knew what a PR gold mine this was for the Committee—he hadn't been pre- pared for how bright the camera lights would be. He hadn't been prepared for the way his entire body perked every time one of those bulbs flashed right at him, a thirsty, neglected plant back under the sun. And while he'd been prepared for the Committee chair's question—*Are you now or have you ever been a member of the Communist Party?*—he hadn't been prepared for how deadening it would feel to give such a lackluster response during what, Alexi was realizing right then, may very well have been his final performance.

And yet he had known that, in the end, he would answer exactly as the lawyers had advised. So he'd looked right into the cameras and said, "Your question, Mr. Chairman, is both improper and illegal." It was precisely the response he was supposed to give, vague and evasive—and, Alexi feared, completely unmemorable. He delivered it exactly as he was supposed to, in a clipped, unemotional tone—everything he'd learned *not* to do in acting class—and, maybe worst of all, the whole thing was over so quickly. The moment his words were out he was excused, all the cameras swiveling away from him and down the aisle to follow the next witness approaching the chair.

✵   ✵   ✵

DOWN THE road now, on the other side of an overpass, Alexi saw blinking lights spelling out MO EL. He pulled into the lot, grabbed their suitcases and led Benny to the lobby. It really wasn't so bad. Moths flitted around a single bulb and the sofa was threadbare, but back issues of *Time* were fanned out attractively on the coffee table. There was an older woman behind the desk doing a crossword, and the radio was broadcasting a baseball game. Alexi paid his eight dollars and got the key and he and Benny walked back outside, around the rear of the lot and up the concrete steps to their third-floor room. It was carpeted and relatively clean. There were two single beds with a desert landscape framed between them, and he and his son put down their luggage and looked at each other.

"You want to play cards?" Alexi said.

"I'm not sure we know the same games."

"You want to read, then?"

"I didn't bring a book," Benny said. "Do *you* want to read?"
Alexi shook his head. "Are you hungry?"

"Not really. Maybe a little."

"Oh my God," Alexi said. "It's ten o'clock. I forgot about
dinner."

"It's okay. We can eat tomorrow."

"No," Alexi said. "You wait here."

He locked the door behind him and ran out to the thoroughfare. He could see his son watching from the window and wondered what he looked like from three stories above. There were
car dealerships on either side of him but not a single restaurant,
so he sprinted ahead to a filling station. He grabbed the first
things he saw and brought them all to the register: two root
beers, licorice, Hershey bars.

His stomach flipped just looking at the food, but when he
returned to the motel and spilled the loot on the bed, Benny's
eyes bugged. "I *never* get root beer."

Alexi couldn't believe this was actually earning him points.
"What's your mom making these days?"

"Meat loaf, tuna casserole."

"So she still has time to cook?"

"She does it on her day off, then freezes everything for the
week."

"She's doing alright, then?"

"Yeah. Okay. Not *great*."

Alexi could hear Katherine's voice so clearly—even Benny's intonation on that last word, as though her thoughts were
being transmitted directly through their son. He'd spent the

past year thinking about what he'd done, wishing he could fix it, knowing he couldn't. Knowing, even, that he was capable of making it worse, of rubbing dirt in her wounds, like earlier that day outside the prison when he'd felt so nervous seeing her that Alexi realized now he hadn't even thanked her for driving Benny up, probably taking time off work to do so. But it was only right then, sitting beside his son, that he understood, even without Katherine in the room, even with the Golden Gate Bridge between them, just how much he'd hurt her. And he knew it wasn't just his arrest, or the affair with Julia Wexler. It was Katherine knowing that all her conversations, even the most painful, private ones, had been recorded. It was the shitty apartment in Palms. It was the fact, as she told him after his hearing in Washington, sitting together in the bar of the Sheraton Park Hotel, that he'd hidden this whole world from her. "The thing with Julia I can understand," she'd said. "I hate it and it makes me want to run you both over, but at least it's something I can wrap my head around. But you swore to me that working with a communist director didn't mean you were getting caught up in that yourself. You kept a *life* from me, Alexi."

And Alexi, at a loss, in a moment of desperation, feeling, for the first time, that the possibility of losing Katherine was so horribly *real*, had tried to reason that acting was his career, his livelihood, it was how he supported his family. That if she really thought about it, he'd simply been playing another part—and that was when Katherine had stood up, buttoned her coat and said, "You're an idiot," and left him sitting in the hotel bar.

Katherine Baker, one of the most politically mainstream

people he'd ever met, one of the only people he'd ever known who had actually voted for Willkie. Katherine, from Burwell, Nebraska, who, when they first met, both in their early twenties and new to L.A., had told him he was the third Jew she'd ever talked to, and Alexi had found something sexy, even thrilling, in that admission, moving her hands jokingly through his hair to prove he didn't have horns. Back then Alexi had been agentless, managerless, spending his days combing *Backstage* for casting calls—and even then, even when convinced of his own impending failure, he'd never doubted that things would pan out for Katherine. Right away she'd gotten a job as a receptionist at a furniture design studio, and though her dream wasn't to answer phones but to be a designer herself, Alexi was certain the moment the company decided to hire a woman, Katherine would be the obvious choice. He used to love driving around with her, watching her point out things he'd passed a million times and never considered, how every lamppost, park bench, stop sign was someone's aesthetic decision. He used to love, once they were married and living together in that bungalow off La Brea, walking out to their backyard and finding Katherine in a sleeveless shirt with a kerchief on her head, pulling apart some dilapidated chair she'd bought at a yard sale and stripping and reupholstering it herself, seeing potential for beauty in everything.

She was the one person he'd ever confided the whole Alexi-Alex-Alexi transformation to, and though she claimed she was impressed with him for coming up with it, Alexi knew, deep down, that she found the whole thing sort of silly. She found the whole *industry* silly: always asking how he could be so enthralled by people like Stella and Jack, who spent their weekends lounging by the pool, drinking expensive wine and discussing immigrants' rights while one of their Mexican workers cleaned leaves from the filter. Katherine was, at her core, so inherently practical and stable and—Alexi found this stunning—*happy*, that he sometimes feared she didn't really get him. His anxieties, while initially cute to her in an ethnic, anthropological sort of way, as if his tendency to expect the worst could actually be traced back to some pogrom, soon seemed to exhaust her. Her own parents, immigrants themselves, had suffered just as much, maybe more, than Alexi's, coming from Norway to an equally harsh climate, the grocery they ran only recently recovering from the Depression, her father's liver disease exacerbated by all those years he couldn't afford a doctor.

That's horrible, Alexi had said when she told him, when they were first together and swapping secrets late at night, more intimate, he had found, than the sex itself. Yeah, well, everybody's fine now, she'd replied, as if there were nothing left to say. And he'd watched the reel of those difficult times flicker across her face for just a second longer before moving on to the next scene of her life story, where as girls she and her sister Ellen would fantasize about moving to California the first moment they could, and then—this was where Katherine's voice went high and clear as a ballad—actually *doing* it.

Katherine was so skilled at blocking out the things she didn't want to look at, and, only a few years into their marriage, she began telling Alexi that his worries seemed self-indulgent and overblown, as though he had the power to turn them off like a switch. Which was one of the reasons he found Julia Wexler so easy to be around. Another Jewish transplant from the outer boroughs, another person who vacillated between the highs and lows of fame and failure at an athletic, almost Olympic speed. Another person whose ambition was fueled by the same paranoia that whatever success she'd achieved could be rescinded at any moment—though in all truth, Alexi knew Julia, one of the only head female writers in the industry, had more to be worried about than he. Even Stella, whom he and Julia both respected, knew she was able to do more interesting work by leaving her name off the credits, giving her husband all the glory. And while Julia was smarter than anyone on the film—no one would argue that—she felt she needed to wear these tailored man-suits to fit in at studio meetings; to crack more jokes than any of the guys; sometimes, Alexi felt, taking the shtick a bit too far by lighting a cigar around the writers' table. But even though, because they worked together, she had no idea about the Alex-Alexi thing, he knew, in his heart, that Julia would have understood that as well. The moment he saw her he felt like he was going home, that all his acts and defenses could be dropped, shrugged off as easily in the doorway of her bedroom as his jacket and shirt and slacks.

Julia was adamant their affair remain casual, not disrupting— let alone destroying—either of their marriages, and she asked about Katherine constantly. They'd never met, but Julia seemed genuinely interested in her. Not out of jealousy—more like Julia was so concerned about her potential threat to Alexi's relationship that she wanted to protect his wife in some way. She was forever inquiring about Katherine's background, her job, always taking her side when hearing about some minor tiff, even when Alexi didn't think he was asking her to choose sides, and he could never tell if it was his wife in particular or some sort of intrinsic loyalty to other women (even if she was, in fact, *the* other woman).

But Alexi always obliged and answered her questions, sometimes talking about Katherine for so long that he could almost see her in Julia's house with them. His pretty, wavy-haired wife, complimenting Julia on her spacious Neutra, on her yard, on the wooden deck that stretched out to a garden filled with juniper and jacaranda trees. He could see the three of them sitting around Julia's bright red patio table, Katherine shielding her eyes from the sun, fielding Julia's queries about Benny, about the design world, Julia doling out advice on how to nudge her boss into giving her more challenging projects, Katherine shooting Alexi a look that this woman was *pushy*. Then Katherine would flip the conversation back to Julia—she seemed to believe sharing anything about her accomplishments was inherently shameful and immodest—and as soon as talk of the movie came up, Julia and Alexi would immediately launch into some mistake they'd made at work and lean in together, trying to untangle whatever knot they'd created. And Katherine would sit back, stare up at the trees and tell them both in the calm, no-nonsense voice she'd perfected even before motherhood, to stop their useless analyzing: no one else on the film was possibly obsessing over whatever slight they feared they'd made, and why couldn't they just enjoy the lovely afternoon?

What Alexi never got to tell Julia, before she'd named names and severed all contact with him, was that she shouldn't have felt so guilty, that a twisted and terrible part of him wondered if the affair had actually made him a better husband. Somehow spending all that time with Julia, talking about Katherine, only reinforced his love for his wife. Plus getting to obsess over everything work-related with Julia meant he didn't need to burden Katherine with any of it, letting him throw all his energy into his family. And Katherine was spared his boring industry stories when he knew, strutting around the set in his military boots with a war-torn, gutted-out backdrop behind him, that Julia was waiting on the sidelines, ready to go out for drinks and pick apart everything that had happened on the movie that day, looking, if not for her pantsuit and heavy script under an arm, like one of her own characters, a dark-haired Soviet beauty pining for Lev back in the village.

He'd always felt so rejuvenated, coasting down Culver from the studio, back home to his wife and son. It was as if he were finally fulfilled. Katherine satisfied him maybe ninety percent but Julia was perfect for that niggling ten. Very little made him happier than pulling into his driveway and seeing, through the window, his family moving around inside, a diorama of his life he could so effortlessly step back into. Katherine's boss had finally agreed to let her take a stab at designing—sometimes at dinner they'd clink glasses to their good fortune—and Alexi used to feel so blessed walking in and finding her on the living room floor, going over sketches, surrounded by fabric swatches and charcoal pencils. He loved listening to her talk about flax and bark cloth, comparing Prouvé to Ponti, words as foreign and beautiful to Alexi as Italian or Portuguese.

Katherine never got a chance to finish the project. When Alexi was called in to testify, her boss, a man they'd had for dinner half a dozen times, whose son used to play with Benny, said he just didn't want to "get caught up in all that business" and fired her as quickly as he'd hired her. Now she was working at a dress shop she'd once frequented in Century City and waiting on, Alexi was certain, the same women she used to shop and lunch with. Women Alexi doubted were calling anymore, let alone inviting her to parties and outings with their children, no one wanting to get their hands dirty, no one believing for a second that the wife of Alexi Liebman hadn't been involved in anti-American activities as well.

※　※　※

"SO THINGS haven't been easy," Alexi said now, turning to his son. Benny was sprawled on the narrow motel bed, clutching his root beer with both hands. "Is she—talking to *you* about this?"

"She said she saw those FBI guys everywhere. So Aunt Ellen told her to see a psychiatrist."

"Benny." Alexi set down his drink. "Have you been eavesdropping on your mother?"

He shook his head. "She tells me. But she doesn't see Dr. Bittman anymore."

"He fixed her?"

"No," Benny said. "Stella, from the movie? She came over a couple months ago. She said she felt bad doing this—and she really seemed to—but that Mom had to stop going to Dr. Bittman. That what she told him could put a lot of people in trouble. Stella gave her the name of a good one in the Party."

Alexi looked around the room, at the frayed carpet and the yellow bedspreads and his son beside him, his tongue licorice-black. So Katherine was being watched from both sides. "And she went to this new psychiatrist?"

"She was pretty upset after Stella's visit. So she isn't seeing anyone." Benny shrugged, but the gesture looked false and exaggerated. This was not the way, Alexi thought, that a nine-year-old was supposed to talk. "During the day she's okay," Benny continued, "but at night sometimes she thinks they're at the window, and it's just a branch. Or she makes me check inside closets and behind doors. But lately she sleeps with me, and that makes it better."

"And those FBI men—*were* they following her?"

"Mostly they'd just park across the street and watch us. Once I went out to the side yard and saw them going through our trash, and another time they threw their sandwich crusts on our lawn, but other than that they were alright," Benny said, as if the whole thing were perfectly normal, as if he were simply describing nuisancy neighbors, and Alexi felt his throat constrict. He stood up. He scooped all the wrappers off the bed and tossed them in the garbage. "Let's get you to sleep."

Benny pulled out a little leather toiletry kit—Alexi could see everything in there, so neatly packed, even a bag of tissues, and a tiny spool of floss Katherine must have measured out just for this trip. His son was a good brusher, working even his back teeth and gums, and Alexi found that he was keeping his own toothbrush in his mouth much longer than he would have were he alone.

Then Benny spit, looked up and said, "I wanted to visit you this year."

"I know you did," Alexi said, slowly. "And I really wanted to see you. This thing with your mother and me—it's complicated."

"I know," Benny said. He walked back into the room, where he stripped down to his underpants and climbed into bed.

"Do you want to talk about it?" Alexi said, wanting very much not to talk about it.

"That's okay. It's kind of nice having a break from her, you know?"

Benny looked somewhere past him, at the wooden night-stands, the brass lamp, finally settling on the desert landscape on the wall, cacti and brown hills and a moon too pocked and orange to be taken seriously. He seemed exhausted. "From it. From the whole thing. That's what I meant." He pulled the covers to his neck and closed his eyes. "You know any good stories?"

"Sure." Alexi was touched by the question. "About what?"

"About jail?"

Alexi stood in the doorway of the bathroom, watching his son. He was so tiny in that twin bed. He thought about Katherine, somewhere in the city, peering out her sister's window to make sure she hadn't been followed. He had not only ruined much of her life, he thought; he had passed on the horrible flu of panic to the one person he'd believed was immune. "There isn't much to say," he said, finally. "You don't do a lot in there."

"But what's it *like*?" Benny said.

"It's not a good place."

"But—"

"It's a place you never want to end up, understand?" That was the way his own father used to talk to him, shutting down a conversation before it had a chance to happen, like watching a storefront's metal grate slide down right in front of him, one of those shop owners who randomly closed up whenever they felt like it, even when customers were waiting outside. Alexi could have been five, ten, fifteen—it didn't matter, it was always the same. Always the feeling that every question he asked his father, even something as innocuous as whether he should set the table, was an intrusion and a burden. That Alexi's presence alone exhausted the man, made him breathe deep as though he were trying hard not to snap. Which of course made Alexi ham it up more, anything for his attention. He had such a clear image of coming home from school and attempting to regale his father with some anecdote about his teacher. Desperately attempting to fatten it into a full-fledged story, impersonating classmates the man might have found more interesting than his son (was that when the performing had started, Alexi wondered, back in that small, bright kitchen in Queens?) while his father closed his eyes and grimaced, as if doing everything in his power to stop his patience from reaching its end, and Alexi wondered now why he couldn't do things differently. Not just to stand in the doorway ruminating about it, but to actually walk across the room and sit beside his son.

So he did it. He perched on the edge of the bed, the green motel sign reflecting off Benny's toothpick arms. But the boy was asleep (to be nine again, Alexi thought, dreaming before your head hit the pillow), his breath low and even, his knees tucked to his chest and his arms around them, as if, even with the bed all to himself, he was still carving out the space where his mother usually crawled in beside him.

✳   ✳   ✳

ALEXI HAD never believed that saying about everything improving with a new day. Usually the moment he awoke, before even opening his eyes, he was well aware of all that was wrong in his life. But the following morning was optimistically sunny, and even breakfast at a nearby diner wasn't half bad, a fruit cup, eggs, free refills on the coffee and toast with three different kinds of jelly. A breeze hit him as they walked back to the car, that perfect California weather Alexi hadn't realized he'd missed until right then, when he was so comfortable he forgot about the temperature completely.

"So listen," he said to Benny, pulling out of the lot. "No filling station junk today. I say we hit up a few vineyards, have a picnic lunch somewhere special." In the daylight, even the thoroughfare was quite pretty. Vineyards combed out on either side of him, and beyond, cows ambled across bright yellow fields. They both, at the same time, rolled down their windows, and all that balmy air filled the car.

Alexi found a jazz station and for about an hour they drove around. They stopped at a cheese shop for the best picnic food he could find: a hunk of Camembert, a Bûchette de Banon and a baguette. Down another road he pulled over at a farm stand and bought a carton of raspberries. He didn't bother to wash them and he and Benny ate as they drove, licking their lips and wiping their hands on their pants and giggling. Alexi was feeling giddy. He was feeling like a kid again, being with *his* kid, and as they coasted through the hills, he felt something opening inside him, a tranquillity he hadn't known was there. This was what it felt like to drive around with your son on a warm day, he thought. He put an arm around Benny's shoulder and his son immediately leaned into him, all his weight against Alexi's chest.

Up ahead was a Mediterranean-style winery, white stucco with iron gates and bougainvillea trailing the walls and the terra-cotta steps. The gardens on either side of the long, sloping driveway were so impeccably groomed that Alexi felt a little guilty sullying the lot with the Plymouth. Gazebos dotted the property, and in the center of the grounds was a pond where Alexi could see, darting beneath the water, Japanese koi that he suspected cost more than Katherine's monthly rent in Palms.

Inside the tasting room, wooden barrels were scattered about with cheese and cracker samples; Alexi was proud when he saw his son take only one, using the little square napkin to collect the crumbs, without him having to say so. He would tell Katherine, he decided, that he noticed the good manners she was instilling in their son. It might be a good excuse to call her.

Behind the counter, an attendant was waiting on an older couple, silver-haired and so alike in their navy sweaters that Alexi couldn't tell whether they were siblings or had simply been married for so long they'd begun to resemble one another. He took a moment to survey the wine. An entire shelf of Bordeaux blends, and there, nestled between two Barbeitos, the pièce de résistance, the crowning glory, the 1936 Georges de Latour Private Reserve. He was filled with a rush of memory: Stella and Jack had introduced him to it back when Alexi was a hack, a novice with an unsophisticated palate, not knowing the difference, even, between a Viognier and a Riesling. Of all his friends, those two had always been ahead of the curve on everything, and Alexi had a flash of their trip together, picnicking on grounds as lovely as these, then driving a couple cases back to L.A. in time for an NAACP benefit they were throwing at their place in Hancock Park. Alexi saw himself standing by their pool with a glass in his hand, surrounded by people, all of whom wanted to be near him. He couldn't remember the story he'd been telling but remembered people laughing and himself laughing along with them, certain that night it would be impossible to embarrass himself no matter how drunk he got—so different from his first industry parties, when he was starting out and never even completely sure whether his invite had been a mistake, every conversation a cause for second-guessing, so afraid he'd say one wrong thing and immediately be outed as a false ally, a false European, a false Alexi.

But there, at Stella and Jack's, he'd felt his life commencing. There people laughed at his jokes, even if they weren't funny, though somehow, when he was feeling that good, when he was riding that high, they almost always *were*. Every story he told seemed to have an arc, a punch line, an effortless, self-deprecating beauty—and he suddenly remembered the tale he'd been telling that night by the pool, about his grandmother's run-in with the NKVD outside her apartment, a story he'd only heard secondhand from his parents, as he'd left Moscow as a baby, but into which Alexi had found, easily enough, a way to insert himself as a character, the young grandson in the doorway with his Babchi, listening to the old woman shout those officers into silence for lurking outside, then inviting them in for coffee and dessert.

"And for you?" the attendant said then. He was tanned, with dark hair combed drastically to one side and pale blue eyes that seemed to boast about the rest of his face.

"A bottle of the Private Reserve." Alexi calculated, after the motel room and the filling station snacks and the raspberries, bread and cheese, that he had a little less than seven dollars left, and he was willing to drop it all on that bottle. He turned to Benny. "I don't care what it costs. Nothing in the world," he said, "is better than a glass of this with that Camembert."

"Agreed," the attendant said. "Absolutely. That will be ten dollars."

Alexi swallowed. The wallet in his hand, his black leather Ferragamo wallet, suddenly felt flimsy, meaningless, another stupid prop in his ridiculous sham of a life. This was, he thought, a thousand times worse than the previous night at the Pinecone, simply because his son was seeing it. He had a sudden, massive fear that this was what every subsequent day would be, a slightly variant, though eerily similar, round of humiliation.

He surveyed the tasting room. His first thought was that he had no idea Stella and Jack were *that* wealthy, carrying that wine out by the caseload. His second thought was that no one, not a single person, recognized him—and they never would. The attendant didn't know he was waiting on a man who couldn't afford that bottle, who could hardly afford the free samples. He smiled patiently at Alexi. He grinned down at the boy. Benny was looking back and forth at Alexi and the attendant, and then he reached into his pocket and pulled out the five-dollar bill his mother had given him. He laid it on the counter. Alexi stared at the bill. He wondered if there was any-thing more excruciating for a child than watching his father shamed. "Put that away," he whispered, and when Benny didn't, when he just stood there, Alexi snatched it off the counter. He shoved it into Benny's pocket and led him toward the door. He could feel the attendant staring. Only this time, unlike the night before, he couldn't come up with a single excuse for why he was bolting back to the parking lot.

He got into the driver's side and covered his face with his hands. Benny slid in next to him and Alexi knew, suddenly, that he was going to cry. The first time he ever had in front of his son—the first time, since he was a boy, that he had in front of anyone. Benny tentatively put a hand on his arm.

"That's a good wine," Alexi said, wiping his eyes.

"I know," the boy said.

"I promise you, we'll share a bottle one day."

"It's okay," Benny said. "I don't even like wine."

"Of course you don't," Alexi said. "You're nine years old."

"Actually," the boy said, "I'm ten. I had a birthday in April."

"My son is ten." He stared out at the windshield, tiny dead bugs splattered on the glass. Beyond that was grass and water and more grass, everything beautiful and still as a photograph.

"The thing is," Alexi said, "you asked me a question last night and I didn't give you a straight answer."

"That's alright," Benny said quietly. He picked at a mosquito bite on his arm, flinging the scab in the air. "Maybe I shouldn't have asked."

"No," Alexi said. "I want to be the kind of dad you can say anything to. That's something I thought a lot about this year. It's just hard for me to talk about."

"Yeah?" Benny said, looking excited.

"Not in the way you think," Alexi said. "I didn't get in any fistfights, no one knifed me in the leg. If anything, life inside was quiet. Most people had done their craziness out in the world and were pretty beaten down by the time they came in."

He shifted in his seat. "But something happened to me in there. I had a lot of time on my hands and so I finally started paying attention to the news." The world, it turned out, was falling apart. Every day, he told Benny, new things came up about Russia. They'd all get together, Alexi and his buddy Karl and a few others, over dinner or cards or sometimes during shifts in the garage, and discuss it all. They weren't so naïve they believed the Soviet Union would be perfect, but in those meetings at Stella and Jack's they *had* talked about how it stood for a better way of life. And yet suddenly Alexi was hearing about the treason trials, how even the supposedly staunchest communists in Russia were turning out to be traitors. It was the most depressing feeling, sitting in the prison yard with all these believers, discussing plans to fix the world while it was burning up around them. Sitting around with all these people who, unlike Alexi, had genuinely devoted themselves to the Soviet model. All these people who had destroyed their careers and their families for an ideology that may, in the end, not have worked at all. "That may have been making life worse for all the common people in Russia everybody was always talking about," he said. "Just like my parents had told me all along."

Alexi's tears were coming so quickly that every time he wiped his eyes a new batch was waiting. He had no idea if any of this made sense to the boy. If Benny was old enough to understand even a fraction of it, if all any of it meant to him was that his father hadn't been around. That he'd missed science fairs and parent-teacher conferences and—Alexi wasn't even sure what he'd missed.

"I'm sorry," he said. "You must think your dad's gone crazy."

"No," Benny said. "I get it. At least I think I do." And then Alexi saw something in his son's face, an expression of pure, unbridled adoration, and he thought about how much he would have killed for a moment like this with his own father. It was all so unfair, he thought. Fatherhood was like one giant free pass. The crying, the rambling, the admissions of weakness: all of it seemed to be making his son admire him more, and when Katherine broke down and did the same thing—the exact same thing—it made Benny want to run from her. He hated himself right then. Benny was the only person he had left, and Alexi didn't trust himself not to set this relationship on fire along with all the others. He thought about his friend's pool house awaiting him in L.A., where he'd begin to grovel for work he didn't even want, now that he could no longer return to the studio, now that all his contacts were still in jail, or hiding out in Mexico, or God knows where.

Alexi had convinced himself all that mattered was that he be near his family. But now even the smallest decisions felt enormous, insurmountable, potentially destructive—and for the first time, it occurred to him that this weekend could be causing Benny even more damage than the past year when he had no father around at all.

He put his keys in the ignition. Alexi suddenly wanted to drive very fast, as far away from himself as possible. "Let's go," he said.

"Where?"

"Back to San Francisco." He'd punished his son so much already. Benny shouldn't be forced to contend, on top of everything else, with the full reality of the disgraced man his father had become. It would devastate him. "I'll drop you with your mother and Aunt Ellen."

"But," Benny whispered, "what did I do wrong?"

"Nothing. It's just time to go."

"But I don't understand," his son said, and when Alexi didn't say anything, when he felt, quite possibly, that he had exhausted every word in the English language and there was nothing left *to* say, Benny mumbled, "Okay. I just need to use the bathroom."

He watched his son disappear into the tasting room. Sammy Kaye floated out from the speakers, and a Cadillac pulled up to the lot and a man got out, followed by an attractive black-haired woman: people Alexi might have known in a life that was feeling so far away it was as if it had never been his to begin with. He could see horses meandering in the distance, and, walking freely through the gardens, a peacock. My God, he thought, where *was* he?

Alexi was itching to go, out of this vineyard, this town, this . . . he could go anywhere, he thought. Anywhere and nowhere. He looked around the property. Benny was taking an awfully long time. Alexi got out of the car and walked up the path where he saw, through the door, his son coming out of the bathroom from the back of the tasting room. Soon, Alexi thought, Benny would be grown, with a wife and a home and maybe a son of his own. And yet all of that seemed so far in the future, watching Benny walk toward him, still so in the process of becoming a boy, let alone a man. There his son was, wiping his hands on his pants, running a finger up his zipper to make sure it was closed. There he was, walking up to the tasting counter, so high it reached his shoulders. The attendant was busy talking to the black-haired couple, and when he turned to the register to ring them up, there his son was, ducking behind the counter. There Benny was, swiping a bottle of the Private Reserve right off the shelf. There he was, slipping it under his shirt, walking past the bar without even a sideways look—a better actor, Alexi thought, than he himself. His pulse kicked. He had no idea what to do. He stepped forward to stop him, to turn him around and make him give it back, to teach his son a lesson while he was still young enough to listen. But Benny was already walking through the doors and into the bright sunny day, pulling the bottle from his shirt and thrusting it at his father: terrified, astonished, ready for his love.

Retrospective

Friends quoted in the obituaries talked about Eva Kaplan in her heyday, back in the sixties and seventies. They talked about the parties she and her husband used to throw in their Jerusalem home, inspired by the secret apartment exhibits Eva had attended in Moscow. A few Russian artists were often in attendance, and friends recalled them standing in front of their paintings, surrounded by philanthropists and U.N. officials and Knesset members, while Eva swept through the crowd in a silky pantsuit, a cocktail in hand, wearing what appeared to be all of her gold at once. The exhibits went on in the living room, but displayed throughout her home was the permanent collection amassed over a lifetime: the Picassos and Légers bought for a pittance back in the thirties, when she was still a young and ambitious art student in Paris; the Kotins and Gottliebs she'd begun collecting in the fifties during her years in New York; and, of course, the works that had made her as famous in her circle as the painters themselves: the hundreds of pieces she'd smuggled out of Russia, right up to the fall of the Curtain.

The art, her friends admitted, wasn't always that great. Of course the whole point, one friend said, was that it was supposed to be edgy and political, but there was no getting around how unappetizing it was to stare at a canvas of Nikita Khrushchev in a compromising position each morning over breakfast. Other pieces had been virtually destroyed by the time Eva exhibited them. It was hard to know if the poor quality had to do with the fact that the artists often worked with anything they could scavenge off the streets, mud and trash and auto paint, or if it was the shoddy way Eva had packed them, so that by the time the smuggled art made it through customs at Ben Gurion and was unveiled on her wall, the canvases, which sometimes weren't canvases at all but paper bags or burlap sacks, were so faded and torn it was hard to see what the artist's original intent had been. Still, friends insisted it wasn't simply the work one bought but the stories that went along with it. Eva had sneaked out several of Litnikov's now-famous labor camp paintings and, more than anyone, had promoted Mikhail Borovsky's work throughout the U.S. and Israel. Borovsky had been one of Russia's best-known painters under communism and internationally prized even after his death a few years ago, possibly the only member of the Artists Union the unofficial artists had respected back then, the only one, they'd said, able to think craftily within the constraining box of Socialist Realism—the only one, as Eva had said, who didn't think membership meant he had to paint "another bridge, or smiling worker, or ridiculous cow."

All over the world, obituaries puzzled over how Eva had managed to perform one of the largest and most dangerous art-smuggling operations of the twentieth century. The only person with a bigger collection was an American economist in Maryland, a friend of Eva's, whose quest to bring as many unofficial Russian works to the western world had inspired her, she'd said in numerous interviews, to do the same for Soviet Jewish art. A curator in Stockholm, quoted in her *Ha'aretz* obituary, believed Eva may have surreptitiously rolled the thinnest sketches into rugs she'd purchased before going through airport inspection in Moscow, while the director of the National Gallery in London thought she may have hidden beneath the canvases of state-sanctioned art—those bridges, those workers, those cows—the unofficial works. But as Eva's will traveled across the Mediterranean and the Atlantic to her family in Boston, the biggest question for her daughter Wendy was what her mother had bequeathed to her. Wendy had spent the past two weeks in Israel, dealing with the funeral and the shiva and sitting through one too many luncheons honoring her mother at the Israel Museum, where Eva had been a board member for nearly fifty years. And while the trip had only confirmed for Wendy what she'd feared most of her life— that these art people knew her mother better than she did herself—Wendy's father had already been dead two years, she was the only family Eva had left and she felt, in her heart, that the woman would have wanted to make her daughter's life as financially easy as possible. The paintings in Eva's house alone, Wendy told her own family as she tossed aside the rest of her mail and opened the executor's letter, had to be worth almost twenty million. But there, typed out clearly and succinctly, Eva's last wishes were stated: she was selling her private collection at discount to the Israel Museum and donating the proceeds, every last shekel, to charity.

Wendy sank into a chair and put her face in her hands. It was so like her mother, she whispered, to map things out to the minutiae. All the money, Eva had decided, would go toward creating the Eva Kaplan Family Foundation, which her daughter Wendy, son-in-law Larry and two grandchildren, Mira and Hannah, would administer. The foundation would fund art education programs at youth villages and immigrant absorption centers from Kiryat Shmoneh to Eilat, places Eva had been supporting for years. She'd use the rest of the money—of which there was millions—to build a new wing at the Israel Museum that would house the Eva Kaplan Mentorship Program, dedicated to granting fellowships to promising young curators from around the world, who would come to Jerusalem to work in the same space, and follow in the footsteps, of Eva herself.

And what could the Kaplans of Boston say?

"It's really . . . amazing," Wendy's husband Larry said slowly, as though rummaging through his head for the appropriate word.

"And sort of tragic," their son-in-law Peter offered. "That she'll never see any of this."

"But is it maybe," their daughter Hannah said, "just a *little* bit tacky, putting her name on everything?"

"What it is," Wendy said, finally looking up, "is so unbelievably *her.*" They were all at the dining table now, which no one had sat at in years—everyone always ate in the kitchen, even with company—but which had felt so fitting to spread the legal documents across, as if they were in a boardroom in some glittery high-rise and not a Victorian fixer-upper on Cedar Street.

"Always flying out to Europe, or lunching with some refugee scholar," Wendy said. "Always—always—letting everyone know just how generous she was," she said, walking into the kitchen to answer the phone. Standing in the doorway, twisting the cord around her elbow, Wendy resembled her late father, with her short, disheveled hair and sleepy green eyes, as if perpetually startled from a nap. Then she hung up, walked back into the dining room and said, "That was the Israel Museum. They're planning another event next month in her honor."

Her eyes filled up, that fast. "We're all invited," she whispered. "The entire foundation."

Larry came behind her and rested his hands on her shoulders, keeping them there as the first cry, and then the second, escaped her throat. "It's halfway across the world," he said. "And you just got back. The museum would understand if you said you were busy."

"Right," Wendy said, swallowing. "I *am* busy," and everyone nodded, though just a few weeks before she'd been talking about how unnerving it was to have both her children grown and married, and to only be working halftime now—that it felt strange and decadent, at fifty-six, to begin cultivating hobbies. But as soon as she said it, it turned out everyone was busy. Mira, of course, was out of the question—no one had heard from her in days. Larry couldn't leave his grad students last-minute, and Hannah couldn't pull the kids out of school so early in the year—it was only October. There would be other events, they reasoned, in which to honor Eva—*many* other events, they were certain—and since construction on the museum wing and the absorption centers wouldn't be completed until summer at the earliest, it made sense, they decided, to wait until then. They could fly out for the ribbon-cutting ceremonies and turn it into a big family trip, maybe rent that apartment in Baka they'd liked so much for Larry's sixtieth, and enroll Hannah and Peter's girls, now that they were old enough, in kibbutz camp in the north. So they'd miss this one event, they said. What was the harm, and really, who at this point was keeping tabs?

Unless—and that was when Wendy turned to her son-in-law Boaz, who had been silent the entire night, sitting at the end of the dining table. Unless he wanted to go. He could treat it as a free vacation, Wendy said, make a quick appearance at the museum, then relax in Jerusalem for a couple weeks. Or get some free research out of it, spend time with that Ladino poet he loved whose name they were always forgetting. And when Boaz, surrounded by all of his in-laws except his wife Mira herself, who, only six weeks along, had up and left him for another man last Monday, calling him and saying she was sorry, but she needed some time away—when Boaz, who had been wondering if there was something seriously wrong with him for obsessing over the life and death of a woman he barely knew, poring over every obituary he could find, then driving here tonight, as if he too had a stake in the matter—when Boaz said he felt a little funny being the only one to attend given, you know, the circumstances, all four present members of the Eva Kaplan Foundation turned to him and said that he was family, always and forever, and that they all just had to be patient while Mira got this last tantrum out of her system before the baby came and she finally had to start acting like an adult.

❋   ❋   ❋

THAT NIGHT, the calls and emails from Israel kept coming. It seemed Eva had given every organization she'd donated to a sneak preview of her will and they all wanted to be the first to extend their gratitude. The director of the Israel Museum, one of Eva's closest friends, offered to pick Boaz up from the airport; the absorption center's development officer wanted to take him to lunch; the youth village coordinator invited him to Afula to tour the grounds. And on and on. By the time he said good night to his in-laws and began the long and silent drive up I-89 back home to Vermont, he'd agreed to eight site visits for the foundation, as well as meetings with the lawyer and the real estate broker and a full morning at Eden Storage, where Eva had an extra unit no one had known about, filled with cast-off belongings Boaz had somehow agreed to sort through. He'd also agreed to stay at Eva's house, however creepy that might be, to keep an eye on the contractors' work before the place went on the market. Most of her furniture had already been sold, but he told Wendy he was happy to sleep on the mattress they'd left for him, that he was happy to do it all. He'd suggested he fly out as soon as possible, and while Wendy kept thanking him for taking the brunt, Boaz knew it was tacitly understood why he was so eager to get on that plane: anything to flee his present situation.

But when he pulled into the driveway, when he saw the darkened windows of his and Mira's little white house, when he opened the door and yelled "Hello?" and nothing came back, he wondered if he wasn't traveling to the one place that might make him feel worse. Not because he'd grown up in Israel—he'd been back half a dozen times since moving to the States—but because Mira had accompanied him on every one of those trips. That was where they'd met, a decade ago, on a graduate translation fellowship in Jerusalem. He was twenty-five, Mira twenty-two. He'd met Eva that year as well—he remembered Mira dragging him along on what she called "the obligatory visit to her royal highness." Boaz had been excited by the invitation—they'd only been together a couple months and this was the first of Mira's relatives he was meeting—but as they walked through the hills of Talbieh and onto Hovevei Tzion Street, every home more coiffed than the last, he'd felt a stab of panic. He was from Kiryat Gat, a tiny city in southern Israel that Mira, who considered herself an expert on Middle East geography, had never heard of and had, only half-jokingly, accused him of making up—and until that day, Boaz hadn't known streets like Eva's existed: not even the prime minister lived like that. Jerusalem had seemed to him a city where people didn't simply live on top of each other, they lived right *on* you, sitting on your stomach, pinning you down by the arms so you had no choice but to smell the soup on their breath and hear their opinions on the bus strikes, the housing crisis, your career choice. And yet here were old stone homes with rosebushes and sculpted citrus trees and gleaming cars visible only through electric gates—not apartments but actual houses, perched so high above the city that even the garbage fumes no longer existed, as if the mayor had allotted these people better air.

Mira must have sensed his discomfort, because right outside her grandmother's house, beige stucco and relatively modest from the street, she turned to him and said, "Fine. They're rich. But that doesn't mean I am." And then she did a strange thing: she patted her jeans, as if her entire life's worth could fit within those frayed, faded pockets, and Boaz wondered if only people comfortable around money felt the need to prove to the world that they had gone without it.

Then Eva opened the door and Boaz stood there staring: it was Mira exactly, if he were to fast-forward fifty years. The same wide brown eyes and tall, muscular frame and cheeks that would never, it appeared, thin with age. The same face (not pretty, exactly, but stately) and the same proud, purposeful stance— shoulders back, head up—even as she kissed both their cheeks, took their coats and flung them across the mail table.

"Sy!" she yelled down the hall. "The kids are here."

Inside, the house had more of an aged than intimidating glamour, the sofas and armchairs faded by the sun, all the heavy mahogany furniture that had probably looked just right in their previous apartment on Central Park West a little stuffy and out of place in the Mediterranean climate, like seeing someone show up at a barbecue in a suit. The really outstanding thing was the art. It covered the walls from the ceiling all the way to the floor, with pieces he recognized—Picasso's pencil sketches, Magritte's bulky nudes—hanging right next to paintings that didn't so much look like paintings but squiggles on playing cards and tablecloths and sugar sacks.

"That's a Rubashkin," Eva said, putting an arm around him. "They threw him in a psychiatric prison to 'shape up ideolog- ically,'" she said, making air quotes. "So he did a portrait of a guard he met there." Eva pointed at what clearly depicted a man being birthed from an anus. She smelled of powder and peroxide, as if she'd just that second returned from the beauty parlor. While Boaz had never been a fan of assumed intimacy, he suddenly wanted to stay there a very long time, listening to stories about artists he'd never heard of, whose fates he'd never considered, as Eva led him from painting to painting, leaning in close as if sharing a secret.

"Eva!" her husband yelled, coming out of the study, the sounds of a soccer game drifting into the hall. He was heavy and balding and wearing a dress shirt and slacks so rumpled he reminded Boaz of an overstuffed drawer. "You're gossiping," he said, and Eva said, "It's not gossip if it's true," and he smiled at Boaz, as if they'd had that exchange a million times and he knew when to concede, and then all four of them walked out to the terrace, where cups and saucers and a tower of little frosted cakes were laid out. Eva poured Boaz a cup of tea and said, in English, "Hebrew or English?" and when he said, "Either," she said, in impeccable, unaccented Hebrew, "You're the only boy this one's ever brought by, so I know you're better than the others. Tell me about yourself."

"I'm a translator," Boaz said. Sy's arm was draped over Eva's shoulder, her hand on his leg. They held each other with such effortlessness that Boaz was touched: there was clearly so much love between them, even after fifty-plus years of marriage. He felt as if he were getting a privileged view into the future, see-ing how the girl he loved would look as an old woman, her own lined and papery hand clutching his knee. "Well," Boaz cor-rected, believing he should only call himself a translator once his work was out in the world, "I'm *studying* to be one."

"Oh please," Eva said. "Say you're one and act like one! I'm sure you're brilliant. What are you working on?"

"A couple stories, from Hebrew to English. And Mira and I are taking a class on Ben Yehuda."

"Ah," Eva said. "You know he built a house forever ago near our old place on Ein Gedi Street, a big stone monstrosity, then died before he moved in."

"Right," Boaz said, shocked that Eva could be so blasé about the inventor of the modern Hebrew language—that to her, Ben Yehuda wasn't a brilliant, revered linguist but some show-off who'd raised the property taxes in her neighborhood. Boaz was trying to take it all in without gawking: the house, the art, the view, which everyone at the table seemed immune to, as if it were perfectly natural to gaze out at the classic postcard shot of the Old City's stone walls, the glittery gold dome and the hills beyond, the cars snaking up the Mount of Olives looking, from that vantage, as tiny and insignificant as toys. This was the first time Boaz had lived in Jerusalem, the first time he had lived outside the Negev, and he'd felt, when he first arrived at Hebrew University that fall, that all his years of working hard had paid off, that he'd gotten the translation scholarship he'd dreamed of, that it could lead so easily to a book, a career, a life—that, in his own private way, he had made it. He'd found that everything, even walking outside his dorm on Mount Scopus and buying a coffee and a roll in the morning, felt thrilling and significant, as if something inside him had caught fire.

But then he'd met Mira, who saw her year there as nothing but another planned rest stop on the map of her life, which had already included a junior year in Cairo and nearly every summer since childhood in Israel, the distance of traveling halfway around the world as trivial to her as the field trips Boaz had taken, as a boy, to the kibbutz water park. It was both exciting and unnerving being with someone like Mira, who talked about Jerusalem with the ease of a native he himself couldn't fake, loving the architecture, the history, the bookshops and cafés near her apartment and the sweet old couple who ran the produce market on her block, but so sick of the traffic, the noise, the religious lady on the bus who yelled at her for wearing a tank top, wishing Tel Aviv University had as strong a translation program, wondering why Jerusalem couldn't have one decent restaurant open on Shabbat—no, scratch that, one decent restaurant, period. Sitting out on the terrace, Boaz was aware his excitement at being there made him seem as eager and unsophisticated as a little boy, and so he sipped his tea and tried to act as though none of this were a big deal, though all of it was, in fact, a very big deal.

Then Eva shifted her attention to Mira, as if she were hosting a talk show and Boaz's segment had ended. Mira set down her cup and began, to Boaz's amazement, performing for her grandmother. Sy was between them, his arm still on Eva's shoulder, piping in now and then, but the spotlight never moved, not even for a second, from Eva. There was Mira, perched on her chair, suddenly talking with her hands, her eyes, her feet jiggling nervously, all that confidence Boaz had assumed was as intrinsic as her breath and hair and freckles, magically evaporated around her grandmother: the one person, he realized, Mira felt she still needed to court. This was so different from the way he'd later learn she operated with her immediate family back in Boston, where she'd walk right through the front door and skulk into the kitchen, finally yelling hello to everyone only after she'd scrutinized the contents of the refrigerator and begun picking at a plate of leftover chicken with her bare hands.

But there, on Eva's terrace, Boaz fell a little more in love with her, seeing, for the first time, that vulnerability. There she was, trying to charm Eva with stories, making their year out to be a little brighter, a little more exciting, than it had been so far, describing her apartment in Rehavia as louder and smaller than it actually was, her project with the Arab poet more dramatic than the reality, as if their meetings entailed some dangerous, illicit journey over the Green Line, rather than just across campus in the literature department, where the poet had been teaching for nearly fifteen years.

Then Eva stood up. She took Boaz's arm and whispered that he was a keeper, and he was so warmed by those words, and by Eva herself, that as she led him through the living room and into the hall, he hadn't even realized she was kicking them out until he and Mira were back on the street, clutching their coats, on the other side of the door.

✻   ✻   ✻

IT WAS still dark outside when the red-eye descended into Israel and taxied along the runway. Boaz hadn't slept a minute on the flight, had spent the entire ten hours with the foundation's site visit materials unopened on his lap, watching terrible movie after terrible movie without even plugging in his headphones, and now, shoving his tiny, useless airplane pillow against the window, he tried to rest for the remaining minutes before the seat-belt sign went off. Only nobody would be quiet. The teenager beside him seemed to be calling everyone on her speed-dial to let them know she'd arrived, though Boaz couldn't imagine who would welcome that call at five-thirty. Across the aisle, a religious man was having a conversation on his own cell while his children piled onto his wife's lap, a toddler on one leg and a baby in her arms, the wife nodding yes, yes to a third child tugging her hand, though everything in her face seemed to be screaming no, no, no. That all used to comfort Boaz, being thrust back home before even walking through customs. But now it felt claustrophobic and overwhelming, and Boaz wondered if he was simply in a terrible mood or if he was beginning to crave space like a New Englander.

Outside baggage claim, the director of the Israel Museum was waiting by the fountain. She was sixtyish and attractive in a stern, no-nonsense way, with cropped gray hair, red plastic glasses and chunky geometric jewelry that could only have come from the museum gift shop. "Roni Ben Ami," she said, extending her hand and grabbing his suitcase with the other.

"It's okay," Boaz said, trying to take his suitcase back, but she was already pushing her way outside, where her driver was waiting. Boaz slid in beside Roni, and as her car pulled away from the curb, she turned to him and said, "I've never picked up a donor at the airport. But I couldn't let an intern do it—not for Eva." The sky was lightening, and the familiar cluster of billboards advertising cell phone plans and yogurt sprang into view. It didn't seem possible that he was halfway around the world now, just four days after Wendy had first opened the will. He still hadn't heard from Mira—and if Wendy and Larry had, they weren't letting on. And though Mira had promised the last time they'd spoken that she was staying at her colleague Sharon's house in Hardwick, Boaz couldn't stop picturing her at *his* house, Eric's house, in Albany. Boaz had no idea what Eric looked like, but he kept seeing someone brawny and suntanned, the type of guy who woke at dawn to do yard work, then came into the bedroom scratched and sweaty with a mug of coffee for Mira, slow and groggy in the morning, her dark hair fanned out against the pillow.

"You should see the collection," Roni was saying. "You know how she displayed everything, in that Eva-haphazard way. So yesterday at work I start lining them up chronologically, and that's when I realized she hadn't just been collecting art from that period—her collection *is* that period. It's a complete retrospective," she said, a little breathlessly, and checked her BlackBerry. It kept going off, and Boaz suddenly sensed how important this woman was: so many people working for her, presumably from all over the globe given how early it was, and there she was, carting him around before breakfast.

"Of course some of it's terrible," Roni continued. "Those Rubashkins? But you know your grandmother—all she cared was that it was dissident, outrageous. People might not get that now." She squinted at Boaz, as if to see whether he got it, and he wondered what she saw: a thirty-five-year-old with bed-head and tired eyes, looking a bit like a delivery boy in jeans and a hoodie, having forgotten, as he'd dressed for the flight back in Vermont, that he'd be meeting people like Roni before getting a chance to shower. "Boaz, forgive me," she said, "but which one are you again?"

"Mira's husband." He coughed, wondering if those words were even true anymore.

"The anthropologist?"

"The family has no anthropologists."

"Oh," Roni said slowly, as if flipping through a mental Rolodex. "The architect."

"That's Hannah. Mira's the translator." There was an ugly part of him that wished Mira were there to hear how little her grandmother's friends knew of her, just so he could see the pain shoot past her eyes. But Mira had always suspected it anyway. It's like she's so obsessed with charming the world that there's nothing left for her own family, Mira had told him once—and

Boaz remembered just where they were when she'd said it, that first year together in Jerusalem, during those early months of dating when they'd lie in bed talking through the morning.

That was the night she'd told him Eva's story: leaving her native Prague to study art in Paris in the thirties and falling in love with Mikhail Borovsky, the famous Russian painter who wasn't yet famous. They lived together for many years. Then his father died and he had to go back to Moscow to sort things out for his mother. He said he'd return in a month. But that summer, Germany captured Paris. Eva escaped on a cargo ship to New York. Her entire family in Prague—never heard from again. Mikhail—still in Russia, impossible to reach. In New York she had nothing, knew no one, but she was like you with languages, Mira told Boaz—they came easily to her and she collected them like badges. So with her English, she finagled her way into the secretarial pool at the Frick, and from there, Eva being Eva, began curating shows at small galleries around the city, until the bigger places started taking notice. Then in the early fifties she met Sy, who at that time was enjoying a bit of fame for that book he'd written, the first to so openly criticize Senator McCarthy's policies, maybe Boaz had heard of it? (He hadn't.) Together they started organizing some of the early American conferences on Soviet Jewry, trying to garner worldwide support for Russian Jews denied exit visas, and then they began traveling to Moscow. By that time, the government had made Mikhail an official artist, known for his portraits of Party officials, so he was easy for Eva to find. He'd married by then as well, so he and Eva left their relationship in the past. She and Sy and Mikhail and his wife all began working together, Mikhail sneaking government-issued paints and brushes to the unofficial artists and shepherding Eva into clandestine apartment exhibits around Moscow, introducing her to virtually every painter whose work she ended up smuggling out and making known abroad.

It's amazing, Mira had said, that my grandmother risked her life for these artists, knowing if caught she'd be interrogated, jailed, probably worse. But then my mom was born, and it was Grandpa Sy who stopped making those trips, it was Grandpa Sy who decided it wasn't worth putting himself in danger when he had a child, and I don't think my grandmother canceled one flight. Imagine how that made my mother feel, Mira said—and while Boaz knew that was his cue to take Mira's hand and whisper yes, he could imagine how hard that must have been, he just couldn't bring himself to do it. The whole story confused him. It didn't seem possible that Mira had lived twenty-two years and experienced no real sadness of her own—that the stories she shared late at night in bed, supposedly the most painful and private of her life, were about other people.

Then Mira had faced him. It was the part he dreaded most about dating, the assumption that he was supposed to turn to the girl he'd just slept with and reveal his own dark stories. So, as always, he gave the shorthand: he'd never known his father, he had no siblings, his mother had passed away when he was twenty-one. All the other girls would whisper condolences, then go uncomfortably silent; and Boaz, afraid he'd ruined their evening, would always say he was fine, couldn't they see he was fine, then fumble for a way to maneuver the conversation back to them. But Mira didn't go quiet—she got angry. She said it was unfair he'd suffered so much. It was a sentiment he'd never considered—that everyone was entitled to a happy life—but Mira felt it vehemently on his behalf. She sat up in bed, and Boaz remembered just how she'd looked that night, a decade ago, headlights flashing through the window and illuminating her broad, pale shoulders. "The whole thing breaks my heart," she said. "That you had to bury your mother when you were barely an adult yourself."

And Boaz wondered how he could find himself loving and resenting a person at the same dangerous, accelerating speed, because while her attention thrilled him, he sensed it had as much to do with Mira's ego as with him—that more than anything, she wanted to crack him open and be the first girl to peer inside.

She'd gotten upset over the wrong thing anyway. He'd spent years preparing for the day he'd bury his mother—she'd battled kidney disease her entire life and was practical about her condition, talked about it openly, wanted him to understand its inevitability. What was hard were the months that followed, after shiva was over, after the phone calls and condolence cards and prepared food stopped, after he'd paid off his mother's medical bills and cleared out the closets and donated all her clothes to Karmey Chesed and Boaz was left with no final tasks to distract his thoughts. He'd been discharged that year and while all his army friends were backpacking through Thailand and India, Boaz was back in his childhood apartment, supposedly studying for university entrance exams but really just wandering the four rooms, bumping into his own furniture. The only real solace he found was in books. When he was younger Boaz had read to escape, but during those months back home, reading consoled him in a way no person at the funeral had been able to—writers who had found language not only to describe the pain he felt but to control it, their books containing the infinite possibilities of a sadness he feared could otherwise consume him. There was one entire week he stayed in bed reading, and when, on the eighth day, he finally walked around the corner for groceries, he was struck by this: no one had noticed he'd been inside. That was when he truly understood he was on his own. And the thing about being alone is knowing that if you want to enter the world again, you have to be a guest in it—people are doing you a favor by inviting you into their homes for family gatherings and national holidays, and the only way to act is cheerful and easy, even when you're so depressed you can barely muster the energy to brush your teeth, and to arrive with wine and flowers and always offer to help with the dishes.

That was when Mira had stood up, and Boaz feared he'd unloaded so much that she wanted him to leave. But she just opened the window, and he listened to cars whistle past as sirens drifted down Azza Street. "No one wants you to fake it," she said. "You know the other day, when it finally stopped raining and I called you from Independence Park and you were working so hard you didn't even know the sun had come out? I loved that," she said. "It was so weird of you to miss the first real day of spring and not care at all." And he could see that the weirdness thrilled her, as if she were catching a glimpse of his real, uncut self, even all the messy footage he'd worked so scrupulously to edit out. He'd never met a person who accepted him so fully, but he'd later learn all the Kaplan women were like that: they laughed and cried and yelled whenever they felt like it, and expected the people around them to do the same. Yet even that night, Boaz understood that while he respected

Eva's utter ease with herself—the woman had lost her entire family at an even younger age than Boaz but refused to act like anyone's guest—he had a hard time admiring the same trait in Mira, when she'd simply inherited it.

He knew that was unfair: it wasn't Mira's fault her parents supported her at every turn, sending her to softball leagues and theater classes when she displayed a modicum of interest, doing everything possible to ensure their daughter's life was a series of smooth, paved roads with endless green lights. It wasn't Mira's fault she'd been taught to be unafraid of failure: taking enormous risks even on her earliest translations, reworking full paragraphs, changing nouns to verbs simply because she believed it "sounded better" her way—so different from Boaz, who found himself growing more timid with each project. Even the good things that kept happening to him that first year—the fellowship; the internship at Hebrew University's academic press that quickly turned into a job—felt precarious, as if he could make one mistake and all the success could be rescinded so easily that he'd be back where he started.

When their fellowship in Jerusalem was over, Mira asked him to come back with her to Boston. She pieced together adjunct teaching, Boaz convinced the press to let him work remotely, they found an apartment not far from her sister. But they kept searching for cheap, quiet places to spend weekends, vacations, summers together, just the two of them, distraction-free with their work, and finally during one excruciatingly humid June day, Mira put down the bowl she was drying, wiped her sticky hair from her forehead and said, "This is disgusting." It was a hundred degrees outside and at least a hundred-twenty in their kitchen, and when Boaz peered out the window down the street, he could see an elderly couple moving so slowly it was like they were wading through tar. "Let's get out of here," he said—and that was the moment, if he boiled it right down, that he suddenly began to feel he too was entitled to better air than the rest of the city.

A month later they were living in the Northeast Kingdom of Vermont, hours from anyone they knew, in a house at the end of a dirt road, a house with a porch and a yard and garden with beds already built by the previous renters. He loved the landscape, so different from anything he'd seen in America: the blue rivers and green fields and red barns, as if children had used the most basic set of crayons to scribble it into being. He loved the fact that he could roll out of bed and into his study to work all day, the days bleeding together so fluidly the distinction between weekdays and weekends no longer mattered. He loved the language he and Mira created up there: a hodgepodge of Hebrew and English half-sentences no one else would have understood, but which made more sense to him than anything else. He loved seeing Mira walking around in old jeans and rubber gardening clogs, her entire closet of dresses and tailored coats instantly superfluous. He loved sitting on the porch with her and imagining a child, their child, brown-armed and goofy, sprinting past them on the grass. Probably he got the whole image from a commercial for coffee filters or fabric softener, but he didn't care. It worked for him—for them.

For many years Mira had said she wanted children in theory but not quite yet—that she needed to sort her life out first: a stable teaching job, a secure paycheck. But a couple months before Eva's will arrived, Mira walked into the kitchen one morning, poured herself a cup of coffee and said, "I'm ready."

Just like that. And Boaz felt his chest swell and said, "Really?" She smiled and nodded, and soon after was pregnant. Though she wasn't supposed to tell anyone so early on, Mira called her family immediately, saying if she miscarried she'd want them to know so what was the point of keeping secrets, and they all drove up to Vermont, Wendy and Larry and Hannah and Peter and their girls, and piled into the ob-gyn office. As the doctor moved the monitor over Mira's still-flat stomach, Wendy swore she saw a penis on the screen and Larry got misty-eyed that he'd finally have a grandson and Hannah snapped that it was impossible to know so early—and Boaz had felt so blessed, surrounded by family. All that resentment he'd once felt for Mira suddenly seemed so self-indulgent when he imagined his child being born into the Kaplans, this child who didn't even have bones or teeth or skin yet but was already so deeply adored by everyone in that room.

There was a night not long after that visit, a completely simple and uneventful night, when they had a fire going and were eating dinner on the couch with a movie on, and he'd had a feeling of being utterly sated, as if everything he needed in life existed right there. He'd pulled Mira close and kissed the soft spot between her eyes and whispered that he loved her, and she'd whispered that she loved him too. "No," she'd said. "It seems like such a bullshit thing to say! How can I when I also love this pasta, this movie, this fire? We need a different word," she said. "We need to exhume Ben Yehuda from his grave and ask for an approximation of what this is—this love." And then she took his hand and squeezed so hard his knuckles popped.

Looking back, he wished he could zero in on the moment things started to falter, the moment he should have suspected

Eric was lurking on the sidelines. But it was impossible. Even her recent bad moods were the ones she'd cycled through the entire time he'd known her, always coming at the end of a project when she was stressed about what to do next, saying she was so far removed from being swept up in a translation that she couldn't even remember how it felt. Boaz would wander into her office upstairs and find her impatiently watching the view from her window; the sun couldn't set fast enough.

Even a couple weeks ago, when Mira announced that she couldn't take the silence anymore, that they must have been insane for isolating themselves up there, away from the world, there in the Home of the Lonely—even that hadn't felt alarming. She always made some similar proclamation when her work wasn't going well, as if the very quiet she'd once craved became a taunting little monster when the open hours of a day loomed. And so Boaz did what he always did when she got anxious: he packed up the car and they drove down to her parents' house in Boston. He loved pulling onto their wide street, with its Craftsmans and Victorians and enormous leafy trees, he loved walking inside with his own key and dropping his bags on the floor, his coat on the banister, as comfortable as one of Wendy and Larry's own. He loved the house, creaky and bright and always messy, as if Wendy were still rebelling against her upbringing of white carpets and polished silverware, her walls not covered with famous paintings but childhood craft projects, every single thing her daughters and granddaughters had papier-mâchéd and glitter-glued in the art shed of Camp Haverim over the years. The art was terrible, but Boaz loved it. He loved it all. He loved the pencil markings on the pantry door, measuring Mira and Hannah's growth as girls, loved the hodgepodge of family photos cluttering the mantel, the endless parade of sweet and dopey dogs. He loved arriving in the middle of the day, when Wendy and Larry were still at work, and napping on the beanbag chair in the base- ment, surrounded by relics of the Kaplan home, the unused exercise equipment and water-warped Beta tapes and boxes of toys Hannah's girls had tired of but which were waiting for their kid, his and Mira's, even labeled that way, *for M+B.* He slept so peacefully those afternoons, the sound of Mira upstairs on the phone with her sister, a neighbor's lawn mower in the distance, the front door opening and Wendy and Larry greeting their daughter, then asking, "Where's Boaz?"—two words as beautiful to him as a song.

※   ※   ※

"MIRA," RONI was saying now, as they snaked up the high- way toward Jerusalem. "Okay, I remember her, maybe from the Bronfman dinner? Tall with black hair, looked a lot like Eva?"

Boaz nodded miserably and Roni said, "It's a shame she's not here. She couldn't get off work?"

"She left me," Boaz mumbled. "The question is why I'm here. Eva's *her* grandmother."

Roni stared. She opened her mouth, then closed it. And Boaz, who had never overshared in his life, who had no idea where that outburst came from and didn't trust what was coming next, cracked the window and looked out toward Mevasseret, at the skinny trees and sun-beaten hills and dis- tant houses blurring past.

She let go of her BlackBerry and slipped it in her purse. It was the first time he'd seen it out of her hand; and gadgetless,

Roni looked different, gentler: not just a museum bigwig but a wife, a mother, maybe still someone's daughter. She touched his arm and said, "Tell me what's happening." And maybe because he was back in a country where strangers found it perfectly acceptable to inquire into other people's personal lives, maybe because he sensed all the doors that had been swinging open the past decade could close in on him at any minute, and maybe most of all because he understood that, while in a normal situation Roni wouldn't even nod to him on the street, the fact that he represented the foundation obligated her to care about his problems, Boaz did something he never would have imagined he was capable of: he turned to this woman he didn't know at all and started to talk. He told her things he hadn't told anyone, not even Wendy and Larry. He said he hadn't even known Mira was unhappy. That when she didn't come home from work the Monday before last, it never occurred to him she was leaving; all he could think to do was obsessively refresh the local news online for traffic accidents. He hadn't even been aware of Eric. Of course he'd known she'd gone to Albany for a campus visit that fall, a trip on which he'd declined to accompany her, not wanting to waste days in a sterile motel room while she gave craft talks, particularly because she wasn't even interested in the position; she simply thought being offered the job would give her more leverage at the college where she already worked. And when it turned out to be an inside hire, the entire thing had seemed to Boaz a nothing story, a trip that didn't even merit an anecdote.

Then that Monday evening, Mira finally called him, supposedly from her colleague Sharon's house in Hardwick. She was crying when she told Boaz about Eric, a guy who ran a restaurant in Albany where she'd stopped for a drink during that long and exhausting campus visit, a guy she'd been emailing ever since. Nothing romantic at first, not even flirtatious. But then they were writing every week, then every day, these long and detailed emails that felt more like letters, all about their families and work and even their childhoods, getting to know each other with such a focused intimacy she'd forgotten was possible. They'd never done anything, Mira promised, not even kissed, and the whole thing had felt so Victorian in its prudishness, though she couldn't deny she'd fantasized about sleeping with him—how could she not, having been with Boaz for so long that she could predict every one of his moves, their sex life more like a race to see who came first. But the whole thing with Eric had seemed so manageable, so predictable, the kind of situation many married people invariably found themselves in, because after a decade together it was hard to feel as thrilled as you did in the very beginning, and she'd told herself she had nothing to feel guilty about because all the situation had amounted to was a pile of emails.

But then she started to call him once Boaz had gone to bed, crossing the yard and climbing onto the rock where they got cell service. She started to feel as though Eric was on her mind all the time and everything she did, even the runs she took in the woods behind their house up to Fox Ridge—suddenly she found herself narrating all of it to Eric, as if these things could only be meaningful if she imagined him experiencing them with her. So they started to meet in Brattleboro, halfway between their houses, just for the day. Eric would plan these elaborate outings. He had two young children from his previous marriage, and she wasn't sure if he'd been this way before fatherhood, but he saw every afternoon as a potential adventure. He was the kind of person, she said, who'd hear about a good diner thirty miles away and make a whole day of it, the kind of person who loved thinking about new things Mira might want to do and see that she hadn't even considered. But those afternoons hadn't seemed worth mentioning, because when she'd told Boaz she was meeting up with some of her colleagues and he'd nodded from his desk and told her to have fun, it really had felt as though she wasn't doing anything technically wrong. The whole thing had felt so textbook, looking for one more exciting distraction before she began the steady gray march into adulthood, and if she was really going to be honest, this entire crush was a big part of the reason she had finally decided to get pregnant—she'd convinced herself that maybe a baby could instantly bring her closer to Boaz and farther from Eric, cutting off these terrifying new feelings before they even had legs to stand on.

And so, that past week when Eric picked her up from the train station in Brattleboro, she opened her mouth to tell him she was pregnant, and that whatever it was they were doing, however harmless, had to stop. But instead she had blurted, it had honestly just rolled off her tongue, that she loved him. And Eric had pulled to the side of the road, cut the ignition and said he'd loved her from that first night she walked into his restaurant and that he wanted to make a go of things, that nothing in his life had ever made more sense, and that was when the entire room went blurry for Boaz and he hung up the phone, ran to the bathroom and threw up.

"So they didn't sleep together," Roni said.

Boaz stared at her. "So?"

"So you know the baby's yours."

"Of course."

"I don't understand what the problem is," Roni said. "You're having a child together. She'll get this man out of her system and come back to you."

"I'd rather she slept with him than fell in love."

An image was coming into Boaz's mind, a photo of Mira from that campus visit to Albany he'd found her looking at one night on her laptop. It was a simple picture, her on a bench somewhere in town. But she looked happier than he'd seen her in years, shielding her eyes from the sun and smiling wide, so he'd asked to make it his screensaver, and it was only now occurring to him who had been holding the camera.

"What did you say?" Roni said.

"When?"

"After you vomited and she called you back. I've known you forty minutes and already I'd bet one of Eva's Litnikovs that you picked up on the first ring."

"Fine," Boaz said. "I told her I felt betrayed. I told her one of the things I loved most about being married was that I felt safe with her, and I didn't think I ever could anymore."

Roni shook her head, sadly. "Boaz," she said. "You tell her you felt safe, and all she hears is that her husband sees the world as dangerous."

Boaz didn't know what to say. He stared out the window and wondered when Jerusalem had gotten so dirty. Garbage everywhere, crumbling houses, cats darting out of trash bins—so many they must have outnumbered humans on the street. The few people outside this early all seemed so gloomy, propped against the bus depot or walking past in a hurried sleepwalk, a group of Filipino women looking as if they'd been up for hours, pushing the very young and the very old down the sidewalk. Even the sky seemed depleted, as if it wished the day would just end already. But then the driver turned off Keren HaYesod onto a side street, and Boaz caught sight of two boys kicking a soccer ball. They were young, six or seven, in t-shirts and shorts but moving too fast to feel the wind that had picked up. They were running and laughing and when one of their mothers yelled something from a window, they laughed some more. Those kids could have been anywhere—Vermont, Boston, Kiryat Gat, probably a million places Boaz had never been— and what struck him was how touchingly naïve they seemed, as if they couldn't imagine anything that could make them happier than what they were doing right then, in that glorious moment. Suddenly Boaz was overcome by it too, a complete and spontaneous happiness. All at once it felt so simple to let go of his problems for just a minute and feel grateful to be a part of something as big and basic as that morning, that city, that street. He felt a lightness inside him, opening wider and wider as they drove through the hills up to Eva's house, and then he climbed the steps, unlocked the door and found Mira inside, waiting on the floor of her grandmother's empty living room.

✻ ✻ ✻

SHE'D GOTTEN in last night, she said. Her parents had told her he was coming and she couldn't stand the idea of him doing this alone. "I can't stand any of it," she said. "All I've been doing is feeling miserable, then feeling worse for even *allowing* myself to be sad."

She stood up and reached for his arm. But she caught the

sleeve of his shirt instead. Boaz hadn't realized he was backing away until he was up against the front door. He heard the
bleats of traffic outside, saw the scratches on the wall where
Eva's mail table had once been. Most of her furniture had
already been sold, and the room was filled with ghostly out-
lines where the walls had darkened and aged around those
wood tables and heavy tweed sofas. He had an eerie, immediate feeling of remembering just where things had been, the
stacks of magazines covering the shiny white mail table and
the large vase that always, always held fresh-cut flowers, and
beside that, the ceramic umbrella stand Eva had brought back
from Marrakesh—

"Boaz?"

He blinked, and everything came horribly into focus. It was
almost unbearable to look at her. Her sweater was rumpled, her
hair a tangled nest, and he thought about her thinking about
him all night, too nervous and keyed-up to check her reflection.
He knew he should feel sorry for her, this mess of a Mira. But
everything, even the very fact that her matted hair suggested
she'd just woken up, made him angry—he'd barely slept at all
the past ten days, too afraid of what he'd dream. It didn't even
make sense that he was seeing her. Her absence had felt bolder
and more intrusive than she'd ever been in person, as if it had
taken on the heft of a dozen women, and now there she was,
just standing there, so casually alive.

"What," he said, finding his voice at the last possible moment,
"are you doing here?"

"I'm physically sick about this."

"What does your boyfriend say about you using up our sav-
ings to fly here?"

"He's not my boyfriend."

"You promise you weren't with him this week?"

"I told you, I was with Sharon. You have to believe me."

"But you told me you loved him."

"I do." She looked so tiny in that enormous room. She still wasn't showing; if anything, she seemed as gawky and nervous as a teenager, biting her lip and stretching her sweater sleeves over her hands. "I can't tell you how much I wish this wasn't happening," she said. "But it's the truth. I love you in one way, him in another. I'm sorry. I can't stand here and lie to you of all people, and say that Eric means nothing to me."

"Do you understand how ridiculous you sound? Like someone we'd hate."

She winced, as if she'd been slapped. "You know what? I *want* you to hate me."

He was still backed against the door, as if it were the only way to protect himself, seeing her from this singular angle, like a sniper. All around him, the bare walls were dirty and gray and riddled with nail holes, and it struck him how depressing it was that Eva and Sy had transformed this empty space into such an interesting and beautiful life, and now a realtor was going to lead a new couple inside and apologize for those holes and then some workman would come and in twenty minutes all of it, the entire history of that room, would be spackled over.

"You don't understand," Mira said, "what it's like to be with someone who exists so fully in his head. Who has no desire to leave our weird little cocoon. And then Eric would put all this effort into thinking about what would make me happy. He'd have plans for us. We'd go to lunch. We'd go on hikes."

"We go on hikes."

"No, Boaz, we'd go on walks outside our house. We'd walk to think, then go back to our offices to think some more. Sometimes I'd feel like we weren't even really living together. It was like we were swimming in the same pool, but I was never allowed in your lane."

"I thought that was part of the deal," he said quietly. "You said it was. That with you I was *allowed* to disappear."

"Right outside your office window," she said, "you can see all our patio furniture knocked on its side, and there's bird shit all over it. Like, it's really covered in shit. And I'd look out your window and wonder what kind of person could see that every day and not just go hose it off."

The entire time they'd been speaking Hebrew, but then something inside her seemed to rupture and Mira blurted, in English, "But I could never be upset about that—about anything—because you've convinced yourself I have no real reasons to be sad. That your pain will always trump mine. It's this fucked-up game you've been playing since we met."

"But I love you," he said, a little helplessly.

She took a long breath and let it out slowly, as if thinking hard about what she was going to say next. "Being in love with my family isn't the same as loving me."

"That's bullshit," he said. But he knew he was lying. Of course he couldn't separate that love. All at once he saw so clearly what would follow. Not just that night, or the long flight back to the States, but beyond. Winter, spring, the baby. Her family would call incessantly to check in on him, they'd probably even take his side, but after a while they'd learn to embrace Eric because there was no other choice: Mira loved him and she was blood. And Eric would be so infuriatingly gracious about the whole thing, he'd probably invite Boaz down to Albany for dinner, and Boaz would have to sit across the table from the two of them, over some elaborate meal Eric had prepared with herbs and vegetables from his own fucking garden, and beer he'd brewed himself. More images started popping up that Boaz couldn't block. Holidays, when he'd have to make that drive he knew by heart, down to Wendy and Larry's to pick up his kid. He'd have to park on the street and walk up their steps, and rather than going right inside he'd have to stand there, wiping his feet on the mat, listening to all their voices through the door until someone heard the bell and let him in.

"You understand this Eric thing is your fault, too," Mira said. "Of course I fell for someone who knows how to be close to me. That's what you do in relationships, Boaz—you try to see the world through the other person's eyes. I mean, look at my parents, my grandparents—they're like these model couples. Maybe what's difficult . . ."

She didn't finish. But the sentiment existed now, there in the room: Boaz didn't have a model, and maybe that was the problem. He'd always believed one of the most terrifying things about intimacy was another person knowing your darkest insecurities and being able to use them against you in your weakest moments, an emotional sucker punch. He realized now how wrong that was—it was much more excruciating for someone to know these things and choose not to say them, as if that person was the only one who understood just how crushing the truth could be.

He walked across the room, right past her, out to the terrace. Even that perfect view of the Old City he'd once admired suddenly looked crass and artificial, and he turned away. Mira came up behind him. "But despite all of this, I really do love you," she said. "And I know we're supposed to be together. That's why I flew out here—it's all I want. To have a family and grow old with you and to one day look back on this whole time as nothing but a selfish blip in my thirties."

"And Eric?"

"I'm willing to never talk to him again if you promise me things will be different. That I'll get all of you this time. That you'll stop keeping some big part of yourself stashed away."

She wrapped her arms around his chest. He smelled her sweat and lotion and hair, this apple shampoo that had always seemed sickeningly sweet to him, but which now made him so nostalgic he wanted to cry. The truth was, Boaz couldn't visualize what exactly it was she needed from him, he couldn't even describe it, but maybe all that mattered was that he'd never wanted anything more in his life than to give it to her. "Just say you'll try," she whispered, and then she stepped forward and touched his face and pulled the "yes" right out of him.

❅   ❅   ❅

IT WAS impossible to forget Mira's comment about sex with him being a race, so Boaz tried to ignore all the shortcuts—but he honestly didn't need to. Naked, Mira *was* starting to show and her entire body felt different, not just her stomach but her hips and arms, and afterward they lay in the guest room and talked. Mira said she'd been reading up on what was happening with the baby, that it was still the size of a blueberry but that hands and feet were starting to form, though in the book illustrations they looked more like weird little paddles. She said she was lucky that so far she'd been spared morning sickness but that she couldn't stop peeing, it was this annoying, ever-constant thing, and then she looked around the empty room and reminisced about staying there as a girl. And maybe because Eva was gone, or maybe because she felt as giddy as Boaz, this time Mira's stories were happy: the Russian political cartoonist who did sketches of her and Hannah, the pancakes Grandpa Sy made when she was homesick, the nights her grandmother let her try on her perfume and beaded handbags as she dressed for a function.

It was 10 A.M. and Boaz could hear people moving around down below on Hovevei Tzion Street, but he had no desire to join them. He wanted to stay in this room the rest of the trip, just him and Mira. But he also wanted to do things right this time, wanted to be the kind of guy who'd listened to everything she'd said and would make her happy now, a guy who'd made plans in between all the foundation meetings, who would take her tonight to that restaurant inside the shuk she'd loved their last trip here, the one he'd complained was cramped and kitschy and pretentious, but he'd enjoy his meal this time and not make a dig about the prices, and then they'd walk through the city and stop somewhere for a seltzer for her and a beer for him, they'd sit up at the bar together and he'd hold her hand, her leg, never, never giving her a reason to swivel away from him again.

Only his cell phone wouldn't stop ringing. The director of the absorption center wanted to know how his flight was, the broker asked if she could stop by in the afternoon, the man at Eden Storage said they were closing early today so the sooner Boaz came, the better.

The day was still gray, but even the exact sidewalks and

buildings he'd seen hours before seemed brighter with Mira by his side, as if the entire city had been sandblasted while they'd been indoors. Even the fact that he had to spend the morning sorting through Eva's castoffs, the task he'd dreaded most—it reminded him too much of doing the same for his mother— seemed less depressing with Mira's hand in his pocket, her head on his shoulder as she led him down Jabotinsky Street and across Emek Refaim to Eden Storage, introducing herself to the owner in that Hebrew so technically perfect she always gave herself away as a foreigner.

"I'm so sorry," the man said. He had a kind face, with a wide smile and a head round as a basketball. "Your grandmother really was one of the good ones."

"You knew her that well?" Mira said.

"She was here all the time." The man sorted through his enormous chunk of keys and led them outside to the row of sheds. "Once, twice a week."

"For how long?"

"My wife and I have been here forty years. So that at least."

"To visit her storage facility?" Mira rolled her eyes, as if this guy were just another crazy in the capital of crazies.

Then she pushed up the door of the shed and gasped. The sound was so dramatic, so unlike anything he'd ever heard from Mira, that when Boaz walked inside, he expected to find a dead animal, decaying under the boxes.

But there were no animals, no furniture, not even any boxes. Just paintings. Covering all four walls up to the ceiling, at least fifty in total. All of them, every single portrait, of Eva. And all, Boaz saw as he looked closer, bearing the signature of Mikhail Borovsky in the right-hand corner.

There was Eva when she was young, pink-cheeked and grinning with a green scarf knotted at her neck, titled, simply, *Paris.* There was Eva more than twenty years later, in a series of almost forty paintings, all titled *Moscow.* Those led up to the *Jerusalem* series as Eva progressively aged, the last one looking so recent Boaz guessed it was the final portrait Borovsky had done before he'd died. And in almost every one, Eva was staring straight at the artist with the widest, most radiant smile.

Mira took a deep breath. "She came here all the time?"

The man nodded, and Mira continued, "Always by herself?"

"Yes."

"She never brought—her husband?"

The man glanced at Boaz, then at the floor. "I'm sorry," he said. "I . . . I didn't know."

Mira looked up at the ceiling and started to cry. The man awkwardly tapped her shoulder, as if all of this were his fault. He stepped out of the shed, kicked gravel around.

Boaz knew his only job right then was to comfort Mira. It was the husbandly thing to do, the right thing, the only thing. To kiss her cheek and whisper that painful as this was, none of it mattered anymore. They were all dead now, Eva and Sy and Mikhail and his wife—all of it was moot. And if she really thought about it, maybe Eva and Mikhail had been smart to keep this a secret. There was no denying she'd loved Sy, there was no denying they'd had a beautiful marriage, and who knew, if things had worked out differently, Mira may never have been born.

But every one of those words felt like a lie. How, Boaz wondered, could Stalin ever have believed realism was the safer solution? He would have done anything to be surrounded by surrealist pieces he didn't understand, paintings he could stare at for hours, puzzling over myriad meanings, because looking at those portraits, there was only one possible message.

Eva's adoration was clear as a photograph, and the Paris painting made him think of one photo in particular: Mira on her campus visit to Albany. That younger Eva was a mirror image of Mira—the same full face and straight eyebrows and thick black hair. But what got him was their shared expression, a joy so genuine the smiles were coming more from their eyes and their mouths had no choice but to follow.

Mira was standing beside him, but he suddenly felt as if they were separated by a vast, impossible distance, and he knew it didn't matter how many promises she made—there was a man she loved more than Boaz, a man who knew how to make her happier than he did. It was something he'd probably known for weeks, but the simple truth of what it actually meant—that this would no longer be his life—was just too painful to look at, it was like staring directly into the sun. He closed his eyes and leaned against the wall. The painting behind him barely rattled, but Mira rushed forward. She grabbed his arm and asked what was wrong. But for the first time, Boaz couldn't think of a single word to describe this kind of loneliness, so scary and real it required an entirely different language, new and strange and yet to be invented.

Author's Note

Some of these stories were inspired by my family history, and I'm thankful to my relatives—among the best storytellers I know—for sharing them with me. I also found the following books particularly helpful in my research: Larry Ceplair and Steven Englund's *The Inquisition in Hollywood*, Friederike Kind-Kovacs's *Samizdat, Tamizdat, and Beyond*, John McPhee's *The Ransom of Russian Art*, and Victor Navasky's *Naming Names*, as well as Roberta Wallach's film *Partisans of Vilna*. Rich Cohen's *The Avengers*, Peter Duffy's *The Bielski Brothers*, and Seth Kramer's documentary *Resistance* inspired scenes and characters in "My Grandmother Tells Me This Story," and I'm grateful to them for creating work that has been so meaningful to me. Additionally, everyone at Libri Prohibiti in Prague and the Jewish Partisan Educational Foundation in San Francisco was incredibly generous with their time and resources. I'm also indebted to Mikhail Iossel and the Summer Literary Seminars for bringing me to Lithuania as their writer-in-residence, where I was able to do essential research at the Vilna Gaon State Jewish Museum. While in Vilnius, I also had the pleasure of talking about Russia's unofficial art movement with Vitaly Komar and about partisan life for teenage girls with Regina Kopilevič. Finally, thank you to the Lifschitz family in Israel, who invited me to a party at their house in Haifa many, many years ago, where I was lucky enough to meet a woman from Antopol who led me to Benzion Ayalon's incredible oral history of the village that first moved me, a decade ago, to begin this book.

Acknowledgments

Enormous thanks to:

My tremendously wise and caring agent, Bill Clegg, whose enduring belief in these stories has meant the world to me. Everyone else at William Morris Endeavor, especially Chris Clemans, Raffaella De Angelis and Shaun Dolan.

My brilliant and thoughtful editor, Jill Bialosky, whose guidance with this book has been immeasurably valuable. The terrific Erin Sinesky Lovett, for her remarkable dedication and enthusiasm. The rest of the wonderful team at Norton, particularly Bill Rusin, Ann-Marie Damian, Julia Druskin, Ingsu Liu, Nancy Palmquist, Rebecca Schultz, Cardon Webb and Fred Wiemer.

The Stanford University Creative Writing Program, for the generosity of a Wallace Stegner Fellowship. My extraordinary teachers there: John L'Heureux, Elizabeth Tallent, Colm Tóibín and Tobias Wolff, for their insights and example. Christina Ablaza, Krystal Griffiths, Ryan Jacobs and Mary Popek, for always having the answer. And Eavan Boland, whose support and mentorship over the years has gone above and beyond.

My teachers and classmates at Columbia University; and the U Cross Foundation, Bread Loaf Writers Conference, Sewanee Writers Conference, Djerassi Resident Artists Program, Mesa Refuge, San Francisco Writers' Grotto, Summer Literary Seminars in Lithuania and Sozopol Fiction Seminars in Bulgaria. Blue Mountain Center feels like a second home, and Harriet Barlow, Alice Gordon and Ben Strader feel like family.

My trusted group of readers, all incredible writers and cherished friends: Sarah Frisch, Skip Horack, Kirstin Valdez Quade and Stacey Swann.

My Stegner workshop-mates, who offered incisive feedback on drafts of some of these stories and remain a group of people I feel lucky to have in my life.

Aimee Bender and Micah Perks, for getting me started.

This long and—I fear—incomplete list of people who provided crucial support along the way, from editing to researching, to letting me sleep on their couches: Andrew Foster Altschul, Adrianne and Michael Bank, Harriet and Richard Bass, Rick Bass, Elizabeth Bernstein, Will Boast, Jeremiah Chamberlain, Harriet Clark, Katie Crouch, Rusty Dolleman, Mike Durrie, Jim Gavin, Maria Hummel, Scott Hutchins, Mikhail Iossel, Ken Kalfus, Tom Kealey, Dana Kletter, Adam Johnson, Yael Goldstein Love, Catherine Lucas, Mike McGriff, Laura McKee, Oren Manor, Haaris Mir, Stuart Nadler, Peter Orner, Jamie Quatro, Victoria Redel, Justin St. Germain, Christine Schutt, Stephanie Soileau, Shimon Tanaka, Jesmyn Ward and Jennie Yabroff.

Jennifer Terk Chance, Julia Ellis, Emily Freed, Brian Garrick, Sarah Grafman, Helen Kim, Shanna Pittman-Frank, Michelle Prats, Dean Vuletic and David Washburn, for being there from the very beginning.

My amazing and ever-growing family of Antells, Antopols, DuNours, Griers, Hirsches, Johnsons, Moskins, Silberlings and Tigays—I love you all more than you know.

Finally, my deepest thanks to Chanan Tigay, best reader and best friend.